PHOTO CREDIT: VIKRAM KHURANA

Tuhin A. Sinha, a columnist and a screenwriter, is one of India's best-selling novelists, with each of his four previous books, *The Edge of Desire*, *Of Love And Politics*, *That Thing Called Love* and *The Captain* (formerly *22 Yards*) breaking new ground in terms of subject and treatment. He is also a screenwriter of several popular TV shows, including the popular *Yeh Rishta Kya Kehlata Hai* on Star Plus. A keen political observer, Tuhin's columns on Indian politics appear regularly in India's leading dailies. He also has a regular blog on ibnlive.com and appears frequently on news channels on discussions of politics and cricket.

THE EDGE OF POWER

TUHIN A. SINHA

hachette
INDIA

First published in 2013 by Hachette India
(Registered name: Hachette Book Publishing India Pvt. Ltd)
An Hachette UK company
www.hachetteindia.com

1

ISBN 978-93-5009-704-5

Hachette Book Publishing India Pvt. Ltd
4th/5th Floors, Corporate Centre,
Sector 44, Gurgaon 122003, India

Typeset in Adobe Garamond 11/13.5
by Saanavi Graphics, Noida

Printed and bound in India
by Manipal Technologies Ltd, Manipal

This book is dedicated to an imagined future Prime Minister of India, who might be able to pull the country out of the mess she finds herself in right now…

Prologue

On an unsuspecting winter night in December 2012, India was shamed yet again…

At 9:30 p.m., after watching a movie in a popular mall in New Delhi, a feisty twenty-three-year-old girl and her male companion boarded a bus bound for Dwarka in west Delhi. The bus had only five other people in it, so they climbed in without a thought, happy to get seats, and began an animated discussion on the movie they had just watched.

All was well until the friend suddenly noticed that the bus had swerved off its regular route, into a narrow by lane. One of the men inside – a boy of seventeen or eighteen – deliberately bolted the door. When the friend objected, the men abused him. He was subsequently gagged and beaten to within an inch of his life with an iron rod.

The men then dragged the girl, kicking and screaming, to the rear of the bus. They beat her with the rod, and gang raped her repeatedly while the bus driver continued to drive. The rod was shoved into the girl's insides at one point. The most savage of the men was also the youngest among them. When each of the men had finished with her, the girl and her friend were tossed out onto the road, with the driver even trying to run them over by reversing his bus into them. Her friend managed to pull her away in the nick of time.

When the details of this horrific incident began to emerge over the next few days, the country was reminded of another ghastly gang rape that had taken place nearly fifteen years ago, a few hundred kilometres east of Delhi in a remote village in the Kishanganj district of Bihar. The victim back then had been Shruti Ranjan, wife of the Deputy Commissioner of Kishanganj, who had been brutally gang raped and left for dead by politically-sheltered local goons. This incident had altered the course of Shruti's life in unimaginable ways. Along with her mentor, the late nationalist leader Sharad Malviya, she had gone on to rewrite the politics of the land.

The rape assault on Nirbhaya, however, was a stark and shameful reminder for the country that nothing – absolutely nothing – had changed in India insofar as crimes against women were concerned.

As Nirbhaya battled for life in the Intensive Care Unit of Delhi's Safdarjung Hospital, the worthies in Lutyens' Delhi were as unconcerned as always. India's aging prime minister, Devender Singh; the forty-eight-year-old president of the ruling Indian Democratic Party(IDP) Mukta Prajapati; and the thirty-eight-year-old president of India's leading Opposition party, the Jan-Hit party, Ravi Nehra, all issued press statements professing their concern and dismay, but remained largely indifferent. They were all engrossed in maintaining the status-quo that ensured them their seats, filled their pockets and fueled their avarice and greed.

Chapter 1

It was 10:30 a.m. on Friday – five days after the gang rape in the capital city of India that had outraged the nation and shocked the world. Ravi Nehra, leader of the Opposition Jan-Hit party sat in the conference hall of his party office on Humanyun Road with fifteen party-members who constituted the Opposition's Parliamentary Committee. Since it was the last day of the winter session of Parliament he had assembled his party to take stock of their floor strategy for the day. The events of the hour were not particularly pressing to him.

Seated to Ravi's right were his two most trusted aides: the bearded, forty-five-year-old MP from Hajipur, Ankur Yadav – who had started his career as a building contractor until his skills at fixing deals had won him Nehra's trust; and the fifty-seven-year-old sugar baron Raghunandan Gupta, once accused of illegally stashing a large sum of undisclosed earnings in the Bahamas.

Even as the group mulled their options, they were distracted by a scene that was unfolding a couple of kilometres away at India Gate, and playing out on the large-screen LED TV of the conference room.

The majestic lawns around India Gate were overrun by a protest march of huge proportions as thousands of angry people, women of all ages among them, rallied against the

Government's inability to curb crimes against women. The rape victim, Nirbhaya, was struggling for her life in hospital. The only words she had whispered to her mother, as she swam in and out of consciousness had been, '*Ma, I don't want to die.*'

As hordes of incensed college girls protested Indian chauvinism and political apathy, a scuffle broke out at one end of the venue and the cameramen quickly trained their cameras on this bit of breaking news. The police instantly retaliated by resorting to a lathi-charge and tear-gas, bearing down on the young girls with characteristic insensitivity. The angry young girls, sick of the patriarchal boorishness of the Indian system, were in no mood to be cowed down; they actively clashed with the men in uniform.

Leading a large group of these protestors was a tall, thin man who was just a few days away from launching his own political organization: the Azad Bharat Party. A journalist turned activist who represented the common man, Daivik had greatly stirred up the political scenario in the country with his fiery, proactive stance on issues that the two leading political parties were perceived as being characteristically compromising on.

Daivik appealed for peace but his pleas were lost in the pouring of outrage. Finally, he took the mike and began to speak. As Daivik began his passionate speech a hush fell on the crowd. Incensed with the policemen's insensitivity in attacking the protestors he lamented: '*Despite all of the Indian Democratic Party (IDP) Government's failures, if there was one thing that had not yet taken place, it was a Jallianwala Bagh kind of massacre... Today, seeing the way the police are gearing up for a massive clash, I fear that even* that *unsavoury chapter from history might repeat itself here...*'

Hearing Daivik's voice, Ravi Nehra looked at the TV screen in distaste. This stupid bugger was becoming a thorn in his side: 'Bastard! He has a penchant for exaggeration,' laughed Ravi Nehra mockingly, as he muted the TV and turned away from the giant-sized plasma set to face his party colleagues.

Ratna Pandey said: 'I think we should forget the issue of Foreign Direct Investment for the time being. Anyway, the common man won't connect with the issue until it has been implemented and he suffers.'

Nehra stared impassively at her face, refusing to comment.

Ratna continued: 'In fact, watching these protests, I feel women's safety can become a crucial election issue… we must raise it to such a level that the protesting public sides with us. It is such an emotive issue that if leveraged well, it will earn us rich dividends.'

Nehra responded to this highly respected female MP with a supercilious sneer: 'Come on, Ratnaji, you know that these protests die out as quickly as they begin. Our public is fickle-minded. One day they protest with the same intensity against corruption, the next day it's against terrorism and now it's about women's safety. Have all these protests made any difference to politics?'

'But don't we have a moral responsibility as the country's leading Opposition party?' she countered, ignoring Ankur Yadav's frown, which was meant to dissuade her from questioning the supreme command.

'What are you talking, Ratnaji? We have two MPs and at least seven MLAs and MLCs facing charges of sexual misconduct. The ruling party has even more. Besides, when you go lower down the order, at the district and shakha levels, you will find many party activists facing charges of sexual offences too. Rape and sexual offences are all about power, Madam. It is common knowledge that many a times women consensually give in to powerful men to obtain favours…and when they aren't returned the favours they expect, they cry rape.'

Ravi Nehra's crass assertion left everybody in the room in queasy silence. His chauvinism was quite unbearable.

A silenced Ratna couldn't help but recall the radical speech that Nehra had given at the national executive of the women's cell of the party just two months ago. The irony of it was appalling. '*Women ought to think and believe that they are not just equal but a step ahead of men. Our party is starting a toll-free national helpline number which any woman who is facing sexual harassment at work or elsewhere can call at any time of the day. Apart from counselling, this helpdesk will even help in initiating legal action against the guilty,*' he had announced.

Nehra's speech had drawn thunderous applause even as he had concealed the lascivious glint in his eye as he had looked at Aparna Kamath – the voluptuous, thirty-something president of the women's cell. Aparna, a social-worker in Pune, had been a peripheral member of the party until Nehra had appointed her to the top-post. Of course, all sorts of steamy stories and speculation had blotted the unexpected appointment, with the commonest one suggesting that it was a one-night stand at a party workshop for farmers in Wai that had paved the way for her meteoric rise. There were many stories of Nehra's womanizing floating around. At one point, early on in his career, a woman had even accused him of rape. But Nehra had used his guile to have the case dismissed. It was the same guile that he had used to worm his way to the top and usurp the leadership of the party, outsmarting more deserving seniors. Ratna Pandey rued her isolation within the party as did many others – like the old warhorse, Ratnesh Prasad.

'Ratneshji, what is your opinion? What should our key focus be today?' Nehra turned his attention to the man in Ratna's thoughts.

'Nehraji, what about the coal scam? We haven't raised that issue since the last session, when we had completely cornered the Government on it...' Though Ratnesh answered, he knew his opinion held little importance.

Nehra barely heard Ratnesh out – his focus shifting back to the TV set. And his handsome Jat features turned dark with anger and disbelief as he watched a familiar figure join the protest at India Gate.

Rhea's entry had made all the media attention shift to her. Her presence would make it all the more difficult for the police to get away with its high-handedness. Because, after all, Rhea was still Ravi Nehra's wife.

After five years of a stormy marriage and a tumultuous relationship, it was common knowledge that Ravi and Rhea were a mismatched couple. They remained together mainly for the sake of their three-year-old son whom Nehra doted on – or so he made it appear. They even went on a yearly foreign holiday together. But beyond that, only a deafening silence marked their relationship. Rhea lived at their Gurgaon home, while Ravi stayed at his official residence in Lutyens' Delhi.

Nehra switched off the TV abruptly, disturbed by his wife's show of rebellion, which he had not got used to over the years. He was embarrassed to have seen her like this with his party-members watching him. The deft strategist in him was still struggling to arrive at the right way in which to deal with his wife – now that her advantages had been fully extracted and she was more of a liability.

Rhea was the daughter of the late Sharad Malviya, who was still referred to in the media as 'the best PM India never had'. A firm, decisive and dynamic nationalist leader, Malviya had died in 2002, in a mysterious plane crash, just on the eve of a General Election that his party had been predicted to win.

Until a few years ago, Rhea, as Malviya's political heir, had commanded a following that had made her both alluring and invincible. And then she had thrown it all away by falling in love. Or perhaps, as Shruti Ranjan had warned her, she had been trapped by Nehra in what had been the mother of all conspiracies.

Glancing at his watch, Nehra ended the meeting rather hastily: 'It's time for the session to begin…let's take stock of things again tomorrow.' The abruptness with which he ended the meeting echoed the impulsiveness with which Nehra took most of his decisions. Very few people actually understood what was going on in his mind but, yes, Nehra never did anything – not even shake hands – without calculating its potential advantages first. Under Nehra, his Parliamentary Committee had got used to the futility of such supposedly important meetings.

'But, Nehraji, what will our key focus in Parliament be today…?' a young MP tried seeking some clarity.

Nehra was casual. 'Fuel price hike…protest against it…'

'But that was done two weeks ago…'

Nehra paused, even as he tried not to lose his cool.

Sensing his leader's annoyance, Ankur jumped in with his suggestion: '*Arre bhai*, is there ever any shortage of issues? *Achcha* do one thing, protest against the peace process being initiated between India and Pakistan. Isn't that a powerful issue?'

'Yes! We must raise the issue of this meaningless peace process,' Nehra ratified his stooge's suggestion instantly, not allowing any room for a counter-opinion. 'Ratneshji, you will initiate the discussion on the matter, okay?' he added.

Ratnesh nodded weakly.

Nehra got up and left. He was six feet tall, with sharp features and a handsome handlebar moustache. His personality had quite an impact on the voters. As they watched him leave, a quiet exchange of helpless expressions was the only means of protest that the party-members had. Ruing the grim state of affairs that existed in the Jan-Hit party today, Ratna Pandey wondered if this was indeed the party that had once been led by Sharad Malviya. She actually missed the very person whom she had distrusted the most when she had been around – Shruti Ranjan.

It was expected that the Delhi gang rape and issues concerning women's safety would dominate the day's proceedings in Parliament that day. Instead, the issue was raised only briefly in passing by a Jan-Hit party MP, who was among the worst speakers in the house. All he said was, '*The Opposition demands to know the steps that the Government is taking to ensure that such an incident doesn't get repeated in future.*'

Indeed, so ineffectual was the statement that the Home Minister was only too happy to spell out a series of safety measures that everybody knew had been cooked up on the spur of the moment. Yet the Opposition chose not to pursue the matter and digressed to another issue.

PM Devender Singh, IDP Chairperson Mukta Prajapati, and Ravi Nehra were present in Parliament when this query was put forth. While the PM sat mum as he usually did – making it difficult to guess for a first-time viewer whether he existed for real or was a wax statue – Mukta Prajapati pretended to be occupied studying a file, while Nehra was seen passing a note to Ankur Yadav, like a bored college student.

No wonder the people of the country had begun to feel increasingly despondent about its political leadership, particularly as a perception of some sort of match-fixing between the Ruling and Opposition party had begun to gain ground.

How they all wished Shruti Ranjan had been around.

Chapter 2

At 9:30 p.m. that night Ravi Nehra was ready for his last appointment of the day. The visitor was ushered in through a discreet back entry, away from the prying eyes of the media, his own staff and other visitors. In fact, whenever he entertained one of his special guests, all his personal staff – except for his most trusted Officer on Special Duty (OSD) Pathak – remained unaware of the secret guest's identity. With time and experience, they had learnt that the visitor had to be one of the four: a top industrialist, a senior ruling party MP, a hawala dealer, or a whore. When rumour was that the guest was the last-mentioned, his staff indulged in a guessing game about the guest's age and ethnicity. Ravi was quite versatile in his tastes.

This time though, the guest in question was B.C. D'Souza, Special Advisor to the IDP Chairperson, Mukta Prajapati. D'Souza – a stocky, bald man in his early fifties – was among the shrewdest power-brokers in Delhi. He arrived in Nehra's sanctum-sanctorum carrying an expensive bottle of French wine. 'Madam has sent it for you. From her husband's collection.'

Rajveer Thakur, the spouse of the President of the ruling party, had his own spectacular rags-to-riches story. Nobody quite knew the exact nature of his business but in the sixteen years that Mukta and he had been married, his assets had multiplied no less than 500 times. He was supposedly in real estate development. Some speculated that he also owned a lottery company in the North-East. It was rumoured that without officially being a part of the IDP, his money virtually ran the entire show. Despite ample evidence of gross financial impropriety on Rajveer Thakur's part, nobody – even from the Opposition – went after his case for fear that the vengeful Mukta would have the crusader implicated under false charges by the unreliable and wholly Government-owned National Bureau of Investigation (NBI).

Ravi uncorked the bottle with the ease of a connoisseur and asked Pathak to serve the wine. Judging from their mutual warmth, it was evident that this wasn't the first such late-night rendezvous between the two.

'Madam is very thankful to you, Raviji...with your support, this Parliament session passed off pretty smoothly.'

Holding his glass of wine in one hand, Ravi rummaged in his pocket for his bidis with the other. Then putting his feet up on his desk Ravi lit a bidi with the panache of a pipe-smoker. The raw smoke emitted by it made D'Souza cough.

'*Desi jat...desi bidi...*hahaha,' Ravi guffawed at his discomfort, then suddenly changed his tone: 'D'Souza Saab, we had struck a deal to let this session be peaceful, remember? I have fulfilled my part of the promise. Now you need to fulfil yours.'

The deal was this: the Jan-Hit Government in Haryana had been reduced to a minority after four of its MLAs had been disqualified for electoral malpractices. If the regional Haryana Janata Morcha (HJM), which had five MLAs and was part of the IDP-led coalition at the Centre, could be pressured into supporting the Jan-Hit Government in the state, then the State Government would easily survive. D'Souza was supposed to play backroom mediator and get the HJM to support the Jan-Hit party.

D'Souza knew Ravi drove a hard bargain. 'We know, but you also know, Nehraji, that the HJM can be a tough nut to crack…'

'I don't care…Just one more year in power in Haryana will help us finance our next Lok Sabha campaign…It's no longer safe to rely so heavily upon hawala money. Already three of our MPs are under the scanner thanks to that honest swine whom you've made the Finance Minister.'

'Oh, Nehraji, you know all our other ministries are corrupt…having one honest Finance Ministry covers up for those,' D'Souza confessed brazenly. He also knew that if the IDP did not fulfil its share of the promise then the next session of Parliament would be a wash-out. He thus left promising that the IDP would do all it could to help a Jan-Hit-led government be formed in Haryana.

This deal was one of the many quid-pro-quo deals that Ravi had got into with the ruling party. He was convinced that in politics there was no victory, no loss. 'Politics is pure business and barter is the best form of business,' Nehra often told his cronies.

For all his failings, Nehra had some noble intentions as well; he was uncompromising when it came to protecting India's territorial interests. He wanted Government to increase the defence budget to 2% of the nation's GDP. He wanted India to open up its economy further. For all the opposition that his party had put up to the proposal for FDI in retail; in private conversations he held a different view.

Complex and multi-layered, Nehra typified the market-driven politician who had as many vices as he had virtues. In this age, when every perception tended to be subjective, it had become difficult to dismiss him as outright corrupt. After all, Nehra had a comprehensive plan for the electrification of all Indian villages. The Jan-Hit party State Government had sanctioned some very aggressive irrigation schemes. However, it was also a fact that most of the companies to whom the irrigation projects were being outsourced were owned by people close to the party. These projects were outsourced at lavish, unrealistic budgets and the beneficiaries in turn were supposed to be funding the party. So it was brazen quid pro quo at its very best.

But yes, in the end, villagers and villages were benefited, even if the cost incurred upon the economy was exorbitant.

Ravi Nehra had always been candid when he spoke of his politics to his close aides:

'Barter is the essence of living. And our politics simply can't wish it away. Come to think of it, with the cluster of regional parties that we have today, you think either of the two national parties can ever come to power on their own? Doesn't it make sense, then, to evolve a system of happy co-existence? In fact, I am open to the idea of ruling by rotation. Let one alliance rule for the first five years, while the next one rules for the next five. Trust me, the country will be the gainer in this.'

Nehra had so many facets and layers to him that, despite all his negatives, the positives in him often managed to camouflage the evil. And he continued not just to stay afloat but also to rule India's principal Opposition alliance.

Even as Ravi Nehra got back to flipping news channels for one last time that night, another thought played persistently in his mind; the thought that the new day was also his fifth wedding anniversary. Taking a long puff of his bidi, Ravi called Pathak inside his cabin. 'I'll be away for the night. Anything significant that I need to know?'

'Two things, sir,' nodded Pathak. 'One, a party MP from Muzzafarnagar, Shadab Khan, has issued a statement to the press saying that the party badly needs Shruti Ranjan back. He has in fact appealed to Shruti to return…'

'Send him a show-cause notice,' Ravi cut him short. 'Anything else?'

'Sir, there are many reports that Daivik Verma is inching closer towards the formation of his new party. 1 January is when he will be launching it. In fact, after this rape incident, public support for his new party is growing by leaps and bounds. It could be a game-changer in Indian politics…'

Nehra nodded uncomfortably and gestured to Pathak to leave. There was something about this young man, Daivik that he had begun to intensely detest. Was it envy borne of the fact that there was another commoner with more ambition and zeal in Indian politics than him? Or was it the fact that a person whom he had casually snubbed a little over a year ago was now set to challenge him and usurp the Opposition space in Indian politics from under his nose?

Nehra, who seldom wasted his time thinking about people, was for a change compelled to think about this underdog who had begun to give him cause for worry. He remembered his first and only meeting with Daivik …

When Daivik Verma had first entered Ravi Nehra's office, over a year ago, he hadn't been especially surprised to see Nehra sitting with his legs up on the table, smoking a bidi, and fiddling with his cellphone. He had after all heard of the unrefined behaviour of the Jan-Hit party president from many a fellow journalist.

'*Aaiye*...*aaiye*,' Nehra had greeted him without looking up from his phone. 'I've just installed *WhatsApp* on my cell... it's fun, yaar, isn't it?' he had beamed.

Daivik had forced a smile. What he had not really cared for was the omniscient presence of Nehra's stooge, Ankur Yadav. The oily man sat on a sofa nearby watching both of them closely.

For the next few minutes Nehra ignored Daivik and continued being besotted with his phone and exhaling smoke. Not realizing Daivik was choking on the acrid bidi smoke, he gestured to his flunky, who offered Daivik a wide choice of refreshments – fruit-juice, tea, coffee, milk shake, soft drink, and beer – from a pre-arranged tray. Daivik refused, indicating he was there for a purpose. This did not deter Nehra from typing into his phone with a suggestive smile, until finally hanging up with a look of great delight on his face. His gleeful expression clearly suggested that he'd managed to make some sort of an arrangement with the female he was engaging with.

Satisfied with this important negotiation, Nehra finally got down to acknowledging Daivik: 'So tell me, Daivik Verma, what brings you here?' he had asked.

'Sir, the Ranchi by-election is due next month. I want to contest the seat on the Jan-Hit party's ticket.'

For a moment, Nehra had not responded, making Daivik anxious.

'Oh that's a great thought...excellent indeed! In a democracy a leader should always be elected at the hustings – not nominated like our dummy PM. Nehru, Indiraji, Atalji were all elected leaders, weren't they?' Then in the same breath, Nehra added: 'So who's your financier?'

'Sorry?' Daivik had been stumped.

'*Arre bhai*, I hope you know that in India, Government doesn't fund elections. In some countries, they do, but not here. Here you've got to have at least 4–5 crore ready with you before you take the plunge.'

Daivik had been shocked. 'But I thought that's what party funds were meant for?'

'That's what outsiders think...Party funds get exhausted organizing our 5-star *chintan baithaks* every few months. Then, we have to spend on organizing mass rallies and ferrying people to them. The rest gets spent on hiring chartered flights for our top five leaders...they never travel by public carriers, you see,' Nehra had laughed cynically.

'So you mean to say that your MPs use their own funds to fight elections?'

'Of course they do – that's why we have so many builders, industrialists and businessmen getting our party tickets...and mind you, they win by spending on freebies for the slum electorates...If *we* didn't get these money-bags in, they would be lapped up by some thriving regional party...'

Daivik was appalled to hear this. Not that he was unaware of the corrupt culture that Nehra had been promoting these last three years; but to hear it from the horse's mouth was shocking indeed!

Nehra then decided to give him some advice: 'That's why I tell intellectuals like you to focus on TV appearances.

Let hopeless creatures like us take care of the dirty world of electoral politics. Still, if you are determined to get into elections, I'll tell you the way to go about it…'

'And what is that?' Daivik had asked.

'Get yourself financially backed by an industrial house. Since you are already popular, it won't be difficult. In so far as Jharkhand goes, the best bait would be a businessman who has interests in mining. Offer him stakes in Ranchi. He will take care of your interests and you will take care of him…Do you understand the game?' laughed Nehra.

By now, Daivik's patience had been tested enough. He stood up and said, 'Interesting games you play, Nehraji! No wonder that despite the Government's endless failures, people are still not ready to trust you.' Daivik stomped out of the room, but not before delivering his caveat: 'Nehraji, the tragedy of this country is that both the Government and the Opposition are in the ICU…But you know what? People are worried that is you remain the President of the Jan-Hit party, it's your party that is going to die first…'

Subsequently, whenever Nehra was apprised of the remarkable political strides Daivik had accomplished in the last year, he couldn't help thinking he had underestimated the bloke completely.

Chapter 3

At 12:15 in the night Gurgaon wore a pretty deserted look. All was still except for the sporadic activity of nocturnal creatures in the posh farm-houses on Mehrauli Road, or in the many five-star hotels that dot this satellite town. That night, however, Ravi Nehra, was spied on the streets, speeding dangerously in his white Porsche. He didn't have a single bodyguard for company, which is the way he preferred it at night. It gave him more privacy and freedom. Besides, he carried his pistol with him at all times. There was a small security contingent following him though, which had been asked to reach the destination directly. Blazing on the car's audio system was Kareena's item number from *Dabangg 2,* 'Fevicol Se…'

Nehra drove straight into Beverly Hills, one of Gurgaon's plushest high-rises. He rode up the elevator to the penthouse suite of the last building. Outside the door he quickly sniffed some white, viscous substance from what looked like a cigarette-lighter and then pressed down on the doorbell. A sleepy maid in her teens answered the persistent ring. 'Madam is asleep…' she informed him.

Pushing past her, Nehra strode in and moved towards the master bedroom, his eyes looking more bloodshot and hooded than ever. Inside the bedroom, Rhea was fast asleep. Ravi was instantly aroused by the sight of her in her skimpy nightie. He turned on a lamp, sat down by her side and started roughly caressing her face with his fingers. Rhea woke up with a shock.

Nehra couldn't help laughing at her. 'Did you think someone had sneaked in and was going to rape you? Sure, Delhi is unsafe…it helps to be on guard,' his laughter grew wilder.

Rhea knew his jokes were tasteless. But she didn't bother to tell this to him for she knew the answer. '*Oh come on… a jat doesn't need to be sophisticated in his jokes. He makes an impact where it really matters.*'

The double meaning in the sentence notwithstanding, Rhea could not dispute its truth. Sure, Nehra was rough and wild. About Rhea's only achievement in the last five years had been to make him stop using the Hindi swear-words he would otherwise unleash at the drop of a hat. Most of these expletives had obscene references to the private parts of women family members.

Rhea thought Nehra would confront her for joining in the protests at India Gate. Instead he had something else on his mind.

'Sex?' he asked her point-bank.

It was this sort of directness that Rhea had found both tantalizing and humiliating about her marriage. Even as she struggled for a way to ward him off, Ravi grabbed her face in his hands and kissed her hard. It was the kind of kiss that Rhea hated as much as she found it hard to resist. Of course, she could tell he was high on cocaine – a fact that too had ceased to bother her.

The maid entered the room just then, making Nehra and Rhea jump apart. Covering up her awkwardness, the maid stuttered, 'Do you need anything or should I go to sleep?' Nehra, who was quite stoned, looked at the maid with livid eyes, walked up to her and slapped her hard. The maid burst into tears and fled the room.

A distraught Rhea wanted to follow the maid but Nehra shut the door. He tried to look at Rhea romantically but despite his efforts, his looks conveyed only lust. He pushed Rhea to the bed and began to roughly kiss her breasts, first through her dress and then without it. Gradually, his kissing got more intense.

Rhea hated his lovemaking because she knew that it wasn't Nehra's love but his hatred for her that he was expressing. Somewhere she knew that Nehra felt a sense of triumph knowing he was raping the woman who had ceased to be his wife long ago; so what if they were still not legally separated. But, perversely, she also enjoyed it because of all the five men she had had sex with, there was none as good as Ravi. Nehra was a stud with a wild animal instinct that drove her insane with desire.

And so it happened. Even as he sucked and pulled on her breasts, Nehra lifted her nightie with his left hand. In one minute, he unzipped himself and in another he plunged in, as deep as he'd ever gone, leaving Rhea gasping.

This wasn't the first time Rhea had been raped by Nehra. This was how their marriage had always been, probably from the second year on – by when they knew they weren't meant for each other. Nehra would not touch her for weeks until his carnal attraction for her was aroused again.

Why did Nehra want sex with her today? Sure, it was their marriage anniversary. But that wasn't the reason. Entering Rhea on the day that she had rebelled against him by joining the protests gave him a feeling of authority and power over her.

Two minutes later Nehra was dressed to leave. 'I'm off in the morning for a rally in Gorakhpur.'

As Nehra opened the door, Rhea stopped him. 'Ravi, I have to tell you something.'

'Shoot!' said Ravi without turning around.

'I want a divorce. I have thought a lot about it and my decision is final.'

Nehra was taken aback, but the cool customer that he was, he didn't show it. 'Anything else?' he asked disdainfully.

'Nope. That's it for today.'

'Divorce is all that you will get! Our son will stay with me,' Nehra warned her, looking menacingly into her eyes.

'Oh get lost! Don't wield your stupid threats…do you even care if he is alive?' Rhea snapped at him as Nehra stormed out of the room oblivious to Rhea's angry tears.

Nehra didn't leave immediately. He went to the bedroom where his three-year-old son, Anway, slept peacefully in his cot. Seeing his son, Nehra's face softened. From the brute that he was a few minutes ago he became the caring father, tenderly feeling his son's face. Three days ago, Rhea had sent him a message saying Anway had a mild fever. Ravi had kept tabs on his son's health through the nanny. Anway seemed fine now, but the father looked worried.

Nehra made some cooing sounds, hoping his son would wake up. He wanted to play with him. But Anway's slumber was so sound that he wouldn't even budge from the position he was sleeping in. Disappointed, Nehra left.

As he sped away in his Porsche, Rhea stood watching him from the balcony. She realized that even these rare encounters with her husband would soon become a thing of the past. She hated herself for what she had reduced herself to; for throwing away her political career to marry this savage brute. Rhea really, really missed talking to Shruti Ranjan, whom she felt was the only person she could bare her heart too.

Chapter 4

In a hazy battlefield, a fearless commander with unusually suave and aristocratic looks, wearing the supreme commander's cap and boots, leads his troops... There's the sound of heavy artillery and the exchange of gunfire as two sets of troops battle each other out... This chief commander leads his men with indefatigable zeal even as the enemy comes charging in from the other side, making his task seem increasingly impossible. Nonetheless, he unleashes a fresh offensive, exhorting his troops to be fearless... He tells them: 'This is your tryst with history. Do, don't die...'

It was 8:20 a.m. the next morning. In her plush Versova apartment in suburban Mumbai, actress Catherine Khan (nee Kapoor) woke up in a cold sweat. This wasn't the first time that this nightmare from a long-forgotten war had tormented her in her sleep. Indeed, she had lived with these visions ever since she was a child. In her childhood, she used to experience the dreams infrequently but lately she had been experiencing them more often: at times even on consecutive nights. The frequency of this dream, she realized, had something to do with her state of mind and the state of the nation...

Catherine had been on anti-depressants for the last two years. At first, it was her failed marriage and career that got her down; lately it was the sorry state of affairs in the country that evoked so much angst in her. She was often surprised herself that the latter could affect her so deeply.

She tried to control her mounting anxiety, not wanting to disturb her three-year-old daughter Nia, who slept next to her, oblivious of the chaos her mother was in. Wiping her groggy, sleep-deprived eyes, Catherine got up carefully, and walked to the front door to get the newspaper.

Ten minutes later, she sat on the living room sofa with a cup of black tea in her hands. She looked tense and upset; her mouth was dry. Well, that was the kind of impact that reading about the Delhi gang rape for the fifth consecutive day had on most people. Ever since Catherine had first read the story, she couldn't stop herself from thinking about the nameless girl whom the whole world knew only as Nirbhaya.

Nirbhaya was definitely fearless to be fighting this terrible battle with such fortitude, but hadn't the rapists in this country become completely fearless too? Brazenly, shamelessly, fearless! Had the fear of the law completely ceased to be a deterrent to these savage bastards? After all, even in the five days that had gone by since this heinous incident, not for one single day had the newspapers not reported fresh incidents of rape – including those committed on children.

Catherine, like most other mothers, couldn't help but feel scared for her daughter. As Catherine thought about Nirbhaya, the other bigger problem in her life seemed to pale into insignificance: her impending divorce from actor Armaan Kapoor. The last year had been very emotionally draining for her; what with the unending court visits and the responsibility of being a single parent.

Catherine's film career, which three years ago had been at its peak, had also hit a rough patch. Her last two movies, made after she had resumed work after Nia's birth, had bombed at the box-office. Despite her best efforts, she hadn't been able get back her Size 0 body, which added to her worries. Even the thought of her much-hyped, first bilingual movie, with Tamil superstar Eeshwaran, which was almost ready for release – failed to enthuse her.

In her agitated state, she tossed aside the paper and listlessly flipped TV channels. Nirbhaya's condition was deteriorating further. Catherine felt a deep sadness. She was in the grip of an intense melancholy that made her even more susceptible to the war dreams she had. She could sense something in her pushing her towards a life-altering decision. Perhaps only Shruti Ranjan could have brought this Government to task for its insensitive handling of the situation.

An hour later, when the nanny had taken Nia down to play and Catherine sat alone with her thoughts, the doorbell rang. Catherine opened the door thinking it would be the milkman. Instead it was her one true friend – Daivik Verma. Daivik hugged her hard and long. It was a robust hug that Catherine shared only with him.

Daivik's appearance at this early hour reminded Catherine of the significance of the day: this was the day, eight fateful years ago, that Catherine had first made a panic call to Daivik at 1:30 a.m. In the next few hours that had followed, they had become the best of friends. This day, thus, marked the birth of a very special bond between them; a bond that neither had the words to define. Daivik and Catherine had since celebrated this anniversary every year, even when they had barely met otherwise.

Daivik had taken time off his packed political schedule and taken the 6 a.m. flight from Delhi to be with her. He had picked up her favourite cake, a chocolate and rum confection, getting which found and packed had delayed his arrival by a good 45 minutes. Like he always did, Daivik just had the two names *Catherine* and *Daivik* written on the cake. The manner in which the two names were placed beside each other, reasonably close yet a little apart, was symbolic of the way Daivik viewed his relationship with Catherine. His love for her had always gone unrequited.

Catherine cut the cake on her breezy terrace garden, with Daivik looking on. As she fed the first piece to him, they both grew nostalgic…

Chapter 5

Daivik Verma, like Ravi Nehra, was a man of many parts. He had grown up almost all over the country, because his father, who worked in a bank, was transferred out every few years. Till the time Daivik was in junior school, the family moved to each new posting together. But once he reached the eighth standard, around the year 1990, his mother decided to move back to their hometown, Ranchi, where she took up a job as a teacher in a well-known public school.

While his father worked away from home in a different city, Daivik and his mom took care of Daivik's paternal grandfather or Dadaji, who was already in his late seventies and suffered from schizophrenia. With no siblings, Daivik ended up spending a good amount of his time chatting with his grandfather, whose moody temperament he had resented as a kid. His grandfather, Mithilesh Verma, was a staunch Gandhian who had taken part in the Quit India movement. He had met Gandhi twice in his life. Later in the early 1970s, Mithilesh had become a supporter of Jai Prakash Narayan.

1990 had been a tough year in Indian history. The nationwide anti-reservation stir, coupled with the Ram Janmabhoomi movement had led to a near civil-war situation. Towards the end of 1990, there were massive riots in various parts of the country. And everytime the Verma family would watch a report of these riots on TV, the septuagenarian Verma would react violently. 'They are killing Gandhi!' he would yell. 'At least I am not a killer. I did not kill Gandhi.'

Daivik's mother, who came from a family with strong Rashtriya Swayam Sewak (RSS) roots, often teased her father-in-law in an affectionate sort of way, 'Relax *Babuji*, there were enough riots even in Gandhi's time.'

Mithilesh would hit back: 'But there was a Gandhi who selflessly sat on fasts to make those riots end, even risking his own life. Does this generation not have anyone who can do that? Is the idea of Gandhism dead?'

Gandhi, for Mithilesh, stood for peace and non-violence; he stood for honesty; he stood for integrity; he stood for equality and sacrifice. He was saddened to see the death of these virtues in the present generation of politicians and leaders. Hence, whenever he'd come across a distressing bit of news which had to do with the country or society, he'd say: 'They are killing Gandhi…at least I did not kill Gandhi.'

After he finished school, Daivik shifted to Delhi to study History at St Stephen's college and followed it up with an MA in Political Science from Jawaharlal Nehru University. His stint at JNU resulted in a big change in his worldview. In a sense, it marked the coming-of-age of his political beliefs. Given an option between his Gandhian grandfather, his pro-RSS mother and maternal relatives, and a perfectly apolitical father, he found himself espousing the Marxist cause.

Daivik's grandfather passed away in 2001, just months before the post-Godhra riots. In a sense, Daivik felt happy that his grandfather did not live to witness the Gujarat riots or else he'd have never said anything else in his remaining years except: 'They are killing Gandhi...At least I did not kill Gandhi.'

After his grandfather's death, Daivik stumbled on a file containing several articles that his grandfather had written on Jayaprakash Narayan. Aptly titled, *'Gandhi Reborn'*, these writings and the thoughts they conveyed were so profound that they made Daivik wonder if the nation had been unfair to the great socialist leader.

Daivik chanced on these writings at a time when he had completed his MA and was still pretty unclear about what he wanted to pursue in life. One rather conventional option was to appear for the Civil Services exam, and the other was to take up teaching. A third – which his heart really desired but which his family was strongly against – was to pursue documentary film-making. The last option was also the most up-hill one considering it required him to take up another course in Mass Communications.

However, after reading his grandfather's articles on JP and living with his persona day in and day out for weeks, he realized he wanted to make a film on JP; not a documentary but a proper feature film. So intense was this calling that he eventually decided to come down to Mumbai. Daivik was well aware that he would have to struggle for years under a known director to learn the ropes. But he was prepared.

The thing about Mumbai, however, is that it has a mind of its own when it comes to shaping the destiny of its inhabitants. Often, the path it reveals is very different from what one imagines. To finance his struggles as a film-maker, Daivik started working for a film magazine called *Gloss* as a freelance journalist. Simultaneously, he also dabbled as a part-time cartoonist with a political tabloid.

In 2004, he had gone to cover the premiere of a so-called 'crossover' film. Among the movie's motley cast of known and unknown actors was a very pretty, London-bred, Austrian-Indian actress, Catherine. Catherine was cast in a blink-and-you-miss-it role of a hooker, but she caught his fancy. The very first time that Daivik met her he knew that she would make it big in Bollywood.

Daivik was clearly infatuated with her. He kept chasing her for the next three months for an interview, surprising even Catherine with his dogged pursuit.

Catherine, for her part, felt a complete stranger in India. Her only India connection, after all, was an Indian father, who had left her mother within a year of her birth. She had wanted to come to India, though she had never imagined coming here in the manner that she finally did.

Catherine was a British TV and stage performer when Indian filmmaker, Yash Mehra who was shooting a film spanning three continents chanced upon her. Her Indian lineage is what excited him enough to cast her in his film. Catherine was to soon realize that apart from being an enterprising filmmaker, Yash was also a compulsive womanizer. He smooth-talked his way into convincing her that she was tailor-made for Bollywood and that she'd become a big star in India. He, in fact, promised to take her as the lead in his next movie, provided she did not work for any other banner for the next two years.

Catherine thought about it a lot. In London, she had a steady career as a TV actress and a boyfriend from whom she had begun to drift apart. Professionally she was satisfied; personally she wasn't. In her heart of hearts, she wanted to be in India to feel and experience a lot of the stuff that she vaguely saw in her dreams. She felt confused and thought India would help sort herself out. Hence, even though the idea of becoming Bollywood's biggest star did not appeal much to her, she allowed Yash to use that as bait to make her shift to India.

Once in India, Yash's intentions became clearer. He gave her a room in his office at Khar, which also had a double-bed and an attached bath. So while the 2BHK apartment was Yash's office during day hours, it doubled as Catherine's apartment at night when she had it all to herself, with a maid to help her with the cooking.

Over time, Catherine started hearing some bizarre stories about Yash – that his marriage to singer Yami Sachdev was on the rocks and that the place she had been given to live in was the apartment where all his latest 'flings' were put up. Soon, Yash started visiting her at night. He'd drop in at 11:30–12, apologizing for the odd hour but nonetheless pretending he had been busy all day. Initially, he played safe by walking in with a female writer. He'd start the conversation, pretending to discuss the script. But when Catherine asked for details about when he proposed to start shooting he would change the subject. Catherine soon realized that after Yash's last movie – which film critics had unanimously drubbed as torture – getting a financier for his next venture was tough.

In the meantime, Daivik had continued his efforts on two fronts: one, convincing Catherine to pose for a cover shoot for *Gloss* and two, convincing his editor that it was not just his infatuation with her that made him think that Catherine deserved to be featured on the cover, which normally only featured established actresses. He tried his best to convince his editor that Catherine would be in that league soon.

Then one day, the expected happened. Yash's 'friendship' ploy had begun to test Catherine's patience. He'd often get DVDs, which he'd make Catherine watch together with him, saying that she'd understand Indian cinema better this way. He had stopped bringing his writer friend along and would invariably persuade Catherine to drink with him too. On this particular night, Yash seemed to have a plan up his sleeve. The DVD he'd brought with him was not a Bollywood biggie but a particularly sensuous film called *About Last Night*. One of Demi Moore's early films, it had some explicit sex scenes between her and Rob Lowe. They watched the movie together, Yash lying on her bed and Catherine leaning uncomfortably against the window. Then Yash patted the place next to him and invited her to lay by him.

Instead, Catherine took the remote and stopped the video, surprising Yash. 'Why are we watching this movie?' she asked with a directness that stumped him.

'Uh...well...we are creative people...watching movies together helps in...'

Catherine stopped him short saying, 'Helps in what? Laying your actresses?'

Yash wasn't prepared for this, but Catherine couldn't stop: 'It's very late in the night. Even creative people ought to be at home at this hour. Would you please...?' She didn't complete the sentence but from her gesture it was more than evident that she had ordered Yash to leave; leave his own 'escape' room!

The suddenness with which all this happened, left Yash dazed. He got up to leave, and then suddenly turned back and tried to force himself on her. Catherine shrieked in disbelief and ended up kicking him hard in the balls. Even as Yash struggled with the pain, she pushed him out of the door and shouted at him to leave.'Go, I said...just go!'

Yash had no option but to leave.

For the next one hour, Catherine was in a huge dilemma. Was her India dream jinxed? She considered her options. What choices did she have at this point, other than giving in to Yash, in order to stay back in India? After all, she knew nobody in the country. She had some relatives from her father's side, but considering that her mother and father had been separated long ago, launching a search for them would mean entering a different pursuit altogether. Instead, she remembered someone who had begun to seem familiar, despite her avoiding him.

She dialled a number at 1:30 in the morning. Daivik was fast asleep when his phone rang, so much so that he didn't notice the number.

'Hello, is that Daivik?' said a sweet voice.

'Yes...?'

'Daivik, can we meet in the next one hour?'

It was then that Daivik realized who the caller was. Though he was sleepy, he did not want to lose this opportunity. An hour later, at three in the morning, Daivik and Catherine sat over coffee at the Taj Land's End in Bandra. Daivik was still anxiously waiting to hear what it was that had brought Catherine to him at this odd hour. His wild fantasies had him wonder if she was feeling horny and needed his help. Realizing that Catherine was about to speak, he cut his fantasies short and looked as sincere he could.

'Daivik, I'm ready for your shoot...'

Daivik was ecstatic when he heard this.

'But I need some help in return. I need you to arrange an accommodation for me, ASAP.'

Daivik was surprised at the unexpectedly pleasant turn his life had taken in the last few hours. The lady he had been chasing for the last three months now sat right in front of him, sipping coffee and seeking a very personal favour.

'How soon do you need this accommodation?'

'Right away!'

It being the middle of the week, Daivik suggested that she shift into his place for the next couple of days and promised to find her a new accommodation over the weekend. Catherine was apprehensive until Daivik said: 'Catherine, I have a very clean record...no history of rape, molestation or sexual harassment, you see...but yes, I am also neither gay, nor celibate. I am all that you are,' laughed Daivik.

Catherine was intrigued by what he said. 'What do you mean I am all that you are...?' she asked.

'A romantic,' was Daivik's cryptic answer, and then he added: 'You can trust me like a friend and I can assure you a safe, comfortable stay in my house.'

Catherine agreed to his proposal, feeling sure that she would find Daivik's place less hateful than her present accommodation. Hence, at daybreak, Daivik had a new flatmate to give him company in his modest 1BHK Andheri flat. Though he tried to put up a calm, restrained front, deep inside he was thrilled. Catherine's toned physique and her exquisite looks had sent his adrenaline on a joyride of sorts.

Daivik had left for work soon after acquainting Catherine with the kitchen and giving her a few numbers from where she could order food. Catherine had spent the whole day alone, thinking about her rather eventful journey from Vienna to London and now here. She hadn't planned her life, yet new people entered it at different points, pulling her in directions that suited their best interest. She wondered if her life would ever get a sense of permanence or whether it would remain as unpredictable as that of her parents and of the army chief who kept coming to her in her dreams.

When Daivik returned home that night, he was accompanied by six other people – a photographer, his assistant, two light-men, a make-up artiste and a stylist. As he introduced them to Catherine, a frown formed on her face as she realized she might be in for some hard work right away. Sensing her annoyance, Daivik took her aside to explain the situation.

'Listen, Catherine, please you've got to do this for me. The cover that was supposed to be used in next month's edition has got ruined. The computer crashed and we can't retrieve a thing from it. The photographer who clicked the earlier pictures has gone abroad and we can't reach him. Now this cover needs to go into print tomorrow afternoon. If you don't do this, then we are doomed.'

He promised a chocolate cake to Catherine for this favour.

Catherine knew Daivik was crazy but had no idea he could be so unpredictable. It took Daivik and the crew almost an hour to convince Catherine to agree the shoot.

During the photo-shoot that took place in Daivik's living room and continued through the night, Catherine was shot as tastefully and sensuously as could be imagined, with Daivik directing every detail. She was given the respect of a Bollywood star, with half-a-dozen people working through the night to make her look like a diva. And when she saw the results she felt for the first time that Daivik was perhaps right: a bright future awaited her in Bollywood.

With the pictures done, Daivik now had to file a story. Normally the accompanying interview would have been about the actress's childhood, her journey as an actress and her last public relationship. Catherine could have answered these mundane queries even in a half-asleep condition but Daivik's special interest in her, had him take her out for coffee to a distant Madh Resort. The coffee session that started around five in the evening, went on well past midnight. Catherine spoke more to Daivik than she had to anyone in her life. Of course, much of what she said was off the record.

The world that Catherine spoke so vividly about, left Daivik mesmerized for life.

Chapter 6

Subhash Chandra Bose will be remembered in history as being among the bravest Indians ever born. Unlike Gandhi and Nehru, Bose stood for unqualified Swaraj (self-governance), including the use of force against the British. This meant a confrontation with Mahatma Gandhi, who opposed Bose's claim to the presidency of the Indian National Congress (INC) in 1939, resulting in the party splitting.

From the early 1930s on, Bose had begun to travel extensively across the globe, with a view to exploring potential military support from friendly regimes and world leaders in his attempt to wage war against the British back home. Most of these visits were to the European nations and one of the potential allies whom he worked on was Adolf Hitler.

In the second week of June 1934, Bose settled down in Vienna, since he had a contract from a publishing company there to write a book on the Indian freedom struggle since 1920. Bose immediately started scouting for a secretary who would help him with his work. On 24 June, a pretty and confident young woman named Emilie Schenkl walked in. There was something about her that made him take an instant like to her. Quite possibly, it was the right combination of looks, intelligence and confidence. For hours, Emilie would take dictations from Bose in shorthand which she'd later type diligently, often remaining awake for nights in a row.

Everytime Emilie heard stories about the Indian freedom struggle, she felt a strange kinship with the land Bose talked about; she felt one with the man who had left his country but who would think of nothing but his country every single moment.

For young Subhash it was an emotionally turbulent phase. He was fighting two major battles: one against the British and the other against a part of his own party, the INC. He was increasingly disillusioned with Gandhi's overly patient and at times even pacifist approach towards the British. While he had drawn up a radical roadmap of his own on how he planned to oust the British, this plan depended upon a lot of things falling into place, some of which he didn't have much control over.

As Subhash ended up spending a huge amount of his time with Emilie, he also confided many of his anxieties to her. A deep bond of mutual trust and understanding soon developed between them and before they realized it, they were in love.

Subhash, however, led a rather peripatetic life. For instance after spending a couple of months in Austria, he'd be off for the next several months either conferring with other important leaders in Europe or taking stock of things back home. Given that Subhash always led life so dangerously, Emilie would fear for him whenever she didn't get a letter from him for a long time. Emilie confided her feelings in her best friend from childhood, Teresa.

'Emilie, can I ask you something?' asked Teresa, a bit hesitantly. 'Are you sure *Subhash really loves you? I mean, a man in his position has more important priorities…'*

Looking out of the window into the frosty horizon, Emilie said something so softly that it almost seemed she was having a conversation with herself. 'I know Subhash loves me. I have seen it in his eyes. Besides, I love him unconditionally and that's more important for me.'

On 26 December 1937 Subhash secretly married Emilie. Their bond was to only grow after their marriage as the couple spent a good amount of time in the hill retreat of Badgastein, sharing thoughts and philosophizing over life's uncertainties. Often Bose and Emilie would just hold each others' hands and walk through the woods of Badgastein for hours without much conversation. Without him uttering a word, Emilie could understand his state of mind. In a sense, Subhash was always stuck in a complicated love triangle that had Emilie on one side and his country on the other. When he'd spend more time with Emilie, he'd get restless to do more for his country. And when he'd be away mobilizing forces for the country, he would miss Emilie the most.

1939 onwards was a particularly tough phase for Bose. First he was forced to resign from the president's post of the INC owing to his sharp differences with Gandhi. Then, he was under house arrest. Subsequently, Bose organized mass protests in Calcutta calling for the 'Holwell Monument' commemorating the Black Hole of Calcutta, which then stood at the corner of Dalhousie Square, to be removed. He was thrown in jail by the British, but later released and put under house arrest. Bose escaped from the country and landed in Germany where he invested three years, aiming for Germany's support in waging a war against the British. In July 1942, when she was five months pregnant, Emilie left Berlin for Vienna to be with her mother and sister. Subhash was in any case scheduled to leave for Asia as soon as travel arrangements could be made. Emilie chose to give birth to their child in her home city, while Subhash pursued his ultimate mission to free his nation from her encroachers.

While her mother and sister took care of her health, it was in her friend Teresa that Emilie confided her emotions...how terribly she missed Subhash during her pregnancy and how she wished he could be by her side.

Subhash and Emilie's daughter Anita was born on 29 November 1942 in Vienna. Subhash was so ecstatic when he heard the news that he left everything to be with his wife and daughter. The three of them spent a quiet Christmas together in Vienna. A few weeks after Anita's birth, Teresa, gave birth to her own daughter called Susan. It was Susan who later gave birth to Catherine.

Subhash's happiness was once again short-lived: when his daughter was barely two months old, he left for Japan, never to meet her again. In late August 1945, Emilie, her mother and sister were sitting in the kitchen at her Vienna home, sipping tea when the evening bulletin on radio broke a news that was to change their lives forever: Bose was no more. It was reported that Subhash Chandra Bose had been killed in an air crash at Taihoku (Taipei).

Incidentally, Teresa had also separated from her husband. And as years went by, Teresa and Emilie, along with their daughters spent a lot of time with each other living as next-door neighbours.

Teresa slogged hard to give her daughter a good upbringing. Susan migrated to London where she studied Economics and later started teaching in junior college. In London, she met a handsome Indian called Nawab Khan at a friend's party. They soon fell in love and were married. However Susan soon got the shock of her life when she realized that Nawab had lied to her – he had a wife and kids back home in Junagarh. Susan got to know this when she was in the seventh month of her pregnancy. It shattered her completely. At that point, Nawab begged for forgiveness, promising that he would divorce his first wife at the soonest. When he failed to do this, even after a year, she walked out on him.

Susan, along with Catherine, came back to Vienna and started living with her mother, Teresa. Aunt Emilie was still their neighbour and her mother's best friend, even though Anita had gone to the U.S.A for her studies. When Catherine was just two, Susan passed away in road accident. Time had now come a full circle for Teresa. She once again, had to raise a child as a single parent, this time it being her granddaughter.

Catherine had grown up hearing stories about Bose from her grandmother and Emilie. Her missing father was another lure. She wanted to visit the land, experience its different cultures and feel its warmth.

Like her mother, Catherine had a rebellious streak in her. Much against Teresa's counsel, she went and settled in London because she wanted to experience the city where her mother had spent so many years. Here, while she was studying, a portfolio shot taken by her friend won her a prized modelling assignment. One thing led to another and soon she went on to become a smalltime TV actress.

All these years, she continued to live the dream that wouldn't cease to haunt her. Somewhere in her heart of hearts, she knew India would call her and so it happened when one day Yash Mehra offered her a role in his movie and she shifted base to India.

And what a decade it had been for her in the country!

The dashing and suave soldier whom Catherine saw in her dreams was Subhash Chandra Bose. In recent months, with her feeling increasingly flustered by the sorry state of affairs in the country, she had been experiencing something very unusual: On at least three occasions, instead of Bose, the soldier who appeared in her dream bore a strange resemblance to Sharad Malviya. The first time this happened, it had left her thoroughly confused. Later she surmised that Subhash Chandra Bose and Sharad Malviya indeed had a lot in common: a radical approach, an unflinching love for the country, obstructed romantic lives and premature, unfortunate deaths.

Daivik found Catherine's past and her sense of belonging to India, quite fascinating. She had two links with India through her growing up years: Subhash Chandra Bose and her own father. While Bose filled her with awe, she obviously couldn't say the same about her father. So, did she hate her father? Did she want to meet him ever?

She wasn't sure about the answer. Looking at her expression, Daivik knew she needed to see him at least once, to get his side of the story.

Daivik thought the story about troubled pedigree and Bose would make a great copy. But then he was committed not to use that portion, nor to divulge it to anybody.

Two weeks later, when the latest edition of the magazine hit the stalls, an ethereal, smoking-hot Catherine in a classic backless velvet gown, her hair wet and her ocean blue eyes looking straight at the reader, instantly caught the imagination of the country. 'I belong to India,' read the cover caption. The cover became a rage, with the magazine having to print twice the number of copies it usually sold.

That month's edition also marked the fifth anniversary of the magazine. And the magazine had organized a lavish party to celebrate the occasion. Among those who attended the bash were ex-superstar Vikrant Kapoor and his son, Armaan. Vikrant had been planning to produce a film to launch his son's acting career and his eye was caught by the reticent and lovely Catherine.

Catherine who was the cynosure of all eyes, felt quite out of place. How she wished men would understand that a seductive-looking actress wasn't necessarily 'available' in real life! She was an extremely reserved person who felt uncomfortable when a person complimented her on her looks. Feeling awkward, she withdrew to the terrace. Noticing her alone, Daivik followed her out. They chatted together with the full moon above lighting their faces with just the right shade of blue and dark until Catherine surprised Daivik yet again:

'Dude, this place is too cramped. Can you take me somewhere else?'

So the two of them sneaked out of the party after telling the editor that Catherine wasn't feeling well. For the next three hours, they danced at Bandra's most famous night-club. At a half past one, when the club was finally shut and the guests were asked to leave, Catherine was eight pegs down. She held Daivik tight and slurred, 'Daivik, my friend, you rock...I've never had so much fun in my life...'

Daivik was as inebriated as her but in better control. With Catherine leaning heavily on his shoulder, he started scouting for an auto. Instead of the auto, a mild, unseasonal drizzle made its entry, making the situation all the more surreal. As Daivik called out to the autos, holding Catherine with one hand, some sort of an unusual realization seemed to dawn upon Catherine. Her blabbering stopped as she looked at Daivik more intently.

'Daivik,' she said tremulously.

Daivik turned to look at her, surprised to see her looking at him so intently. Without uttering another word, Catherine brought herself close, really close to him, and kissed him on his lips. It was a kiss as gentle and soft as one could be. In the next minute though, they were locked in a passionate lip lock, which was disrupted only by the sound of an intrusive auto-wala, enquiring if they wanted to be dropped home. Catherine pulled herself back, realizing what she had done. Was she just drunk or did she actually feel something for this guy? she wondered.

The next morning a sober Catherine had apologized profusely to Daivik for kissing him – much to his disappointment. Catherine thought of him merely as a friend, nothing else. Daivik, on the other hand, had been smitten with her from the moment their paths had crossed. He was pretty confident that the kiss would not go in vain and that sooner than later, he'd work his way into her heart.

Unfortunately for him, that very evening, Catherine had an unexpected visitor: Armaan Kapoor. Though she was astonished to see the film-star's son in her house, what he said left her in a bigger daze. 'Will you act in a movie with me?' he asked. 'Dad and I want you to play the lead in our home production…'

It took a while for Catherine to assure herself that what was unfolding in front of her was not a dream. Indeed, the offer was for real! She could well be a big Bollywood star; a hunch her buddy Daivik had had all along! Catherine couldn't believe her luck; given the clout that the superstar father-son duo held in the industry, all top actresses would have given an arm and a leg to act under their banner. And here she had made it so effortlessly – all thanks to Daivik!

Eventually, the catalyst of this change, Daivik, gradually resigned himself to being just her good friend. As Catherine's Bollywood career took off, he felt the dual emotions of happiness and forlornness, which at times really baffled him.

During the shooting of Catherine's first film, she fell in love with Armaan and eventually married him three years later. However, the marriage was doomed from the start, mainly on account of the disparity in their professional status. While Catherine went on to become a leading actress, Armaan's career never quite took off. He never became more than his father's son.

With Catherine out of his life, Daivik decided, much to his benefit, that he had little option but to move on. With his film-making dream seeming as distant as ever, he dabbled in political cartooning, another skill he had a natural aptitude for; and one which again turned his life around quite unexpectedly.

Daivik deliberately distanced himself from Catherine realizing that she belonged to someone else. Catherine got busy with her film shoots and with Daivik no longer in film journalism, their interaction reduced. Of course, they never forgot their special day and observed it by making sure they were together to cut a cake and spend a few hours of one-on-one time.

As the years went by, Catherine and Armaan began to drift apart. While Daivik sort of knew that all wasn't well between Armaan and her, he wasn't sure if Catherine wanted him to be privy to the details.

Daivik's hard-hitting cartoons, which fearlessly took on the Government for its all failures, gradually made him a household name among the readers of India's leading English daily.

Chapter 7

In 2008, Daivik became an instant celebrity when the Government arrested him on drummed-up charges of 'sedition'. Depressed over the Government's soft stance on terror and its greed for vote-bank politics, Daivik had drawn a rather contentious cartoon.

In this cartoon, he showed the PM, Devender Singh and the IDP chief, Mukta Prajapati holding a weighing scale in their hands. On one plate of the scale was the map of India and on the other were different, torn portions of the Indian map, each portion alluding to a particular community with their total percentage in the country's population. The plate which had the divided India was much heavier, even as the PM and the IDP chief celebrated the divide for their political gains. The cartoon was controversially captioned: *Who's the country's bigger enemy: the terrorists or the IDP?*

Within hours of the cartoon being published, Vijay Singh, a senior IDP leader and a die-hard sycophant of Mukta Prajapati held a press conference demanding Daivik's arrest under the contentious National Security Act. In a midnight arrest, Daivik was dragged out of his home and put behind bars. What followed were two days of nationwide protests until the Government realized its folly and had him released.

When Daivik came out of jail, he was surprised to see the sudden change in his popularity. In just two days, people seemed to recognize him on the streets. He was invited as a panelist for all important debates on the news channels, which he was only too happy to participate in. (What he found bizarre was the proposal to take part in a Reality show on TV, which he flatly refused.)

Daivik utilized his new-found popularity to intensify his campaign against a weak, ineffectual and corrupt Government. He soon became an RTI activist and filed a few queries that shook the Government again. For instance, post 26/11 when the Government was only too keen to make people believe there was 'no local involvement' in the attacks, Daivik filed an RTI query demanding that the Home Ministry reveal the local involvement, arguing that an attack of this magnitude was impossible otherwise.

Soon, he started a weekly column in India's leading anti-establishment paper, the *Indian Express*. So vehement and unsparing was his criticism of the Government's policies that soon enough, the Government had begun to contemplate other ways to shut him up. So, in March 2009, he was arrested again, this time for aiding Maoist insurgency. The Government had hoped that such a grievous charge would ensure a longer stay in jail; at least till the elections were over.

However, once again, the Government's machinations fell flat, when much to its shock, Shruti Ranjan took the issue of Daivik's persecution to the masses. She had started a mass campaign to have him freed. Soon enough, a massive signature campaign was launched to set Daivik free. With almost a million signatures seeking his release, the Government had to retreat on the back foot. Daivik was released as hastily as he had been arrested.

Daivik had sought an audience with Shruti Ranjan after his release.

'You are my inspiration, Ma'am,' he had told her with reverence. 'The country needs more leaders like you.'

'I think the country needs more intrepid fighters like you as well; individuals who are prepared to take on a flawed system,' Shruti reciprocated the praise.

This meeting between Shruti and Daivik had taken place on the eve of the 2009 elections when Shruti was hopping from one constituency to the other, campaigning for her party's candidates.

Sadly, after her party's shocking defeat in the 2009 elections, Shruti went out of the scene and Ravi Nehra became the president of the party. While most supporters of the Jan-Hit party did not approve of his high-handed, venal ways, given that in India the choice between its two national parties is often akin to choosing between the devil and the deep sea, there wasn't much erosion in the party's support base.

After their unexpected 2009 victory, the complacent, ruling IDP were emboldened enough to take the public for granted. Hence, what followed was a slew of financial scams, uncontrolled price rises and a general collapse of governance. Besides, Prime Minister, Devender Singh goofed up the only thing he claimed to know: the economy.

Even though Daivik had never been a great fan of Ravi Nehra, like many others, given the difficult choice between IDP and Nehra, he opted for the latter.

Driven by an intense desire to join the system and play a more proactive role in changing it, Daivik met Nehra in

2011 with an offer to contest the Ranchi Lok Sabha by-polls. The meeting was hugely disappointing, what with Nehra asking him to get a financial sponsor.

That night, when Daivik returned home after meeting Nehra, he couldn't sleep. He was hounded by words he thought he had forgotten, spoken in a voice that he could never forget. He would hear his grandfather's voice all night telling him, '*They are killing Gandhi...at least I did not kill Gandhi...*'

Over the last few months, conditions in the country had grown worse. A string of scams and scandals kept tumbling out of the IDP's cupboard. The Opposition Jan-Hit party would make a hue and cry about them for the first couple of days then conveniently sidestep the issue for something more frivolous.

And this trend continued.

Daivik kept up his crusade through his fiery column. But even he was getting disillusioned. How long could he keep up the tirade by himself? In the process, his professional life had gone for a toss. His film-making dreams were history, while his political activism was taking its toll on his work opportunities as journalist. People were wary of hiring a hot-headed crusader who had a penchant for rubbing the current establishment the wrong way.

And then, the 'coal allocation scam' or the 'coal-gate' happened.

In mid-2012, the Government of India was accused of allocating coal blocks in an inefficient and ad-hoc manner. The loss thus incurred to the public exchequer was to the tune of Rs 1,85,000 crores! Instead of following a process of competitive bidding, the Government allegedly allotted coal blocks in a partisan manner. The obvious speculation for the reasons for this, once again, was a possible quid-pro-quo arrangement. The beneficiaries must have offered something substantial to the ruling party in return.

The back-to-back 2G and coal-gate scams incensed Daivik. He was possessed by an intense hatred for the Indian political system. There was not a single political party that escaped his wrath, not even the regional parties, which he felt posed an even bigger threat to national interests. The absence of Shruti Ranjan – the idealistic leader of a betrayed nation – was being felt like never before. How Daivik wished she would return to the fray.

'These regional parties are like cheating wives. They will sleep with you or your neighbour depending on whoever is willing to spend more on them,' he wrote in one of his articles. So upset was he on the day he wrote this piece that he didn't even realize he sounded outright misogynistic. Soon enough some women's groups were up in arms against him, until he took great pains to withdraw his remark and tender an unconditional apology.

By now, despite his growing frustration with the system, Daivik was more determined than ever to fight the scourge.

On 2nd October, Gandhiji's birth anniversary, Daivik visited Raj Ghat. He stood in front of Gandhi's samadhi for nearly half an hour, just breathing deeply and trying to put his thoughts into perspective. Daivik was a bit nervous as he was set to embark upon the biggest challenge of his life.

An hour later, he stood at the Jantar Mantar surrounded by a few hundred people he had managed to gather through a Facebook campaign. With a determined look on his sleep-deprived face, he made a profound announcement:

'Gandhi is not dead. Not yet. They tried to kill him but he still lives in all of us. He lives in me, you and all of us who are assembled here... On the day of the Mahatma's birth, I hereby pledge that in exactly three months from now, that is on the first day of the new year, the people of India will have a new political party to serve them. This party will provide the real alternative to the IDP and the Jan-Hit party. It will be called the Azad Bharat Party (ABP).'

The crowd roared in applause.

Chapter 8

It was noon. Daivik and Catherine sat on her terrace reminiscing about their lives and the twists and turns that had brought them to this point.

Catherine couldn't stop talking about the depression that had lately engulfed her life. Now with her marriage over, and her career uncertain, so was her stay in India. The only thing that held her back were the recurring dreams that had now become an integral part of her psyche. Sharad Malviya had now almost completely replaced Subhash Chandra Bose as the soldier leading his men on the battlefield, with Catherine being entirely conscious of the inherent symbolism in it.

In the last eight years Catherine had allowed her larger India agenda to take a backseat. Now, with the prevailing chaos in the country, she wanted to revisit it.

At this point, the red light flashing on her phone indicated a BDTV update. *'Nirbhaya, the gang rape victim battling for her life in a critical condition, is being flown to Singapore for treatment.'*

Daivik was as aghast by the news. It was a weak Government's wicked gambit to avoid escalated protests and violence should she die here. Catherine broke down, and Daivik realized it was her overall state of mind that was causing her depression – just about nothing seemed to go right for her! When she regained her composure, he said, 'Catherine, frankly, I am getting sceptical of the plan to launch this new party…'

Catherine was surprised to hear her friend sound this diffident. 'But why? I think the timing is so apt…People want an alternative,' she said.

Daivik laughed dismissively. 'People don't know what they want. They'll still keep voting for the existing creeps.'

'But what is it that's making you so sceptical, especially now that the launch date is just four days away?'

'Catherine, I've been thinking about it, I don't have a single leader of stature with me; I don't have a cadre base; I don't have funds. Well, the internet is no doubt a powerful medium. But I'm not sure it can win an election in a country as vast and diverse as ours. What other option do I have?'

Catherine suggested solutions for the next one hour, all of which Daivik didn't find convincing enough.

'You need a public face to lead your campaign, right…?'

Daivik nodded.

'You need someone who is perceived as incorruptible, has a proven credibility and enjoys public support, right?'

Daivik nodded again.

'And what if the person is just as well-equipped to champion the present burning issue – women's safety?'

Daivik wondered what she was getting at.

'Shruti Ranjan!'

Daivik dismissed the option when he heard it. 'Catherine, you are so naïve. The whole country knows that Shruti will never come back. She had sworn not to…'

Daivik's negativism didn't deter Catherine: 'I think she will. I have a hunch she will; provided we reach out to her now.'

Daivik was unconvinced, but seeing his best friend's optimism, he felt his hopes lift despite himself.

Chapter 9

(Dhar, Madhya Pradesh)

The 80-km-long drive from Indore airport to a small village called Ramti in the district of Dhar in the Malwa region of south-western Madhya Pradesh was an unexpectedly picturesque one. Amid the lush green farmlands were scenic views of beautiful lakes at the bottom of ruined fortresses, which stood testament to the district's tryst with history. However, these sights, which Daivik and Catherine would have enjoyed immensely on any other day, failed to spark their interest. Today, there was just one thought on their minds: *what would the outcome of Mission Shruti Ranjan be?*

The Tata Indica cab took a left turn off the highway. For the next 3 or 4 km, they drove through a narrow village road. There was no farmland along this stretch. In fact, it seemed quite barren.

'I hope someone isn't deliberately trying to mislead us,' said Catherine.

'Are you sure we are going in the right direction?' Daivik asked the driver.

He smiled: 'Don't worry.'

Finally, another ten minutes later, the first semblance of civilization came into view. A broad wall and a gate became visible. They couldn't make out much except that it was not a concrete structure, but made of wood or bamboo.

It was a modest ashram, with an equally modest nameboard that said, *Aatma Nirbhar Mahila Ashram* (Self-Reliant Women's Ashram). The boundary walls were made of bamboo with just two lathi-carrying security guards keeping vigil over the property.

Once inside, Daivik and Catherine were astonished by the expanse of the place. All 100 acres of it! They were led into the front office, where Chhavi Gupta, Shruti's personal assistant, was waiting for them. After a quick exchange of pleasantries, Chhavi said, 'Daivik, shouldn't you have sought a prior appointment with Shrutiji instead of just calling me from the Mumbai airport and saying you'll be here in three hours?'

Daivik thought to himself that if he had done that there was no way this meeting would have happened.

'Won't Shrutiji meet us today?' he asked, playing down his confidence.

'Well, let me speak to her...she is in a meeting with an NGO...but if you tell me your agenda, it might help...'

Daivik was about to speak up when a look from Catherine stopped him. 'Umm, there's something we want to talk to Shrutiji about...we'd like to tell her directly,' he said.

'Okay, I'll go and speak to her but it might take some time. In the meantime, why don't you have a look around the ashram? I'll ask one of the ladies to show you around.'

Daivik had briefly interacted with Chhavi in a meeting he had had with Shruti in 2009. Chhavi had been Shruti's trusted confidante for the last five years and doubled as her official secretary. Besides that one meeting, Daivik had spoken to her a couple of times when he had wanted to convey his thoughts on certain issues to Shruti. So, after the previous afternoon's brainstorming with Catherine, when Daivik had finally decided to reach out to her, he knew it would not work if he sought a formal appointment. Hence, he had used his access to Chhavi to try and force this meeting.

With their fingers crossed, Daivik and Catherine strolled around the ashram campus with a lady to guide them. Even in their preoccupied state, they were enchanted by the planning and design of this one-of-a-kind ashram.

One half of the ashram was a gurukul with classes till the sixth standard. Here, any girl who was deprived of education – either because she was an orphan or because her parents were unable to finance it – was provided a free education. The girls were from different parts of the country and at any given point of time, the gurukul had 300 students. There were six, modestly-furnished classrooms, each accommodating a batch of approximately 35 to 40 students. The dormitory was behind the classrooms and comprised 100 bamboo huts, each accommodating three students. To the left of the dormitory was a play area and a library cum common room. The canteen was on the right.

The attendant informed Daivik that Shruti personally held some of the classes here, besides being involved in all aspects of the development of the students. Catherine looked deeply impressed when she heard this. Even as they were talking, the school-bell rang and a crowd of happy, chattering girls filled the compound.

'It's 12:30; that's when classes for the day get over,' smiled the attendant.

'Yeah, that's such a happy time in the day of a student… when she knows she's done with the school for the day…' laughed Catherine, recalling her schooldays in Vienna. Daivik too had a couple of memories to share from his junior school days in Harazibagh.

'So what sort of schedule do these students follow at the gurukul?' he asked the attendant.

The students' schedule was strictly marked out: wake up at 5:15 a.m., be ready for yoga by 6; breakfast at 7:30, prayer Assembly followed by classes between 8:30 to 12:30; then lunch between 12:45 and 1:45; rest till 3; physical exercise and games between 3:15 and 5:30. Homework and studies between 6 and 8. Dinner between 8: 15 and 9. And every child had to be in bed by 9:30 to wake up at 5:15 the next day.

'That's a tough regimen!' exclaimed Catherine.

'Well, when your leader leads by example, everybody around is encouraged to maintain standards. Shrutiji herself follows a very demanding schedule, often sleeping for just four hours at night…'

Daivik was pleased to hear this. It made him think that Shruti would be battle-ready. The very next moment, though, he cautioned himself knowing they were still not beyond the realm of wishful thinking – not until they had had their conversation with Shruti and Shruti had consented.

Catherine's thoughts were interrupted by a news update on her cell: *Doctors in Singapore not too optimistic about Nirbhaya's chances of survival.* The update immediately brought back the grim reality of the day.

The attendant, in the meantime, took Daivik and Catherine to the other side of the ashram. This section housed the adult inmates. Here, women worked during the day making papad and candles that were sold in the nearby villages and towns.

The more talented among these women made handicrafts that were lapped up by customers in bigger towns like Indore, Gwalior and Bhopal. The revenues thus generated were put back into the ashram for more advanced skills. For instance, those who were interested, got training as nursing attendants. Still others were educated in organic farming techniques, and found employment with NGOs working in the rural sector. In fact, the ashram had even tied up with a well-known Madhubani artist who came and stayed in the ashram twice a year and taught this ancient art style. A few of the women, in fact, had shown a great aptitude for Madhubani, what with their paintings even making it to Delhi's Dilli Haat...

'Wonderful...I can't believe it...Shruti has been doing so much for the country even when she's not in politics...' exclaimed Catherine.

'Well, I always knew she was a genius...an underestimated one...I don't think anybody else would have managed so much in just three years,' added Daivik.

A female voice responded to this from behind. 'I didn't have an option, Daivik. I was a failure in Delhi...As such I had nothing but this to do,' smiled Shruti.

'Sh...Shrutiji?'

Daivik and Catherine were overwhelmed. Just seeing Shruti standing in front of them after all these years filled them with awe. When she had suddenly decided to quit public life three years ago, the news had left the country shaken. Daivik himself had been very depressed that night. But, luckily, destiny has a mind of its own! Here he was, facing the woman whom he considered next only to Goddess Durga.

Shruti looked very different from the way they remembered her. Her long hair, the soft smile on her face, and the basic personality were the same but there were other, more subtle, changes. She had lost weight and in fact, looked a lot fitter and more radiant than she had when she was in Delhi. Daivik thought it was the result of the *ashtanga vinayak yoga* that she was practising religiously that had brought an extra glow to her face. Her dressing had changed too. She was dressed in a simple white saree with a navy blue border and a blue blouse.

Fifteen minutes later, they were seated over cool glasses of nimbu paani in a sparsely furnished room. Chhavi sat with them. 'Frankly, I've been quite lucky in being able to set up all this. It's all thanks to a supportive, Jan-Hit party government in Madhya Pradesh. The CM, Dheeraj Singh has always held me in high regard. Even after I quit the party, he was the first to meet me and offer this 200 acre government land and free electricity to set up this ashram. And that was such a god-send. Without his support, I wouldn't have been able to do any of this. But,' she continued with a sigh, 'the future is a bit uncertain. Assembly elections are round the corner. If Dheeraj Singh does not come back to power, then the IDP Government could possibly create hurdles for me…vendetta politics, you see…'

As the conversation proceeded, Daivik and Catherine were still undecided about how to broach the issue they were here to discuss.

'So Daivik, tell me, what brings you here?' asked Shruti, looking at her watch.

Daivik looked down for a brief moment, to gather the courage to look into Shruti's eyes when he spoke. 'Shrutiji, the country...well, the country needs you back in politics...'

For a moment Shruti's face registered no expression. Then she smiled sadly: 'So *that's* all that you've to say and for which you've travelled all this way?'

'Shrutiji, you must be aware I am floating my Azad Bharat Party...'

'Yes, I know...I don't read newspapers or watch much TV but every morning Chhavi briefs me on the latest that's happening in the country. I am happy for you...you've come a long way...' Shruti sounded consciously detached.

Daivik didn't know how to proceed with the conversation. After all, there wasn't the remotest hint yet of Shruti even being partially ready to consider the idea.

'We have a very special *khichdi* prepared today for lunch. You guys go with Chhavi. I'll join you in a bit,' said Shruti, turning away from them.

'Ma'am, have you heard of Nirbhaya, of the gang rape that has shocked Delhi? A beautiful, innocent girl was raped... her attackers will go unpunished if...' Catherine stopped talking as suddenly as she started, her eyes welling with tears.

Shruti turned to face Catherine. 'I am,' she said softly, looking into her eyes.

'Ma'am, at this time – now more than ever – the country needs a woman leader like you! Please, Ma'am, shouldn't you come back?'

Shruti smiled wryly. 'If you ask me, it is women leaders who have failed the country. One corrupt woman leader spent her term as CM erecting statues of herself; the other spends her time abusing one and all, while her party-workers dismiss rape incidents as 'deals that went wrong'. Isn't Mukta Prajapati a woman leader too? With such obnoxious examples, this country should actually dread women leaders.'

'Ma'am, the country needs you.'

'No, it doesn't...If it did, it wouldn't have let me down twice in successive elections...Every country gets what it deserves and this country deserves a Ravi Nehra...' Calming herself a bit, Shruti added, 'I have been a failure, Catherine...All the years that I was active in politics, was I able to bring down the crime rate for violence against women? Then what gives you the confidence to think that I can make a difference now? On the other hand, I feel responsible towards these 600 ladies staying in my ashram...I can't abandon them...'

'But, Shrutiji, aren't you also answerable to all those people who have pinned their hopes on you?' exhorted Daivik.

'Look, Daivik, today I am too inconsequential to make any change in the system. In fact, you are better equipped than me to pull and move a crowd...and that's what really matters.' A deep sense of betrayal was evident in Shruti's words.

Daivik and Catherine exchanged a dejected look. Perhaps Shruti was too fixed in her stance to consider a rethink. 'Shrutiji...I think you're just happy in your comfort zone. I think you're being selfish!' Catherine accused her all of a sudden.

The insinuation worked pretty well in provoking Shruti. 'How dare you presume to understand my reasons...?'

'Well, that's what I think...you're being selfish.'

Catherine's words made Shruti flare up further. 'Do you realize who you are talking to? Politics took away everything that belonged to me – my husband, my mentor, my family. Yet I did not quit because of them. I quit when the country insulted me with the most humiliating defeat...And you call me selfish? Wow!' Shruti was stung by Catherine's accusation.

'Defeats are meant to be avenged, Shrutiji, aren't they? At least this is what I heard you say in one of your speeches in the last elections,' Daivik joined the fray.

Shruti's anger hadn't subsided. 'Yes, they ought to be avenged, but not necessarily by the losers...change is the order of the day...even you can avenge my defeat, Daivik.'

'Daivik can't, Shrutiji. He can't do anything on his own and that's the sad truth...He needs someone of your stature,' Catherine said emphatically.

Catherine's calculated barbs were by now enough to really offend Shruti. Looking her straight in the eye she said, 'By the way, I can understand Daivik's involvement in politics...he's been an RTI crusader for the past many years...but what makes *you* so active all of a sudden, Catherine? How much do you know about India, anyway? How much do you understand of the political system here? Are you even familiar with what a map of India looks like?' After a pause she added rather rudely, 'Or is politics a last-ditch effort to remain in the limelight? After all, aren't you already past the retirement age for Bollywood heroines?'

Catherine responded with complete calm. In fact, she *wanted* Shruti to question her motives. 'Shrutiji, I know

India as much as any ordinary citizen here does, perhaps even a little more. How many Indians actually know that the country has 629 districts in all? How many of them know that the country has a coastline as long as 72,000 km? How many of them know that the existing bilateral trade between India and Pakistan is estimated at $ 1.94 billion for 2011-12? I know these facts because I care for my country. I know about the total number of districts because two years ago, I wanted to understand the distribution of poverty across the country. I wanted to understand if there were specific districts and states that are worse off in education, basic health care and electricity generation. I was concerned about the country's coastal security and hence dug up umpteen articles to learn more about India's coastline. And last year, when the Pakistani army brutalized some of our soldiers, I wondered why India couldn't penalize Pakistan by cutting off all bilateral trade. If we did so, who would have been more at a disadvantage – India or Pakistan? I never spoke to the media about this as the media knew what it wanted to write about me! If I tried too hard, they would have probably passed me off as a fake.'

Shruti was surprised when she heard this. 'Interesting! Quite interesting! And what is it that evokes so much interest in the country?'

'A dream!'

'Dream?'

'Yes, a recurring cluster of war-time visuals where I see an Indian army-man leading his troops, fighting against humongous odds with nothing but a dream and his determination to spur him on…I have been getting this dream for the last 27 years!'

Shruti was intrigued.

'Who is the Indian soldier who comes in your dream?'

'Subhash Chandra Bose.' For the next half an hour Catherine spoke about her inspiration, her love for India and that childhood dream that never set her free.

Shruti was impressed by Catherine's passion. 'Interesting; very interesting! So it's Subhash Chandra Bose who has propelled you into Indian politics...?'

'Well, Bose certainly inspires me. But there is someone else who inspires me even more.'

Shruti looked even more curious.

'Sharad Malviya.'

Shruti looked askance when Catherine said this, so she went on to explain: 'Isn't Sharad Malviya in many ways a reincarnation of Subhash Chandra Bose? I mean, the same valour, the same selflessness towards the country, the same radical approach, the same single-minded focus and, sadly, the similar way in which they both met their deaths...'

Shruti went quiet when she heard this. Perhaps she didn't like being reminded of the circumstances of Sharad Malviya's death.

'Shrutiji, trust me, Sharad Malviya reminds me so much of Bose – the way Emilie described him,' Catherine said.

Daivik added: 'Shrutiji, along with you, we want to keep Sharad Malviya alive in this country. We can't let his ideals die...'

Shruti went numb. As she sat pensively in her chair, her face cupped in her hand, she couldn't prevent herself from becoming emotional. She knew Daivik and Catherine were quite brilliant at emotional manoeuvring; otherwise they wouldn't have succeeded in bringing her to the point where she felt guilty of letting Malviya down if she stayed away from politics. But she also knew that this was not the truth. Would she once again give herself to being a part of other people's agendas? No, she did not need to do so.

'Are you finished?' she said brusquely, disappointing her guests.

'Shrutiji, are you...?' Daivik asked hesitantly.

'No. I am not getting back to politics. And my decision is final.'

Saying this, Shruti walked out of the room.

Chapter 10

By 10:30 p.m. the gurukul and the ashram had shut down for the night. Everyone was in bed, but sleep eluded Shruti as she sat at her table, her silhouette illumined by the light of her table lamp, her mind deep in rumination of the past. She had been deeply disturbed for the last week, ever since she had first heard about Nirbhaya's gang rape but after today's meeting with Daivik and Catherine she couldn't help feeling guilty.

Did the country need her? Was she letting down the women of India by choosing to distance herself from the power-brokers of the country?

She deeply regretted not having pushed for the death penalty for rapists while she was around. But today, was she really capable of making a difference to the situation, as Daivik and Catherine wanted to make her believe? Even as these thoughts floated in her mind, Catherine's words, drawing a parallel between Bose and Sharad Malviya echoed sharply in her ears:

Isn't Sharad Malviya in many ways a reincarnation of Subhash Chandra Bose? I mean the same valour, the same selflessness towards the country, the same radical approach, the same single-minded focus and the similar way in which they died...'

Right then, there was a knock at her door.

'Chhavi?'

'Ma'am, before he left, Daivik gave me a CD for you. I was so caught up in work during the day that it slipped my mind. Here it is!'

Chhavi handed a CD to Shruti, wished her goodnight and then turned to leave. Shruti had been feeling an unusual forlornness all evening; the sort she had experienced in the dark days immediately after Sharad's death. She wanted to tell Chhavi to sit with her for sometime but Chhavi had already left.

Shruti slipped the CD into her laptop. What she saw deeply shocked and disturbed her.

The CD had minutely detailed, day-to-day coverage of the seven days following Nirbhaya's gang rape – including some particularly graphic details of the five accused confessing to the atrocities they had committed on her. Daivik had been rather astute in assembling this CD as it evoked an immensely strong reaction in Shruti. As Shruti watched the CD, she was besieged with doubts about the country. If the capital was so unsafe, how terrible must it be for women in small towns where incidents like these didn't even get reported?

Had Delhi become this unsafe at 9:30 p.m. in the evening? Could depraved men brazenly hunt for their hapless prey, disguised as bus drivers and conductors? Had society become so sex-starved that it brutalized a woman whose only fault was that she did not give in to the demand for sex by strangers? Was this the new punishment for not giving in to forced sex – getting beaten and prodded with iron rods in your private parts, then being thrown out of the bus naked, and finally almost being run over by the bus?

It had been three years since Shruti had actually watched a news bulletin on TV or read a newspaper. She would just tell herself that what was happening in the world outside her ashram didn't concern her. But today, for the first time, she regretted her ignorance. She tried hard to understand whether a Nirbhaya-like rape was an aberration or whether it mirrored the stark truth of a society that was too meek and cowardly to prevent Nirbhaya-like instances from happening.

As Shruti watched the CD again, she began to feel queasy. It reminded her of her own Nirbhaya moment, fifteen years ago. It brought back memories of the January night she had wished so fervently had never existed for her. She could recall everything so vividly: the foggy winter night as she sat alone in her car waiting for the driver to get a mechanic; a jeep stopping, and four men pouncing upon her. She was violated by four beasts who forced themselves upon her turn by turn, each trying to be one up on the other by doing something more depraved. Shruti had felt like a deer captured by hunters, but instead of killing her at once, the hunters chose to inflict the most unthinkable barbarism upon her, rejoicing at the sadistic pleasure it gave them.

Shruti knew what young Nirbhaya must have gone through because Shruti was also a Nirbhaya.

Half an hour later, Shruti was seated with a huge pile of newspapers from the last two months. As she scanned each one of them attentively, the creases on her forehead increased: there was a factor that she found deeply disturbing: in the last 60 days' papers, there were 33 days when a brutal crime against a woman had been featured on the front page. This, she felt, raised a big question mark over India actually being called a 'civilized' nation.

Shruti felt a primal anger that she didn't know still seethed within. She wanted to do everything she could for Nirbhaya; or if it was already too late for Nirbhaya, then for the millions of other Indian girls who suffered all sorts of abuse at the hands of men. But, sitting here in her ashram, she was no longer in a position to do anything. Would Nirbhaya survive? Given the massive damage to her internal organs, would she ever be able to lead a normal life? Would her psychological scars ever heal?

Shruti knew that for Nirbhaya surviving death was only her first battle. If she did live, getting her life back to normal would be a much more daunting challenge.

As Shruti thought about Nirbhaya, she was reminded of her own days immediately after the tragedy; how she'd closed herself off from the world and cried for hours, agonizing over her fate; of Rohit and her running from pillar to post to get justice; of her discovering that her husband was too weak to be able to trust her implicitly; of her attempting suicide and finally of Sharad Malviya entering her life and giving it a different direction.

Fortunately, Shruti's life soon saw a rise as meteoric as the fall prior to it had been steep.

However, what baffled her at this point was not her steep rise but her unceremonious fall after the rise – which had eventually made her quit everything. Even though Shruti hated herself for doing so, she couldn't help thinking about the man who was the exact antithesis of Sharad Malviya: Ravi Nehra.

She disliked him with all her heart.

Chapter 11

In December 2004, the Delhi High Court had sentenced Shruti Ranjan to three years imprisonment for plotting to have five terrorists killed. The penalty for a crime of such magnitude would have been much higher but it was thanks to Ved Kaushal, one of the country's top-most lawyers and his brilliant defence, that Shruti's sentence had been significantly reduced.

Ved's defence had been simple: the killing of five terrorists was in the national interest. He put forth intelligence reports received by the Home Ministry that said that terrorists across the border had drawn up a comprehensive plan to intrude the tiny southern-most island of Minicoy in Lakshwadweep. Around 100 terrorists were supposed to enter Minicoy from Male, the capital of Maldives, which was just 110 km south of the island. These terrorists were then supposed to quickly distribute themselves along the 10 km length of the island and take its 10,000 odd population captive. They would subsequently have demanded the release of the five terrorists languishing in Indian jails or started killing the inhabitants of Minicoy in instalments.

Thus by killing these five terrorists, Shruti had actually ensured the safety of 10,000 lives. How then was Shruti's offence heinous? Instead, it was in the best national interest. The Government lawyer argued that the intelligence reports notwithstanding, killing of terrorists was still no option; the Government could have easily sealed off the Minicoy island.

To this, Ved argued that what if the terrorists had changed their plans at the eleventh hour and attacked another island of Lakshadweep, say Kalpeni or Agatti, each one of which was just as isolated, and as vulnerable to intrusion?

Despite some obvious flaws in Ved's defence argument, the one advantage that Shruti enjoyed was of public perception. Even as the trial was on, Ved's argument won huge support from the public. In a poll conducted by a leading news channel, a record 83% of the respondents felt that what Shruti had done was truly patriotic. Finally, when the court passed its judgment, taking all aspects of the case into consideration, it gave a lenient three- year jail term to Shruti. As Shruti had already spent fifteen months in jail by then, her sentence was completed in 2006.

Rhea had wanted Shruti to appeal against the High Court's verdict in the Supreme Court, but Shruti had been against the idea.

'But what happens to our plans of launching our new party?' Rhea had asked.

'Big battles need more time for their planning and execution. Let us bide our time…' was Shruti's reasoning.

And hence it was decided between Shruti and Rhea to defer the launch of Nationalist League (Sharad) to 2006 end, after Shruti was released from jail. Shruti, in the meantime, got down to passionately reading up all she could on electoral and governance systems across the world. She would spend a good ten to twelve hours of the day in jail reading books and write-ups which her friend and lover from her college days, Abhay, would send her.

'I think I was plain lucky in my first innings. I managed to achieve whatever I did without any hard work or preparation. This time I don't want to leave anything to chance. I want to come fully prepared,' Shruti would tell Rhea when she visited her.

Inspired by Shruti, Rhea had got down to writing a biography of Sharad Malviya. For a daughter who barely knew her father when he was alive, it was a journey of self-discovery. Sharad's friend from the Communist Party, Mohammad Salim, spoke to her about Sharad's vision of starting a post-graduate college for developing political leaders. 'The dearth of quality leaders saddened Sharad no end. Often during our private conversations at parties, he would lament how the land of Swami Vivekanand, Gandhi and Bose did not have leaders anymore. He held the IDP's dynastic politics responsible for the malaise,' Salim had informed her while adding, 'Though we opposed him publicly and in Parliament, *secretly* we all admired Sharad's guts. He was a born leader.'

Every time, Rhea would hear someone talk about Sharad with such regard she would regret not having spent more time with her father.

Even as Rhea worked on the book diligently, she kept her social life alive. Like other young people her age, she'd occasionally go to pubs and nightclubs where she didn't mind letting her hair down. In fact, battling her own forlornness, she made some new friends at one of the nightclubs she frequented. They included a young MP from Rohtak, Ravi Nehra.

Time flew as it is prone to do. And on Sept 25, 2006, Shruti was released from jail after completing her prison term. Rhea, Abhay, and her parents were there to escort her out. They did not tell Shruti about the scene outside the jail as they wanted her to witness it first-hand: a good 30,000 plus people had assembled outside the jail to greet Shruti! They continuously raised slogans of: *Desh ka neta kaisa ho, Shruti Ranjan jaisa ho!* Shruti was simply overwhelmed; not for the first time was she confronted with the self-doubting query: did she really deserve this adulation?

She still did not have an answer to this except that the adulation had strengthened her resolve to do whatever she could to reciprocate the love of the people.

23rd January, 2007 was to be the D-day: the day Rhea would formally launch the biography of her father Sharad Malviya. This was to be followed by the formal launch of their new party, the Nationalist League (Sharad).

A massive ceremony took place at the Siri Fort auditorium, where the country's president, Swati Oak released Sharad Malviya's biography. '*Sharad Malviya was the best PM that India never had,*' said Oak.

Speaking on the occasion, ex-PM, Yashwant Modi said, 'Even when I was the PM, I think Malviya was a busier minister than me...He just wanted to do so many things for the country.'

It had then been Shruti's turn to speak.

'While everybody raves about Sharadji's leadership skills what mesmerized me about Sharadji was his rare ability to inspire even someone as passive as myself...Sharadji is not dead. He is alive in me, in Rhea, and in countless other Indians who want India to adopt his style of hands-on, aggressive, uncompromising leadership...He is alive in all of us who truly care for our country...'

With Shruti's impassioned speech, the Nationalist League (Sharad) was formally launched, with ten office-bearers. Shruti was its working president, while Rhea its general secretary. Even as the politicos present at the venue watched the developments with anticipation, every time Rhea's name was announced or when she spoke, the loudest claps came from her new friend, Ravi Nehra, the glint in whose eyes was hard to hide.

It was also here that a student who had just passed out of IIM Kolkata, Chhavi Gupta, first met Shruti. Chhavi was so inspired by Shruti that instead of taking up a corporate job, she wanted to assist Shruti in setting up her new party. Shruti was reluctant to take Chhavi on initially as she would not be able to pay her a quarter of what Chhavi would derive from a corporate assignment. 'It doesn't matter, Ma'am. Someone has to sacrifice for the larger good,' Chhavi had told her with a selfless smile. Within weeks of working together, Chhavi, with her hard work, dedication and work ethics, had become indispensable for Shruti.

The evening after the book launch, Rhea had decided to chill at her favorite disco. Giving her company were Ravi Nehra and some other friends. That night the DJ played an eclectic mix of some very catchy retro numbers in both English and Hindi. Both Ravi and Rhea were particularly fond of this kind of music and had a blast dancing to it. In no time, they were several pegs down. And in that inebriated state, Ravi, out of nowhere, started shouting: 'Three cheers for Sharad Malviya! Three cheers for Sharad Malviya!' Ravi, the wily bastard, knew exactly where to fake what. Here he knew the advantages of faking his reverence for Malviya.

Rhea was moved when she heard him cheer for her father. 'Hey, Ravi, what are you saying?' she queried, flushing with pride.

Ravi pretended he did not realize what he was uttering: 'Gosh! I am so drunk.'

That clever bit of play-acting helped in earning him a private dinner with Rhea where the conversation treaded more personal ground. 'I am in politics because of Sharad Malviya,' professed Ravi, with the confidence of a corrupt minister who attests his honesty time and again. 'Whenever I am in doubt, I draw inspiration from his speeches.'

Rhea confessed that she missed her Dad a lot. 'Sharad Malviya' thus helped the two break the ice. It gave them a common topic for conversation and bonding. It bred a sudden familiarity that seemed too innocent for Rhea to realize its repercussions.

Soon the conversation veered to Rhea's plans of promoting her father's biography. 'I so wanted to visit the Jaipur Literary Festival this time to try and promote the book there. Besides Salman Rushdie, whom I just adore, has a session today,' Rhea had mentioned in passing, even as she added ruefully, 'Sadly, my friend with whom I was planning to go, ditched me at the last moment…'

As a new author, Rhea knew how important a literary festival was for networking and promoting her book; for his part, Ravi knew how to exploit the slightest emotional weakness he spotted in her.

'What time is Rushdie's session?'

'At ten in the morning.'

Nehra looked at his watch. It was 2:30 a.m. 'Come on, then, there's no time to waste...'

Half an hour later they were speeding off on the Jaipur Highway in Nehra's SUV with Nehra abandoning his security cover, like he often did.

Rhea was fairly surprised at the way she had behaved in the last few hours. She had befriended a near stranger and was now driving with him to Jaipur all alone! Was Sharad Malviya, to whom the stranger professed his loyalty the only reason for this bonding or was there something more?

She tilted her face slightly to steal a better look at the man whom she'd suddenly opened herself to: brooding eyes, stubble, sharp features, a tall build and long hair that was deliberately a bit unkempt. Nehra was just that wee bit unsophisticated; he still faltered with his pronunciation of certain English words. But then he would more than make up for it with his other style statements: driving the latest BMW SUV, wearing the most exotic cologne and the most expensive Tag Heuer wristwatch.

His tastes in music though were perfectly desi. He liked soft music in private and loud dance numbers at a party. With the pretty Rhea by her side though, he played some Bryan Adam numbers, thinking she would appreciate them better than Hindi music.

As they sped along, Ravi didn't talk very much; he seemed to be lost in his thoughts. And Rhea was completely intrigued by this desi jat who was driving her all the way to Jaipur !

Chapter 12

In 1991, when the Government opened up the economy, it drew massive investment from foreign countries. Some of the biggest MNCs subsequently set up shop in India; in the years to come India became an IT hub and many satellite towns came up near bigger cities just to accommodate the economic boom.

Around 1991, large areas not far away from where the City Centre stands in Gurgaon today, were farmland. The Nehra family owned one such plot of approximately 3 acres, where they grew jowar, bajra and mustard since time immemorial. Ramesh Chandra Nehra, Ravi's father was an only brother with four sisters to marry off. As such, he had a tough time catering to his familial responsibilities. Each time the family had to marry off a daughter, it would have to mortgage something or the other. The first time it was jewellery, the second time it was their modest house, and the third time it was their farmland.

However, Ramesh showed a clear disinterest in pursuing the family profession. He was a dreamer who wanted a lavish life. At the same time, there was little by way of education (tenth class failed) that supported his big dreams. He would thus vent his frustration by beating up his wife after getting drunk with his friends. Along with his friends, he'd often indulge in petty thefts to finance his drinking needs.

Two good monsoon years in the late eighties when Ramesh's father, despite his old age, took the entire onus of farming activities in his hands, helped the family recover partially from its financial mess. Ramesh had two sons – Rajinder and Ravinder (Ravi). Rajinder was dull, unintelligent and lazy, while Ravi was the more promising of the two, often surprising his father with his street-smart ideas, which gave an indication of his wily genius. As such, while Rajinder was made to discontinue his education and help in the family's farming activities, Ramesh took great pains to ensure that Ravi studied for as long as it was possible.

Thanks to Ramesh's sheer lack of interest in farming, a stage came when the farmlands were rendered unproductive. Driven to the point of desperation, Ramesh collaborated with two of his cousins in the infamous Mewat region, south-east of Gurgaon, to rob highway passengers. They indulged in this misadventure every once in a while and made enough to help them survive the next couple of months. On two occasions, they stole cars which they later illegally sold in Rajasthan.

Due to their infrequent indulgence, they managed to evade the police as well. On one occasion, when a local police inspector had pinned Ramesh down, he gave half his booty to the inspector. The inspector was more than happy to close the case. On another occasion when Ramesh went underground, he stayed with his cousins in Mewat as they lived in an area so notorious that the police dreaded raiding it. Another time, Ramesh was bailed out by an estranged second cousin of his, Harjit Dangi, who was an MLA in the Haryana Assembly.

At least the booty thus made helped Ramesh's younger son appear for his matriculate exams. However, tragedy struck once again when Ramesh lost his wife to a cholera outbreak in the district.

The family's misfortunes thus continued. Though Ramesh was making a decent amount of money, he led an uncertain existence. A new Superintendent of Police had taken charge in the area. He was known to bump off petty criminals – particularly those with a history of bullying the administration – in fake encounters. For the first time, Ramesh feared for his life. He wanted to live at least till the day he had ensured that his son Ravi would not have to do the same things for survival as he did.

However, miracles do happen; and very often they happen in the darkest phases of life, when they are least expected. While Ramesh Nehra grappled with his unending troubles in his small world, he had no idea of the changes taking place in India's financial world. He had no idea that the barren land which he so detested would make him a millionaire overnight.

In late 1992 the Government decided to buy out Ramesh's land to develop a Special Economic Zone. Ramesh bargained hard for nearly six months until he got an extremely lucrative deal that earned him Rs 11.5 crore, which was an amazingly exorbitant amount in 1993, when the deal was finalized.

This deal changed Nehra family's life in a way he would not have imagined. Ravi Nehra who was sitting at home for two years after completing his matriculation was quickly enrolled in a leading public school to complete his Plus Two. For this, Ramesh doled out a hefty donation, besides hiring two tutors – one to hone Ravi's mathematic skills and the other to help him speak English. Ramesh had a clear vision for his son. In two years' time, Ravi was packed off to London to do his graduation in business management. It's another thing that Ravi took an extra year to complete the course as he wasted a year, partly in jail on charges of drug peddling and partly in a de-addiction centre!

All along, Ramesh's confidence in his son remained unfazed. By the time Ravi returned to India, Ramesh had created a huge real estate business of his own, facilitating land deals similar to the one that had changed his life. Ravi, at 23, with a degree from a foreign university and vastly improved English- speaking abilities, inherited this business.

Of course, beneath that veil of sophistication, Ravi's true self would often spill out, like the time when he made a pass at someone at a disco without realizing that the female in question was the daughter of Delhi's commissioner of police; he had to thus spend a night in jail. On another occasion, he got into a traffic brawl with another hot-headed youngster. Ravi had hit him so hard that the youngster had to spend nearly two months in hospital.

Ramesh spent a good amount of money on Ravi's anger management. He enlisted the services of a spiritual guru, Yogi Maharaj, who operated out of an ashram in Mehrauli. Ravi would visit the guru thrice a week to practise yoga and other methods to calm down.

All along, Ramesh had a larger plan for Ravi and, more importantly, he had full confidence in the plan bearing fruit. Finally, the time to execute his big plan arrived.

Harjit Dangi, a five-time MLA and a minister in the Haryana Government, who happened to be Ramesh's Chandra's second cousin was clearly going through a rough patch. One year ago he had to quit as Minister after a sting operation showed him as being the kingpin of a major money-laundering scam. Now Assembly elections were round the corner. Even though Dangi was determined to contest it, if not as his party nominee then as an Independent, things really seemed to be going against him. Dangi had been recently diagnosed with cirrhosis of the liver whose treatment required an immediate liver transplant. To add to his woes, Dangi was childless and didn't have a political heir.

This is when Ramesh, bolstered by his new financial clout, approached Harjit with his son. Ramesh had a plan up his sleeve. 'Let my son contest this election. He will keep the seat for you till you return,' Ramesh had suggested confidently.

'How will that help me?' queried Harjit, taken aback.

'You need immediate treatment which is not possible in India. The Enforcement Directorate is keeping a strict vigil on your spending while your own party is waiting for the right opportunity to completely dump you. In this situation the odds are stacked against you from all sides.'

'Talk about the deal.'

'Make my son your political heir. I will personally fund your entire treatment in the U.S. with my personal money, besides settling and converting all your illegal hawala money and routing it back into India as white money.'

Harjit was still in two minds until Ramesh rubbed it in further. 'Actually you have a simple choice to make. You have to choose between death and life.'

Harjit agreed reluctantly and thus kick-started Ravi's political career when he won his first Assembly elections as a Haryana Janata Party candidate from the Assembly seat of Badshahpur in Gurgaon.

Harjit eventually died within days of checking into the U.S. hospital, while Ravi's father Ramesh Nehra was shot dead in Mauritius a year later where he had gone to explore and fix some hawala channels. It was speculated that Ramesh in his mad greed for multiplying money, had double-crossed the Dubai gangster, Aslam Bhai.

Ravi took to his career in politics effortlessly, almost like a fish takes to water. With the necessary guile, money and muscle-power required in contemporary Haryana politics, he continued to rise higher and higher. From the real estate agency that Ramesh owned, Ravi later expanded into the hotel and aviation businesses as well. Ravi's business empire would finance his political career while the clout gained via his political career would help him expand his business manifold. It was a new form of a mutually beneficial businessman-politician, co-existent, double role that he had discovered and was determined to exploit to the hilt. Much after Ramesh's death, people close to the family finally acknowledged what a genius Ramesh was to have foreseen such promise in the black sheep, Ravi.

Three years after becoming MLA, the ambitious Ravi contested his first Lok Sabha polls, from the unfamiliar constituency of Rohtak. This was a dicey seat for the party and the party wasn't finding the right candidate for the seat, when Ravi audaciously volunteered to contest, giving the first clear hint of his national ambitions. Even though Ravi won the seat only by a slender margin, he later consolidated his position by winning the seat a second time five years later, this time with a record margin.

There was something that really worked for Ravi, despite his dubious sources of funding: it was his deft posturing as a pro-development leader. In his constituency Ravi had facilitated some exceptional irrigation schemes, besides improving the electricity supply considerably. From a normal 12 hours average load-shedding at the time he first became an MP, the constituency now experienced only 3-4 hours load-shedding a day.

Thanks to these positive changes, Ravi was hailed as a hero in his constituency and enjoyed immense popularity.

At 33, even though Ravi had tasted and adequately enjoyed every material pleasure in life, including having sex with more than 550 women besides experiencing nearly all forms of alcohol and party drugs, deep within, he was an unsatisfied man. True to his irrepressible ambition which he had inherited from his illiterate father, he wanted to tread beyond Haryana politics. He wanted to be a key player in national politics.

Ravi, in fact, had been relentlessly scouting for the catalyst that would make his shift to national politics a reality.

Interestingly, Ravi Nehra's father had committed a major blunder earlier in his life, whose repercussions continued to haunt Nehra even after his death.

After Ravi Nehra had been sent abroad to study, Nehra senior's life had only become lonelier and he had taken refuge in alcohol, gambling and women. He took to picking up call girls and taking them to a famous South Delhi hotel. His favourite room number was 205 as he swore by the number 7. One day, he waited in his hotel room for a call girl to join him there, but the woman ditched. So Ramesh tried making a pass at the gorgeous receptionist. He tried flirting with her without much success except for finding out her name: *Anu Dangi*. The surname only increased his fondness for her as she belonged to the same community as he did.

Ramesh visited the hotel several times before Anu had a change of heart and accompanied him to his room. Once there, he was about to kiss her when she firmly pushed him away. She then unzipped him and massaged his organ with her hands, her confidence indicating that perhaps she wasn't doing something like this for the first time.

Ramesh was quite surprised by the woman's confidence. Of all the women he had slept with, none took charge like Anu. And the domination continued right till the end when she had pushed him away, saying: 'Only my husband will enter me.'

Ironically, Anu was a divorcee with a two-year-old daughter, Diya. Ramesh was completely fascinated by Anu – her sexual brazenness coupled with her ability to say a firm no when she wanted to.

Ramesh was so enamoured that he ended up professing his love for her. And when she still played hard to get, he cut his palm and wrote her name in his blood. At times, he wondered if he was doing all this just to have sex with her, but the fact was she had become an obsession for him. He thought about her day and night. Three months later, Ramesh had married Anu.

Ravi Nehra never liked his stepmother. Ramesh too, within months of his marriage, also realized what a blunder he had committed by marrying the whore. Anu was involved with at least two other men at the same time and her interest in Ramesh was only in his wealth. Her act of not allowing Nehra sex was a tricky ploy to make him fall for her, which only further showed how well she knew the psychology of men.

When Nehra had confronted Anu over her other affairs, she denied them vehemently. But one day, the senior Nehra laid a trap and caught her red-handed. Two weeks later, Anu died a mysterious death. When the senior Nehra was out of town, she supposedly committed suicide by consuming phenyl. It was rumoured that Ramesh Nehra had had his wife killed by getting her poisoned, and had then used his clout to manipulate the case in his favour. Diya was taken away by Anu's sister to live in Mumbai.

Diya grew up to become a model who shot into the limelight when she stripped nude for a men's magazine. Later, she began posting outrageously revealing videos of herself on her website, besides giving scandalous quotes. She was desperately trying to make a career in Bollywood. Unfortunately, the only offers that came her way were for C-grade, low-cost films or TV shows like Big Boss. Diya knew that if she had to make it big in Bollywood, she would have to star opposite at least one of the top ten heroes. Until the time that happened, she had little option but to live without her clothes.

Diya nursed a strong grouse against the Nehras as she was pretty sure from what she had heard from her aunt that her mother had been killed. When Ravi Nehra became an MP, she tried getting in touch with him. Ravi avoided her like the plague until she got the better of him on one of his Mumbai trips. Much of Ravi's hatred for her was also on account of the fact that his astrologer and spiritual guru, Yogi Maharaj had predicted that Diya would create major problems for him one day.

Chapter 13

Ravi and Rhea reached Jaipur at around 8 a.m. – the early morning fog delaying their travel time considerably. Once there, they quickly checked into a hotel room, freshened up, and left for the venue of the literary festival; Nehra for a change content to let Rhea decide the flow of events.

It was a sunny, pleasant day on the front lawns of Diggi Palace in Jaipur, the best that a winter morning in the Pink City could get. Salman Rushdie addressed a large crowd of book-lovers with Rhea Malviya and Ravi Nehra seated in the third row from the front.

Rhea was ecstatic to be there; she listened to Rushdie attentively hoping to catch up with him later and present him the biography she had penned on her father. Ravi, on the other hand, looked a little out of his depth, trying to keep up an amiable smile, both for Rhea and for the people around.

As the session ended, Rhea headed towards Rushdie, while a section of the media made a beeline for Nehra: 'Nehraji, such a pleasant surprise to see you here…we didn't know you were such an avid lover of literature…'

Only Nehra knew that he hadn't ever read a novel in his life – in English, Hindi or Haryanvi.

'So tell me Nehraji who is your favourite author?'

Nehra was in a fix; until his eye caught Rhea chatting with Rusdhie. 'Rushdie! Who else?' was his hasty response. 'There's no one better than Rushdie.'

'And which is your favourite book?' queried another journalist.

'*Five-Point-Someone*,' was the prompt response. Nehra remembered seeing the book lying on his table. A well-wisher had recommended the book saying it would help improve Nehra's English. Nehra had read the first few chapters before putting it away – like he had every other book.

Just then, Rhea came gushing up to him. 'Ravi, you should have come with me, see this...' Rhea showed him a picture clicked with Rushdie on her cellphone, then hugged him spontaneously. 'Thanks for making this possible,' she said, oblivious of the press people lapping it all up.

After attending the morning session of the literary festival, the two of them decided to go sight-seeing. Ravi had always wanted to visit the famous Amer Palace in Jaipur. There was a reason for his yearning which he could not divulge to the world: one of his distant relatives was a *mahaut* (elephant trainer) who ferried tourists at the palace on his elephant. Ravi had grown up hearing stories about this rebellious relative who had run away from home to chart out a destiny of his own. In Amer, Ravi suggested they take an elephant ride around the fort. And as they rode the elephant, Ravi felt a joy only someone in his position would understand. He felt proud to have graduated to riding on top of the elephant's back, when until now the family's biggest achievement had been becoming an elephant trainer! This time, it was Ravi's turn to exude childlike excitement, and Rhea's turn to be fascinated with him.

In the time Ravi and Rhea spent together, what she liked most about him was how uninhibited he was. His telephonic conversations with party-workers were generously flavoured with rustic invectives, which he used as a habit. Apparently, he also had a female admirer or two, who called repeatedly until he ticked them off saying, 'Sweetie, *kahaa na, aaj nahi*...call you tomorrow.' She wondered what it was that he wanted to deny her today! Ravi, for his part, did not feel the need to hide any conversation from her; which she appreciated. At least, he was not a put-on, she thought. Rhea even found Ravi's penchant for smoking bidis cute: 'It gives a kick which even an imported cigar does not,' Ravi had explained to her.

'But what about the crude nicotine content in the bidi...that's very high...' Rhea had cautioned, with an amused laugh.

'Who cares? Nobody lives forever. Neither you, nor me,' Ravi had shrugged, before adding on a more serious note, 'Anyway, I have a hunch I will be assassinated – like your dad was!' Ravi knew exactly how to win Rhea over; the last sentence was calculated to affect her.

'You think my father was assassinated?' Rhea asked tremulously.

'Well, I can't think of any other way his plane would have crashed like that. It was clearly sabotage...everybody knew Sharadji would be our next PM.'

Rhea's eyes welled with tears. Ravi knew how sensitive Rhea was about Sharad's death and the astute manner in which he played her was all part of his guile. Seizing the opportunity, Ravi hugged her; their second hug of the day, this one much more confident and familiar.

By the time, Ravi and Rhea started on their journey back to good old Delhi, they shared the comfort level of friends who had known each other for years. This was surprising considering both were polar opposites. Perhaps it was this that attracted Rhea to him. Rhea also admired Ravi for being the self-made man that he was. To have made his mark as a politician, with no pedigree, was no mean task in the Indian scenario. Rhea wanted to know more about his world: who were these people, supposedly his followers and activists, who had direct access to him and could call him anytime of the day? Who were these women who seemed to enjoy greater preference in his scheme of things?

Ravi had another reason for wanting to win over Rhea. He had always been in awe of Sharad Malviya and to woo and win over his daughter marked his ascent into the privileged strata of society – whom his folks had only dreamt of serving in the capacity of drivers, peons and the like. Could he woo a girl from a world that had ostracized him and his clan all these years? This, for him, was a true measure of success in life; it was another manifestation of the inferiority complex that refused to leave Ravi and which he was too arrogant to acknowledge.

A massive traffic jam on the highway caused by an accident led to Ravi and Rhea getting delayed by a few hours. At 10:30 p.m. Delhi was still over 50 km away. This was when Rhea spotted a cosy looking dhaba and on an impulse asked Ravi if they could have dinner there. Ravi was only too happy to oblige.

Ravi felt completely at home in the dhaba, throwing himself upon the charpoy and humming a Haryanvi folk song. Within minutes, they sat over a sizzling meal of tandoori chicken and butter naan, with plenty of beer to wash the food down and a bonfire to add to the atmosphere. That night the temperature had suddenly dipped, leaving both shivering.

High on beer and the presence of the lady, Ravi suggested they play a game of *antakshri.* However, like everything else he did, the game was to be played on his terms. 'You can sing English or Hindi songs, while I will sing only Haryanvi songs...' Rhea consented, thinking it would be fun. And fun it indeed was! She couldn't comprehend a word of what Ravi sang, but was completely charmed by his wild dance moves! They had a blast singing and fooling around, completely unmindful of the people staring at them. When they finally sat down, Ravi's phone rang again. From the way he spoke, Rhea could tell it was one of his women admirers. As he cut the call he was confronted with a weird query: 'Are you a womanizer, Ravi?' Rhea asked him sweetly.

For a moment, the question left Ravi struggling for an answer; then he grabbed the beer bottle lying next to him and started shouting, 'Three cheers for Sharad Malviya! Three cheers for Sharad Malviya' – in a rather obvious attempt to side-step her inquiry.

When Ravi started his SUV for the final lap of the return journey, he noticed Rhea was shivering as the January night was quite nippy. In true chivalrous style, he took off his jacket and draped it over her shoulders. A few minutes went by. Ravi drove the SUV at average speed, not getting the right momentum. Sensing something amiss with him, Rhea realized *he* was trembling. 'Hey, you're shivering, Ravi...take this jacket...you need it.'

'It's not the cold...it's something else...' Ravi said.

'What?'

Ravi pulled the car up on the side of the road. 'Will you slap me for what I do now?' he asked, feeling too shy to look into her eyes directly. Before Rhea could answer, Ravi leaned over and kissed her on the lips. Then, scared of the consequences, he retreated immediately, until Rhea held his hand and said, 'Do it again...and hold it for sometime...' guiding him with the confidence of a woman who knew exactly what she wanted and how she wanted it.

Ravi and Rhea indulged in a long passionate kiss, which when it happened, only seemed a logical extension of the way things had been shaping up between them since the night before.

After they kissed, Ravi got back to the wheel and started driving. No words were exchanged in this last hour of the journey. Both were lost in their thoughts and needed time to figure out if the last 24 hours had been a fantastic dream or if the things that had happened between them were for real.

Chapter 14

Rhea and Ravi did not meet for a fortnight after their trip to Jaipur as Ravi was first travelling abroad and then got busy with the Budget Session of Parliament.

Rhea wondered what it was about Ravi that was making her so enthusiastic about him. She wondered if it was her loneliness. She was sure it was not a rebound relationship; after all, it had been four years since her boyfriend Derek had been gunned down before her eyes, and she had not been with a man since. She had consciously chosen this long phase of abstinence to make sure that the next man who entered her life, did so for the right reasons. For a girl who had had her first kiss at fourteen and had been in a relationship with four men, it was indeed a long gap. But then, the thing about the heart is that it is used to defying the mind when it decides to. Rhea wanted to meet Ravi again. She was very attracted to him and wanted to get to know more about the good-looking desi jat.

Ravi, on the other hand, was playing a mindgame of sorts by making himself unavailable; besides he simply hated the idea of falling in love. He had always been clear that if he'd marry someone, the gap between their first sexual encounter and marriage had to be erased. He detested the idea of courting someone and 'being in love', which he found alien to his worldly pursuits. 'Love is the most bogus thing in the world – made believable only by Hindi films. Stop watching those silly films and you will never fall in love,' he'd quietly brag to his male buddies.

Rhea found her feelings confusing. She desperately wanted to share them with the one person whom she could turn to in a situation like this. But Shruti Ranjan had been spending most of her time travelling across the country. And Rhea wasn't sure if she could have a conversation as sensitive as this on the phone.

Being a true ideologue and the inheritor of Sharad Malviya's politics, Shruti knew that the Indian elections couldn't be won over news channel debates or by scoring brownie points in Parliament; they had to be won where they were actually fought: in the villages and smaller towns that constituted the real India. Hence, she was on a 120-day tour across the country to whip up momentum for her new party and help it form local cadres. On this campaign tour, she intended to cover as many as 300 constituencies in two phases of 65 days and 55 days respectively.

She had just completed a tough day, holding three back-to-back rallies in Cuttack, Bhubaneshwar and Konark in Orissa when she got a long sms from Rhea.

'Methinks I'm falling in love again...don't know if it's illusion or for real but things have been different these last few weeks...'

Shruti called Rhea immediately, more out of concern than joy – which also made her wonder if she had indeed grown too old. The first thing that Shruti wanted to know was who the guy was.

'Ravi Nehra, the Haryana Janta Party MP from Rohtak.'

Ravi's reputation preceded him, and Shruti was not unaware of it. Hence, the name did not evoke a positive reaction from her. Instead, she waited to hear more. Rhea told her all that had happened in her life these last few weeks: the Jaipur sojourn where it had begun, followed by two weeks of separation, followed by two more weeks of late-night musings over coffee in Lutyens' Delhi's five-star watering holes. Rhea and Ravi had met four times now, including once when Ravi had dropped in at Rhea's residence at midnight after completing his day's work. They had talked late into the night, sharing their strong antipathy for the ruling Government and discussing ideas and plans to de-throne it.

Ravi was now more forthright about his political initiatives and his vision for the country, which Rhea found quite impressive. His generous praise of Sharad Malviya, whenever possible, had only made the association more robust. Rhea and Ravi had begun to see the possibilities of a synergy between their political plans, which in turn increased their personal proximity.

'That's good news, Rhea, that's really good news... Listen, I'm concluding the first phase of my yatra in the next two days...after that I'll be in Delhi for a week and we'll have a long chat over this, okay...?' said Shruti, trying hard to mask her worries. The first thing that struck her, when she heard Ravi Nehra's name, was his alleged involvement in a major irrigation scam, besides his closeness to a dubious industrialist speculated to be involved in hawala money transfers.

That night, when Shruti finally lay down to sleep, she recalled the first intimate conversation that she and Rhea had shared, many years ago, on a roof-top restaurant in south Delhi. Seeing her mentor Sharad Malviya upset over his daughter's rebellious attitude, especially after the death of her boyfriend, Derek, Shruti had tried to make Rhea see reason. In a surprisingly candid heart-to-heart conversation, Shruti had tried convincing Rhea to find a guy and move on. Rhea, on the other hand had surprised Shruti by suggesting that Sharad and she get married.

At that time, Shruti had a felt an unusual maternal instinct take birth in her. She felt the same protective instinct towards Rhea now. Like a mother, she wanted to be sure Rhea was taking the right decision. In the very next moment, though, she hated herself for arrogating upon herself an authority she wasn't entitled to. Why did she want to behave like Sharad Malviya's wife when she wasn't? The thought revived memories of the father–daughter turmoil that she had been privy to. It made her wish yet again that the man who had meant so much to her had not left her all alone.

Three nights later, Shruti and Rhea met at the very same roof-top restaurant; their favoured spot for meaningful conversations.

'Shruti, I have no idea what's happening to me, but there's something about this guy that makes me want to meet him again and again…Maybe it's just that he is so remarkably different from all the other guys I've met; he's so cool about being desi…He is so damn confident about himself…He lets me be the way I am. Despite me wanting to meet him more often, he seems so calm and detached…I guess that's what attracts me to him,' Rhea explained.

'Are you aware of the guy's antecedents?' Shruti asked abruptly.

Rhea looked a bit surprised, wondering what Shruti was getting at.

'Ravi's uncle, whose political legacy he was bequeathed, was forced to resign as minister in Haryana over allegations of involvement in a money-laundering scam; Ravi's father was shot dead in Mauritius under the most mysterious circumstances; his 'stepmother' was bumped off in a supposed suicide. Ravi is very close to two very controversial people: Godman Yogi Maharaj and rags-to-riches industrialist, Vicky Bhalla.'

'Shruti, aren't allegations a part of public life? I mean even someone like Dad was not spared. Besides, trust me, Ravi is just too simple to be the rogue that the media projects him to be,' Rhea said.

'Are you also aware that Ravi has a reputation for being a womanizer? And that someone from his constituency had once accused him of rape?' Shruti played the Devil's Advocate.

'I am,' smiled Rhea. 'And he has been very candid about his past. The rape accusation was dismissed by the court in its first hearing. But, more importantly, I asked him why he was not married yet.'

'What did he say?'

'That he never found love, nor had the time for it. He says he has probably found it now.'

Shruti couldn't help a wry smile at the uncanny resemblance of the situation to the one she'd witnessed Sharad in, over Rhea and Derek, many years ago. Was Rhea really that gullible or was she just a habitual rebel?

'So when can I meet Mr Nehra?' Shruti had asked her quietly.

On the following Sunday, Shruti, Rhea and Ravi Nehra took a two-hour drive to Rohtak, Ravi's constituency. Ravi had, somewhat persuasively, invited them to have lunch with him there. He wanted to show them the work he had undertaken for its development. Over the last seven years, Ravi had invested most of his MPLADS(MP Local Area Development Scheme) in developing a 50-acre plot into a skill development village.

'In India, demand for unskilled labour is huge, but because of lack of training and erratic supply, they are seldom utilized optimally. They often can't deliver quality work and as such continue to remain unemployed or under-employed. What I've tried to do here is to set up a skill development centre for as many as fifty different skills for which training perhaps does not exist in India…' he explained proudly.

Ravi's work was indeed impressive. While on the one hand, there were farmers, industrial workers, drivers, carpenters, plumbers and construction workers, on the other, there were women who were being trained to become beauticians, cooks, and masseuses. Another section had young boys who were being imparted sports training, especially in athletics and archery. Each of the unskilled workers enrolled in four-week courses, with lessons four hours a day. Upon successful completion of the training, they would get a certificate. Bolstered with this training, these trained workers were encouraged to travel to nearby towns and cities like Delhi, Gurgaon, Noida, Faridabad, Ghaziabad, etc. In each of these cities, Nehra had tied up with several NGOs and low-end employment bureaus to help them provide employment.

'In the last seven years, I have helped at least 70,000 to 80,000 poor people from my constituency find employment,' he had boasted.

He then took them to a small hospital, which he had constructed through private aid. In this hospital, named after his father, Ramesh Nehra, any cancer patient suffering from any form of the disease could avail of consultation for just Rs 2. Depending upon the patient's financial status, Ravi would then fund half, or at times even the full amount, of the treatment through his NGO, *Upchaar*. This NGO was funded mainly by his friend, Vicky Bhalla.

'Again in the last seven years, we have helped as many as 10,000 cancer patients by bearing the cost of their operation, either partially or fully. More than 70% of them have survived. One of them, a pandit, even constructed a small temple for me in his village. I demolished that temple when I visited the village last year,' he laughed boastfully.

Shruti, who was battling a mental block against Ravi Nehra, thought it ungracious not to compliment him on his good work. 'Impressive!' she said, politely.

'Thank you, Ma'am.' Ravi's intention behind being so demonstrative about his altruistic pursuits was to convey to Shruti that their sensibilities weren't that dissimilar. Like her, he too was doing his bit for the poor and needy. He knew that the thought, once seeded, could grow in Shruti, perhaps making her more receptive to him in the future.

An hour later, Ravi played the gracious host over lunch, serving his guests the best of Mughlai cuisine, prepared by his personal chef. Mutton Durbari, Mughlai Chicken Pulao and Keema Mattar were some of the delicacies that adorned the table.

'I'm a vegetarian,' Shruti said quietly.

Ravi profusely apologized for not knowing this and immediately asked his chefs to make some Navratan Korma, which they hastily rustled up.

When Rhea excused herself to go to the washroom Shruti took the opportunity to frankly ask Ravi, '*Do you love Rhea*?'

For a moment, it seemed Ravi did not have an answer. Then he rolled up the left sleeve of his shirt, revealing a large tattoo, with four letters encrypted on it: RHEA.

'What about all the allegations that keep surfacing against you... at times of money laundering, at other times of financial impropriety in your business and your sources of political funding?' Shruti remained unrelenting.

Ravi put his right hand on the tattoo and swore on Rhea's name in typical oath-taking fashion: 'There's no truth in these allegations. The truth is what you saw today. That's why these allegations haven't affected my political journey at all.'

On their way back to Delhi, Rhea felt relieved and Shruti reassured. 'So what do you think of him now?' Rhea asked Shruti curiously when they were alone.

Shruti knew Rhea well enough to know that she would eventually do her own thing. So she replied: 'From here on, it's going to be your decision all the way.'

Rhea knew that for someone as guarded about her emotions as Shruti was, this was her way of giving her the go-ahead.

That night Ravi stayed back in Rohtak and spent the evening boozing with two of his childhood friends, Gopal and Raju, who were now handling his work in the constituency. Despite his obvious success in wooing Rhea, he seemed nervous and anxious.

'Oye, what are you worried about now? You've almost got her, haven't you?' queried Gopal.

'Almost! There's often a slip between the cup and the lip, especially when the girl in question is Sharad Malviya's daughter,' he replied.

'*Abbe yaar*...the truth is that you don't love the girl, you love Sharad Malviya's daughter,' chided Raju.

These words ruffled Ravi for a moment before he gathered himself and brazenly spelt out his agenda: 'The truth is that I neither love Rhea, nor Sharad Malviya's daughter...I love power; the greater the power, the greater my love,' he laughed as he drained a glass of whisky on the rocks.

'But are you sure about the marriage bit? Such girls don't mind romance, but marriage is different stuff. She's supposed to be a rebel, isn't she?' Gopal sounded a note of caution.

Ravi turned towards him, smiled, and spelt out his plan, 'There's a way to deal with such women...Make sure there's no gap between sex and marriage.'

Four days later, it was Rhea's birthday; the day Ravi had chosen to kick-start the 'foolproof' plan that he already had in mind for her.

Rhea had woken up at around eight and sauntered into her living room to find it decked with the most gorgeous decorations that she had ever seen. There were twenty-seven bouquets of red roses in the room – one for every year of her life. A huge banner adorned her living room with *'Happy B'day, Rhea!'* painted on it. And then, as she came to the centre of the room, in true filmi style, flower petals showered down upon her! Ravi had planned everything to perfection. His staff had got in touch with Rhea's maid to allow them in at four in the morning to do up the place. Ravi had personally supervised every bit of the surprise and then made them all leave.

Now as Rhea took it all in, he stood behind her, thrilled to see her respond with such joy.

Rhea had still not seen him. Ravi, though, eyed her longingly – at the red thong rising above her micro-shorts; at the scanty night shirt that didn't hide the fullness of her breasts. He walked up to her from behind, pulled her by her thong and kissed her hard. Rhea could feel his erection and couldn't stop herself from unzipping him. In no time, they had made love on Rhea's sofa, abandoning all restraint. For Rhea, these twenty minutes had been the most blissful start to her birthday ever.

'Thanks Ravi,' was all that Rhea said once they were done, with it seeming pretty clear what the gratitude was for.

'Hey, that's not all,' said Ravi. 'I have a surprise for you.'

'What?'

'Get ready...we'll go on a drive. But listen, can I make a small request? Will you wear a saree?'

'Have you gone crazy?'

'Please, Rhea, for me?'

Ravi drove Rhea straight to a secluded spot on the banks of Lake Damdama, 40 km away from Delhi, surrounded by the Aravalli Hills on all sides. Rhea was mesmerized by the beauty of the spot; she could never have imagined a place as serene as this existed such a short distance from home. A few steps away stood a small, ancient Shiva Temple. Ravi held her hand and led her towards it. What Rhea saw here left her nonplussed.

There were two priests waiting for them, with all the paraphernalia needed to perform a wedding ceremony – including a small makeshift mandap for the pheras. At that point, two boys came in, one carrying two massive flower garlands for the bride and groom, while the other carried an elegantly simple kurta and pyjama for Ravi. Rhea looked at Ravi in shock. Before she could ask him anything, Ravi had the answer ready. 'I want to marry you, Rhea. I want you to be my wife.'

Rhea tried to make sense of the hasty marriage. Ravi said his *saadhe-sati* or the seven-and-a-half year spell of Saturn was starting next week, making it an inauspicious phase for marriage. Besides, he was madly in love with her and found it difficult to be away from her. What better day than her birthday to make her his wife?

'Raviji, the auspicious mahurat for the day is getting over,' warned one of the pandits.

Ravi turned to Rhea. 'Listen babe, don't worry. We will make our marriage public only when you are ready for it, okay? But trust me, I've got both our horoscopes studied and we won't find a better day than this for many years.' Saying this, he hugged Rhea. 'You stay here for a bit. I'll quickly change into the kurta and come.'

Rhea, left to herself, looked out into the horizon, into a seamless firmament where the sky met the earth. She quietly stepped aside and imagined having a chat with her father.

'Dad, I'm getting married. I don't know whether I'm taking the right decision or not. But as you always told me, it's better to do something you believe in and fail, rather than not do it and regret it all your life. I believe in marriage; I believe in the man who wants to make me his wife. Dad – I so wish you were alive to witness this moment. I need your blessings, Dad...'

Rhea and Ravi exchanged the seven vows of Hindu marriage on the banks of the lake. Then Ravi put some sindoor in the parting in her hair. 'You are husband and wife now,' declared the pandit.

Rhea just looked into the horizon, nervous and unsure but also happy deep within.

'Why hasn't Guruji reached yet?' she heard Ravi ask someone on the phone.

After the marriage was solemnized, they waited for a good half hour for the 'guruji' to arrive. Rhea wondered who this guruji was, but Ravi wanted it to be a surprise.

And then they saw a car approach. As the car drew closer, Rhea saw it was a Mercedes. The tinted windows though gave no idea of who sat inside. The silver-coloured car finally drew up in front of them, and out stepped a saffron-clad, heavily-bearded entity with two gun-toting bodyguards in tow: it was the controversial Godman, Yogi Maharaj, who was only recently out of prison for alleged FERA (Foreign Exchange Regulations Act) violations. Ravi instantly touched his feet and asked Rhea to follow suit.

'Guruji is my spiritual mentor,' he informed her. 'No important deed of mine is ever formalized without his blessings.'

As Rhea touched the guruji's feet, he blessed her by putting his right palm over her head. And when he did so, she got a closer view of his eyes: one bloodshot and the other probably of stone; both capable of scaring away the faint-hearted.

'May you both have a very successful marriage with lots of children,' blessed Guruji.

As Ravi got down to chatting with his guruji, Rhea felt her first tinge of apprehension. She wondered if like the sudden marriage and the equally sudden entry of the guruji, there were more surprises in store for her. Her thoughts were interrupted by Ravi asking: 'Rhea, have you informed Shrutiji about our marriage?'

Shruti was holding a rally in a small village in the Medak district of Andhra Pradesh, rooting aggressively for the creation of the Telangana state. 'We have always favoured the creation of smaller states, especially when such a move helps meet the legitimate aspirations of the people of the given region. Besides, such a move strengthens the federal structure of the country. As such, I promise you all today that if you vote the Nationalist League (Sharad) to power in the next elections, we will create a separate state for Telangana within ninety days…'

As Shruti was speaking, she saw Chhavi gesture to her, indicating an urgent phone call. Shruti excused herself to take the call.

'Shruti, I just got married,' Rhea said without ceremony.

Shruti's heart sank.

'Ravi and I just took our marriage vows in this beautiful place… I can't tell you how wonderful it feels… but it's gradually sinking in that I am a married woman now.'

Shruti congratulated her, then hung up, promising to call back.

'We will have to put all our efforts together to uproot the IDP Government in the next elections…Jai Hind!' she said, ending her speech abruptly. She had reasons for the sudden disorientation.

Chapter 15

When Ravi and Rhea bent to touch Shruti's feet and take her blessings, she found the whole experience alienating. Ravi was only a couple of years younger than her. But then Hindu tradition considers touching an elder's feet the most accepted and preferred means of seeking their blessings. An 'elder' here need not be so in terms of age; Shruti was elder to them by virtue of her personal proximity to Rhea's father. But that remembrance did not make Shruti particularly comfortable, perhaps because, despite her 'elder' status, she had very little say in Rhea's marriage.

Shruti, thus, quickly got over the formality, wishing them luck before the three got down to having dinner at her place. 'I am sad you both didn't wait for me to complete my yatra before you got married,' she commented, trying to gauge Ravi's reaction.

'Well, Shrutiji, I was getting into the inauspicious *sadhe-saati* phase you see. And I didn't want to delay my marriage for that long. I didn't want to lose Rhea.'

Shruti was not impressed by his answer and said as much. 'I mean, you're not quitting politics for the next seven-and-a-half years, are you?'

That Shruti did not particularly like Ravi was pretty apparent. What surprised her was Ravi's efforts to reach out to her. As they got chatting, it was but natural for their conversation to veer towards politics. 'All through my yatra, I could feel the winds of change. Seldom has the anti-establishment sentiment been as strong as I see it today. People want change. They are determined to throw out this government,' she noted enthusiastically.

Ravi did not share her optimism. 'I feel the Opposition needs to organize itself better if the IDP Government is to be dethroned next year,' remarked Ravi, before elaborating further: 'I mean, right now the Opposition is fragmented. The Nationalist League and the Nationalist League (Sharad) are going to cut each other's votes and then there are the Left parties. The divided Opposition will only help the IDP sail through again.'

'Hmm, I understand what you're saying, Ravi. But what's the solution? We were forced to create a new party because the Nationalist League had begun to behave pretty much like the IDP.'

Ravi spent the next few moments pretending to think about it, before he uttered his solution: 'Merger. The Opposition parties must merge to dethrone the IDP… that's the solution!'

'You think that will be possible?'

'Politics is the art of making the impossible happen. Let me think this through.'

Shruti's sixth sense had warned her that there was a much larger agenda attached to Ravi getting married to Rhea. She hoped though that her hunch was wrong; she hated the thought of Rhea being used by her husband for political motive. But then it doesn't take long for a person's intentions to reveal themselves. In Ravi's case, it took a mere two weeks.

'I have a master-plan, Shrutiji,' he said confidently to her, dropping in unannounced two days later. 'One that will ensure a change in Government next year; and make you the next PM.'

The first prospect definitely interested Shruti; the latter reeked of Ravi's attempt at sycophancy, which she did not care for. Ravi, nonetheless, went on to spell out his ambitious plan. Ravi's proposal aimed at bringing all non-IDP parties together on one platform. It required parties to let go of their individual identities and to merge together to form a new party by the name of the 'Jan-Hit party'.

'Think of it. Conditions today are as bad as they were during the Emergency. We can't beat this IDP Government by fighting our battles separately. It is a well known fact that after heading the Government for five years, there is no way we can match the IDP's resources. What we can do is come together and consolidate the anti-IDP votes under one block. That's how the Janata Party Government was formed in 1977. And that's precisely what I am suggesting now: an amalgamated Jan-Hit party that can form the Government next year.'

Ravi's plan was too ambitious and idealistic to find Shruti's favour immediately.

'What you say makes sense, but only theoretically. The 70s was a different era. The present-day leaders don't have enough fire in their bellies. They'd much rather continue to sit in the Opposition than take the kind of risk your plan entails,' Shruti noted.

'What if I make it happen?' responded Ravi.

Ravi's plan was contingent upon two factors. The first was Shruti agreeing to be the Jan-Hit party's PM candidate. The reason for this was simple: in a recent poll conducted by a news channel, as many as 42% respondents felt that Shruti was the best-suited candidate for the PM's post. The octogenarian ex-PM, Yashwant Modi followed with 14% votes, whereas Ratnesh Prasad and Ratna Pandey could manage support from only 9% and 7% respondents respectively. Current PM Devender Singh was favoured by less than 5% of the respondents.

Being the rationalist that Ravi was, he was doing no personal favour to Shruti; he was merely making his task easier by letting Shruti's goodwill work on the masses. He wanted to use her as a cover. After all, his own reputation was sullied with allegations – to have someone with credentials as impeccable as Shruti's at its helm would be a huge advantage to the party.

The second factor upon which Ravi was relying heavily was the behind-the-scenes support of the two most shady and controversial figures of recent times: Yogi Maharaj and Vicky Bhalla; a fact he had decided to conceal from Shruti, lest it negated the whole plan.

Yogi Maharaj was a small-time tantrik and astrologer with whom Ravi first came into contact when his father had sent him to the yogi's ashram many years ago for a course in anger-management. In the years that followed, the yogi's stock had shot up rather dramatically. It began with him accurately predicting an election result in Haryana that nobody believed would come true. His prediction was not based on his knowledge of electoral trends; it was based on the personal horoscope of a relatively lightweight MLA, Chaudhary Sundar Lal. After studying Sunder Lal's horoscope, Yogi had predicted that he would be the next CM. When Yogi first made the prediction, people laughed at him; they said he had gone mad. Two months later, though, Sundar Lal, indeed, became the CM of the state, superseding two very senior CM candidates. This was a shocking result that nobody except the yogi had predicted.

After being sworn in as CM, Sundar Lal publicly acknowledged Yogi Maharaj's genius and the maharaj's stock grew overnight. In fact, four years ago, when Mukta Prajapati had realized that it would not be possible for her to become the PM, she was in a big dilemma about whom to appoint to that post. That was when a friendly journalist set up a meeting between Mukta and the yogi. Mukta provided him the birth details of three contenders: Arnab Chatterjee, Abhimanyu Yadav and Devender Singh. Yogi studied each of their horoscopes in detail before drawing his conclusions. 'Arnab is the most competent, but his horoscope paints a poor character. You can never trust him fully and he might just backstab you at a crucial juncture. So best avoid him,' the yogi inferred.

'Abhimanyu?'

'There is a negative yoga looming over him which might make him die in two years' time, leaving the government unstable.'

'I see, and Devender?'

'He is the most meek, loyal and trustworthy of them all, qualities that personally suit you. Besides, I see one more advantage with him.'

'Which is?'

Yogi looked at the horoscope closely again before adding, 'His raj yog starts very soon. If you make him the PM now, he might continue for the next ten years.'

Thus Mukta's choice was made and Devender was made India's PM.

From that time on, there was no looking back for the yogi. His small ashram in Manesar was soon shifted to a sprawling 100 acre plot, provided to him by the government. Yogi became a champion-fixer. Politicians would throng to him to have their horoscopes shown. And in many cases, he was known to exorcize astrological impediments by performing long and very expensive yajnas. Thanks to his political contacts, he began to wield an authority that was clearly disproportionate to his means.

Yogi, as the cunning 'deal-maker' was rumoured to be instrumental in the formation or fall of at least half-a-dozen state governments in India. Moreover in 2006, when the Government faced an uphill no-confidence motion in Parliament, it was again the yogi whom Mukta came calling on, to save the Government. And Yogi did so by convincing the regional satrap, Bunty Paswan, to abstain from voting at the eleventh hour.

However, as often happens, Yogi soon got caught in his own web of deceit. A month after bailing the Government out on the no-confidence motion, Yogi was arrested by Interpol on charges of defrauding a London-based businessman of $200,000. Besides, several charges of repeated violations of the Foreign Exchange Regulation Act were levelled against him. A much-delayed income-tax raid on his ashram uncovered original drafts of payments to one of the world's most notorious illegal arms dealers, Abdullah.

Pressured by a massive Opposition onslaught led by both the Nationalist League and Shruti Ranjan, the Government was left with no option but to dump the yogi. The yogi was arrested and charges of FERA violations were aggressively filed against him. Two months later, when the yogi was released on bail, there was no one to receive him at the ashram – except Ravi Nehra.

Ravi, having known the yogi for years, knew that the yogi was down but could never be out. The betrayed yogi, on his part, saw an able natural ally in Ravi. 'Ravi, I want this Government out. The IDP threw me away like a used condom. I want to avenge this humiliation. I want to teach Mukta Prajapati a lesson. Will you help me?'

Ravi answered in the affirmative, after which the yogi laid out his comprehensive plan. It's strange how an enemy's enemy is a friend; the more powerful the enemy's enemy, the more his stakes increase in your scheme of things. It was the yogi who had first come up with the theory that the only way the IDP could be dethroned was if the Opposition stopped fighting among itself and chose the right PM candidate! Yogi had shared his thoughts with Ravi Nehra.

The other key player in Ravi's master plan was the liquor baron, Vicky Bhalla. Vicky and Ravi had first met in school where they did their Plus Two together. If there was something that brought them close it was their nouveau riche backgrounds; their families' rags-to-riches story. Vicky's father sold gol-gappas from a small stall in old Delhi. The family's fortunes changed the day they managed to obtain the licence for a liquor shop. From then, there was no looking back. When the second generation took charge, Vicky expanded into liquor distributorship, multiplying the family's income several times.

But the real game-changer was Ravi introducing Vicky to the yogi. The yogi used his influence over the Haryana CM, Sundar Lal to work out an incredibly lucrative deal for Vicky. In an attempt to control the trafficking of spurious liquor, the Haryana Government abolished the system of multiple wholesale dealers for liquor. Yogi helped Vicky's company acquire sole wholesale rights for distributing liquor in the entire state. This led to the monopoly of the Vicky Bhalla group, who often sold liquor way above the MRP, multiplying their profits over more than a hundred times.

Bolstered by this success, Vicky ventured into mining and constructions as well, and along with the yogi and Ravi formed an unholy nexus that used the power of money to tweak unfavourable situations to Ravi's political advantage. As Ravi Nehra's covert financial partner, Vicky Bhalla had a significant influence upon his politics. In fact, it was speculated that the real reason why Ravi never pursued charges against Rajveer Thakur seriously was the fear that the IDP would do the same with Vicky. Vicky, for his part, had successfully managed to hoodwink the tax authorities. As such, there was nothing that could be established against him or Nehra.

Whenever he was questioned about his links to Vicky, Ravi Nehra would always maintain a consistent stand: 'We are friends but I have nothing to do with his business interests and he has nothing to do with my politics.' The truth, of course, was just the opposite. When the yogi spelt out his master-plan to Ravi and Vicky, Vicky didn't sound too confident.

'I am not sure if Shruti Ranjan would agree...She's just too patriotic to be a part of our plan,' he cautioned.

Ravi had different ideas brewing in his mind. 'Do you know how Mountbatten convinced Nehru to refer the Kashmir dispute to the UN General Assembly in 1948?

Through his wife, Edwina. That's what wives are meant for. Rhea will convince Shruti to be a part of our plan.'

'You mean you are using Rhea?' Bhalla had asked in surprise.

Ravi Nehra's slimy expression had given Bhalla his answer.

Shruti, however, had remained unconvinced of the plan. 'Rhea, the whole idea seems too wishful. I mean, why would Ratna Pandey, who has opposed me all her life, suddenly support me as the PM candidate?' Shruti had countered Rhea when she had spoken in favour of the plan.

'She will. Ravi has created a stake in it for everyone,' Rhea had reasoned.

Ravi's plan was simple. It was to make everybody an important stakeholder without letting the real control slip out of his hands. Thus, for the first time in the history of Indian politics, the Opposition would form a shadow cabinet. All major Opposition leaders would be given important stakes. Ratna would be the shadow Home Minister; Ratnesh the shadow Defence Minister; Shruti would be the shadow External Affairs Minister besides being the overall head of the shadow cabinet and hence the shadow PM. On the other hand, ex-PM, Yashwant Modi who was past eighty and in frail health, was promised support as the country's presidential candidate if the Jan-Hit party came to power.

If convincing the top leaders required doling out hefty stakes, getting the second-rung MPs to fall in line with the plan was relatively easier: modest estimates suggested that over Rs 2000 crore were spent by Vicky Bhalla and another mining baron from Goa to buy out more than fifty MPs, making them agree to be a part of the Jan-Hit party, and having them root for Ravi to be the working president of the new party.

Ravi's intentions were clear: while Shruti would be the 'mask' of the party or the 'mukhota' as it is rudely referred to in Indian political parlance, the real control over the party affairs would lie with the party president, i.e. him. There was another factor that aided Ravi in becoming the party president: there was such a history of bitterness between the two Nationalist Leagues that it made it easier for him to emerge as a consensus candidate for the post. After all, it was his brainchild and initiative that was instrumental in the formation of such a grand alliance.

Even on the night before the party was to be formally launched with a massive rally at Delhi's Boat Club, Shruti remained in a dilemma. She sat is a dark room with none except her thoughts for company. And there, she could feel herself conversing with the man whose opinion mattered the most to her, despite his not being around:

'Sharadji, I should be feeling happy today, instead I am sad…I don't think I am associating with the right people. They seem like opportunists; they are apparently corrupt…I might become the PM tomorrow but what if that comes at the cost of all the values that you and I have stood for…?'

She could sense Sharad, in his white khadi kurta and pyjama and a beige shawl sitting in front of her. He heard her out, before responding:

'Don't think so much, Shruti…Remember I had always believed that if doing something wrong can help you attain a larger positive objective, then the impact of the wrong deed

gets decimated. Today, the country desperately needs to get rid of the IDP. If you have to forge an unethical alliance to make that happen, do it. No matter what you do, your intentions are noble. And you will provide a much better Government than the Devender Sigh-led IDP... Don't let go of this opportunity. Don't let go of your tryst with history.'

For Shruti, Sharad's counsel was the last word.

The next day, the Jan-Hit party was launched at a massive rally at Delhi's Boat Club which was attended by a record five lakh people. Twelve different state and national level parties merged together to form a grand alliance that swore to uproot the IDP Government and replace it next year. Ratna and Shruti still shared cold vibes; most leaders gave fiery speeches that spewed venom upon a 'weak' PM. The focus of the media, though, remained on Shruti – her expressions and her body language were captured minutely on camera. Shruti, for her part, felt as out of place as she had felt in her initial days in Delhi.

Two days later, when she was told that Ravi had spent more than five crore to gather the crowd he had collected at the rally, she had felt extremely hurt.

The 2009 Lok Sabha elections were now only six months' away. Shruti, even though she continued canvassing for the party aggressively, could clearly smell something foul insofar as the party's funding was concerned. She wanted an erudite party ideologue, A.V. Krishnamurthy, who was also a renowned chartered accountant, to be made the party's treasurer. Instead, Ravi duped her by first agreeing to her proposal and then appointing someone else when she was abroad. Ravi's appointee was far from being a politician, besides having a case of financial fraud registered against him.

Shruti was offended by Ravi's wily tactics. In a press conference upon her return, she arbitrarily declared that the Jan-Hit party would make all donations received by it, public; that an account of its receipts and expenses would appear on the party's website; and that all Jan-Hit party MPs would declare their assets within the next seven days.

By evening, Shruti was negated once again when Ravi told reporters that what Shruti had said was her personal opinion; the Jan-Hit party would do all that she said only if the ruling IDP did so simultaneously.

In the Jan-Hit party's parliamentary party meeting held two weeks later, a majority of the party MPs supported Ravi's stand, saying that it would be suicidal for them to reveal their sources of funding and their assets, unless the IDP did so first. In this meeting, however, Ravi promised to personally acquaint Shruti with every major contribution exceeding Rs 1 crore that the party would receive henceforth.

Shruti found herself in a rather ironical situation. As the PM designate, she should have been upbeat and confident; instead she found herself increasingly isolated. It hurt her to find that most politicians in the country had indeed become indifferent to corruption. What made Shruti lonelier was Rhea's absence from the scene.

Rhea was now six months pregnant; a health complication had resulted in her being on bed-rest for the last two months. Shruti, at times, wondered how Rhea could put up with someone as power-hungry and corrupt as Ravi Nehra. Or was he a different person as husband and lover? When Shruti went to enquire about Rhea's health, she tried probing in a subtle way, to see if Rhea was really happy in her marriage. Shruti's guess was right: she wasn't.

'I don't even feel we are married,' was Rhea's blunt reply. 'Sometimes I don't see him for a week. That too, when he is right here in Delhi and when I am carrying his baby!'

Shruti felt bad when she heard this; she also felt helpless. What Rhea told Shruti was only a fraction of what she had discovered about the real Ravi, post marriage. Cocaine, sex-addiction and abusiveness were what defined the real Ravi Nehra. Nehra must be an accomplished split-personality to cloud these vices so effectively from his public persona. While people knew he was corrupt, no one had a hint of his other vices; not even his wife, even six months after marrying him! In as much as Shruti felt sad and helpless, she knew there was nothing she could do about the situation. Rhea made her promise she would not broach this topic with Ravi; not until she had given birth to her baby. Shruti thus got back to doing what she was meant to: campaigning with full fervour, now that the elections were only three months away.

Shruti had hoped the brewing cold war between her and Ravi would die out if they maintained a cautious distance; instead it soon boomeranged into a full-fledged war that witnessed never-ending stand-offs and skirmishes.

The first stand-off between Shruti and Ravi occurred over the Rajya Sabha elections. Ratnesh Prasad, who had been a RS MP for two consecutive terms, besides being the leader of the party in the upper house, was obviously the party's natural choice for re-nomination from UP. Instead, Ravi sprang a last minute surprise by proposing the name of his friend, Vicky Bhalla.

Now shady businessmen like Vicky who fund political parties, don't do it with philanthropic motives. Sooner than later they can't resist extracting their price, which invariably is a political position. And in case things don't go their way, they are always in a position to employ blackmail as a means of forcing things on the party.

Vicky, apparently, had subjected Ravi to some similar blackmail. He wanted a price for fixing the 'master-plan'. And Ravi was forced to justify why Ratnesh Prasad should not be re-nominated to the Rajya Sabha. 'Seasoned and mass leaders like Ratnesh Prasad should fight Lok Sabha elections...Rajya Sabha is meant for lesser leaders and party funders,' he explained at a parliamentary committee meet of the Jan-Hit party.

'So what's the price that Vicky is paying you for the Rajya Sabha seat?' Shruti had asked with a directness that had left Ravi speechless.

'Come on, Shrutiji, whatever I am saying is for the good of the party. Lok Sabha elections are just three months away. It will serve the party better if a senior leader like Ratnesh fights the Lok Sabha polls instead of a comfortable Rajya Sabha election.'

'Fair enough! But in that case, I want a written assurance from you that for the vacant Rajya Sabha seat we will nominate either a leading academician, a scientist, a legal luminary or a senior journalist, who has espoused social causes through his or her life.' Even as Ravi struggled for an answer and fifteen members of the parliamentary committee looked on, Shruti continued her tirade: 'The Constitution has clearly stated that the Rajya Sabha, which we refer to as the Upper House, should draw representation from erudite intellectuals whose knowledge and wisdom can benefit the country's policy-making apparatus. Instead, we now sell the Rajya Sabha seats to the highest bidder. If this is what you want to do, go ahead. But if Vicky Bhalla is nominated to the Rajya Sabha, I will step down as the party's PM candidate!' Saying this, Shruti stormed out of the meeting.

Ravi, for want of an option, eventually nominated Ratnesh Prasad for re-election to the Rajya Sabha. But this entire episode left a bitter aftertaste.

In order to avoid another confrontation with Ravi, Shruti tried keeping her distance by increasingly operating out of her official residence, whereas Ravi held charge from the party office. But then 'physical distance' if at all, could only provide stop-gap peace.

Soon it was time to draw up the party's election manifesto. Not unexpectedly, Shruti's and Ravi's fundamental comprehension of the importance of an election manifesto was very different from each other's.

Shruti wanted the manifesto to incorporate concerns that went beyond politics. She wanted the manifesto to have a more layered approach. According to her, on the one hand, the manifesto ought to promise concrete steps to curb inflation, combat terror and fight corruption; while on the other it ought to list concrete measures to combat crimes against women and children; fight malnutrition among children, and lay out a comprehensive plan to conserve the environment.

For Ravi the manifesto was a mere formality. He never gave it the importance it deserved. He wanted to weave the entire campaign around Shruti's charismatic persona. For him the one and only campaign line had to be: a weak PM *vs* a strong 'woman' PM.

There was a design behind Ravi keeping the campaign this nebulous. Most of the people he would be giving party tickets to, would be first-time contestants: builders, contractors, gold merchants, etc., who would come loaded with their own sources of funding. Hence, by creating this new political class, he would ensure its loyalty to him.

Moreover, by keeping the manifesto nebulous, he hoped that local issues would play a decisive role in deciding election results. After all, the new breed of politicians that he was creating had no appeal or presence beyond their home constituencies; hence they were unlikely to be taken seriously if they focused on larger national issues. Fighting Lok Sabha elections over local issues was a huge gamble, but then, given the stakes involved, Nehra did not mind being the gambler he had always been. His real motive remained clear: to weaken Shruti's authority so that at an apt moment he could drop her, and emerge as the PM candidate by default.

While Ravi was eventually forced to incorporate most of Shruti's suggestions in the manifesto, the duel worsened their equations, quite irreparably.

When Ravi, Yogi and Vicky met one evening to take stock of the situation, they didn't seem too optimistic, either. 'Boss, Shruti is a harder nut to crack than we'd thought. I doubt if she will let you have your way in the distribution of party tickets,' rued Vicky.

At this point, Ravi who had been getting a call from his residence number finally took the call.

'*Kya hai?*' he said gruffly.

'Sir, Rheaji has gone into labour...She is expected to deliver anytime.'

'*Theek hai*... I'll be there by midnight.' He cut the phone rather abruptly and turned towards the yogi. '*Haan,* Yogiji, you wanted to say something?'

'Well, in that case, the whole plan will fail. If we don't have our people elected, your chances of being a proxy PM candidate go for a toss.'

For once, Ravi heard them all out before he had the final word. 'I have been very patient in letting Shruti have her way twice before, but not anymore. The campaign committee has drawn up plans that will keep her away from Delhi most of the time till the elections get over. And I will make it very clear that the distribution of party tickets is solely the party president's prerogative.'

At two in the morning, when Ravi finally reached the hospital, his son was already eight hours old. What put him in a really awkward position, though, was the presence of Shruti in Rhea's hospital room. It was in fact Shruti who held his baby in her arms even as the new mother lay fast asleep. Shruti too found herself in an equally awkward situation. No words were exchanged between the two as Shruti held the baby out to him.

It was only when Ravi held his son in his hands that it seemed to dawn on him what a special moment it was. Ravi's expression changed; he looked moved, which he rarely did. In some corner of his mind, he also seemed to realize that his political heir had arrived; he held the baby close to him and kissed him on his forehead. Shruti stepped out of the room to let father and son enjoy a private moment. For the next 15 minutes, Ravi gazed at the baby intently; but not once did he look at his wife or try to wake her up. Then he took the baby to where Shruti sat on a sofa, gave him to her, and left.

Shruti was baffled at how insensitive a man could be to his wife; even at the most emotional moment in a married couple's life.

The first phase of polling was just a few weeks away. But Shruti instead of being enthusiastic about these last few weeks, had to virtually drag herself out to campaign. Her hectic schedule and frantic travel across the country, reminded her of her campaigning with Sharad in his last few days. Every time she sat on a chartered flight, she missed Sharad more acutely. She imagined herself talking to him and being reassured by his sage counsel. And at the end of these 'conversations', she'd often break down and then quickly gather herself before the flight landed. After all, the whole thrust of the campaign was to project her as a 'strong' leader. And a strong leader is not supposed to shed tears – no matter what!

Even as Shruti hopped from one part of the country to the other, she kept getting complaints about major irregularities in the distribution of party tickets. Old-timers who had worked at the grassroots level for years were sidelined and new entrants with better resources were rewarded. The aggrieved party-workers tried seeking an appointment with her, which she declined with a heavy heart, realizing that a confrontationist stand with Ravi at this point would erode the party's chances further.

Hence, Shruti decided to cut herself off from other activities and merely perform her 'karma' which at this stage, was to reach out to as many people of the country as possible.

On the morning of the first phase of voting, the country's leading newspaper carried out a damning front-page story, which reported that as many as 35% of the Jan-Hit party candidates had criminal antecedents, with as many as eighteen of them having serious charges of murder and rape against them. This report created a furore in the country. Shruti was on her way to cast her vote in Kishanganj when media persons confronted her on the newspaper report. Initially, she tried to ward them with off with 'no comments' until the media turned hostile.

'You could be the next PM. How can you turn a blind eye to such blatant criminalization of politics?' a lady journalist demanded. 'Come on, Shrutiji, if someone like you, who has suffered rape, can support criminals in politics, then this country is doomed.'

Shruti finally shot back: 'If I indeed become the PM, I will make sure that all my party MPs with criminal charges have to quit – even if that means losing majority in Parliament and even if it means losing the PM's chair.'

Shruti's response was probably impulsive but in Indian politics, her statement amounted to hara-kiri. It exposed her differences with Ravi like never before. Contrary to what Shruti's campaign claimed, this episode showed her up as a weak leader who had very little say even within her own party, and for the first time, the voters started realizing that the 'khichdi' government of the Jan-Hit party might be even more fragile and self-defeating than the Janta Party Government of 1977. This turned the tide against the party.

On the day the results were announced, the Jan-Hit party suffered a humiliating defeat.

The party won a mere 122 seats, whereas the IDP-led coalition garnered 300 plus seats on its own. For Shruti, this was her worst moment in politics and she had none except her secretary, Chhavi, to see her through it.

What was worse was that within hours of the results being announced, Ravi Nehra was seen on one TV channel after another, giving his own inferences about the defeat.

'The voters have rejected Shruti Ranjan. Let's accept that they feel that a weak Devender Singh is a better option than Shruti Ranjan...For us, it's a huge shock, but we accept the mandate with humility...'

Ravi's words were the last nail in Shruti's coffin. Shruti hated herself for landing up in the position she found herself in.

Two days later, on the same day that Devender Singh was sworn in as the PM for a second time, the Jan-Hit Party's parliamentary committee met to discuss the reasons for the party's defeat. Shruti, who had been seen at the swearing-in ceremony of the PM, only two hours ago, was now conspicuous by her absence. Her phone was switched off. Even as others waited for her to arrive, tongues had started wagging about her attitude.

'Now, what's happened cannot be undone...but at least Shrutiji ought to be a graceful loser...' Ravi commented sagely.

'Shruti is quite gracious, or else she'd not have gone for the new PM's swearing-in...If she has not turned up now, it could very well be because of *your* lack of grace... after all, with your irresponsible comments in the media, you've already put all the blame on her,' Ratnesh chided Ravi, exuding the courage that he was known for at the start of his political career.

At that point, the giant TV screen announced more breaking news: the TV channels had just received a letter which Shruti had sent them in her own writing:

'I accept the people's verdict with all humility. I think I was wrong in pushing myself to do something I did not believe in and which I was temperamentally not suited for. I was never suited to be the PM of this country but I let myself be a candidate because I didn't want to betray the people who in various opinion polls had been rooting for me. But alas, I have betrayed them. I therefore apologize to my countrymen, supporters and well-wishers for letting them down. I am hereby quitting politics and public life forever. I wish my country and her people the very best.'

Simultaneously, Shruti also sent her letter of resignation as MP to the party president.

For the next six months, Shruti completely disappeared from public view. It was speculated that she was spending her time meditating in a small ashram on the foothills of the Himalayas.

And then six months later, she was seen on news channels again. The Madhya Pradesh CM, Dheeraj Singh, who was a fierce critic of the party president, Ravi Nehra, and a big-time supporter of Shruti had managed to convince her to spearhead one of the most ambitious projects ever undertaken by a state government for the upliftment of women. While Shruti did speak on the occasion, she stuck to talking about her basic role in the project and refused to answer any queries not concerning the project.

In six months' time, Shruti appeared on TV again when the ashram was finally inaugurated by the President of India. She sat on stage with the President and the CM, quietly watching the proceedings. When her time to speak came, she only said, 'I am thankful to the CM for giving me this opportunity. I hope I am able to live up to the faith that people still seem to have in me.'

What Shruti achieved in the last three years was of course phenomenal, giving her an iconic status and adequately compensating for her failure in politics.

Chapter 16

Dhar, Madhya Pradesh

It was 4:30 a.m. Shruti was lost in her reveries, still recovering from the memories she was forced to revisit, against her own volition. It was the call of the rooster that made her realize the time. Her heart was heavy; only partly by the remembrance of what had happened with her, but mostly by the helplessness she felt.

Nirbhaya's rape, much like Shruti's, had once again brought home the fact that the next victim could be just about anybody – it could be Catherine on her way back from the ashram; it could be any of the ashram inmates, or the little girls who came out chattering and happy at the end of class. Are women really in so much danger in our society? Much like gold coins or jewellery left in the open? But then gold coins and jewellery did not lose their worth… but a woman? She was tossed aside like an old shoe. The thought saddened Shruti no end. Her chain of thought led her to remember Daivik's and Catherine's persuasive argument – exhorting her to get back to politics, the day before.

Politics had been destined for her; as had her failure in it. She never had to work her way up to get into politics;

nor did any of her efforts prevent her from the repeated failures that were thrust upon her.

In comparison, the social work that she was involved in now was purely her choice and she felt a greater satisfaction being successful at it and improving the lives of so many women directly.

No, she would not re-enter politics. Never. She felt sure about it. She did not want to revisit a jinxed chapter of her life simply because others wanted her to.

In her restlessness, Shruti stepped out of her room and meandered aimlessly about the ashram till she reached the common room. She stood outside for two minutes before deciding to go in. Shruti was anxious to know Nirbhaya's fate. Hence, she abandoned a three-year-old rule she had imposed on herself and switched on the TV.

The news was what she had been dreading: *Nirbhaya was no more.*

Shruti felt silent tears course down her cheeks. Chhavi who entered the room just then was moved to see Shruti in such a devastated state.

A little over 24 hours later, in a nondescript crematorium in south-west Delhi, amidst the winter fog and low visibility, Nirbhaya's father lit her funeral pyre. All around, there were teary eyes, heavy hearts and faces frozen in grief. Given that the Government had tried its best to ensure that the last rites of the girl were performed quickly and in isolation, not more than a hundred-odd people were present at the venue. Most of them were people from Nirbhaya's locality, though there were a few politicians as well. Daivik and Catherine were present at the site too – as a mark of respect.

Even as a small pooja was performed and Nirbhaya's pyre was about to be lit by her father, a cab arrived outside. Two women, dressed in woollen cardigans over their saris and draped in thick shawls that covered their faces almost completely, walked in and joined the crowd of mourners.

The pyre was lit. In the light of the fire, Daivik who was standing across from the two ladies looked at them closely. Was that Shruti? But when he looked for the women after the funeral, they had vanished.

It was only 9 in the morning and still quite foggy. Shruti's return flight to Indore was in the afternoon. With nowhere to go, Shruti and Chhavi sat in the cab parked on a desolate street. The driver of the cab fed her some more information about Nirbhaya's fate that terrible night. As Shruti absorbed these morbid details, she experienced a revulsion she had never felt before. Trying hard to calm herself, Shruti asked the driver to take her towards Ashoka Road.

For some unknown reason, Shruti wanted to take a look at the places familiar to her: the roads of Lutyens' Delhi where she had once stayed. She wanted to see if the garden of the bungalow she once occupied was maintained as well as it had been when she lived there.

What Shruti was unaware of was that a news channel had already broken a story speculating about her presence in the national capital and at Nirbhaya's funeral. No sooner had her car reached India Gate, that she witnessed an unusual sight: some fifty people stopped her car. They were not sure if Shruti was inside, till one of them took a closer look and shouted: 'It's Shrutiji.'

'Shrutiji you can't leave us like this...We won't let you go.'

Shruti came out of her car to reason with the crowd. 'Look, I understand your feelings of hurt. Thankfully, India still has an effective justice system...besides, the Government is doing its bit...what else can I do in this situation?'

One protestor shot back: 'You should know better what else can be done in this situation...after all you have the experience of being raped, don't you?'

Shruti was shaken when she heard this, yet instead of anger she felt an empathy with the crowd. After all, everybody had a right to feel angry at this point. Wasn't she better off and more powerful than the protesting man on the street? Then what was wrong in the people expecting more from her?

Shruti thought a moment before speaking to the crowd: 'Will you do what I ask you to?' she said, her expression hard to decipher.

'Shrutiji, you lead us...we are behind you,' the crowd roared instantly.

'Can you arrange for fifty large-sized iron rods?'

'Fifty?'

'One for each of you...'

Exactly an hour later, Shruti, followed by these fifty protestors, each with a rod in his hand, barged into the narrow lanes of the basti where Nirbhaya's rapists lived.

Once they reached the centre of the basti, there was a massive commotion. On the one hand, the inhabitants had no clue what was happening; on the other the protestors looked all set to unleash violence.

At this point, Shruti took charge.

'Have you got their addresses?' she asked the protestors.

'Yes, Shrutiji!' replied the man leading the group.

'Then get all the five houses vacated, destroy all the belongings, and demolish the houses.'

The basti inhabitants were aghast when they heard this. As were Shruti's own supporters at this unprecedented display of belligerence.

Shruti repeated her instructions once again.

'You can't do this! There's something called law and order, Shruti Ranjan...we won't allow you to break it again like you did many years ago...' warned a basti elder.

Two of the protestors shut him up as the others moved towards the houses of the rapists. Right then, the mother of one of the accused came running towards Shruti: 'We will not allow you to destroy our homes...don't forget that my son has still not be proven guilty...besides, forget what my son did, what have *we* done to deserve this fate?' she demanded to know.

'You gave birth to a son who thought he could look you in the eye after raping a woman,' Shruti shot back.

Interestingly, while the police were nowhere to be seen, one news channel was already present at the venue, and was telecasting live.

For the next half hour, the protestors had the five houses forcibly vacated. Shruti surprised herself and the people around her by remaining unmoved by the violence she had instigated. In fact, when the affected families came pleading to her for sympathy, she said, 'Now your boys will know how it feels when something precious to them is destroyed in a moment. Remember, the trauma of a raped girl and her family is far worse...If this is what happens to every rapist's family, then they will think a thousand times before harming another.'

Before any damage could be inflicted, though, a police team finally arrived and took Shruti and her supporters into custody.

The TV journalist reporting the story concluded his story with:

'The last few years have seen Shruti in many different avatars: from the reluctant deputy minister who went on a long leave when she disagreed with Malviya, to a stop-gap CM who proved her mettle by winning the state elections, to a Minister of State who engineered a fake encounter that killed five terrorists, and finally to a PM candidate who allowed Ravi Nehra to manipulate and mar her career. But this avatar – which we saw just now – is unprecedented! This is the avatar of a furious Goddess Kali who will wreak havoc upon society if it doesn't mend its ways and stops sinning. Shruti Ranjan is back – and with a bang!'

After many years, Shruti had to spend another night in jail. Thankfully she had Chhavi for company.

'Ma'am, I still can't believe what you did today!' said Chhavi, partly in shock and partly in admiration, as they sat together in their cell.

'Even I find it surprising. But at that moment, when the protestors surrounded me and demanded I do more, I found it cathartic...I mean, how do you fight a flawed and insensitive system? At times, you've just got to break out of the system and do what you feel provides instant justice. I know what I did was wrong but somehow I don't regret it. Sadly, most Indians are too intellectually challenged to understand any other language but this. I guess I had to employ a language the masses understood.'

Listening to Shruti speak, Chhavi was left wondering if there was a side to Shruti still unknown to her…or if Nirbhaya had invented a new Shruti!

Chapter 17

The next morning, almost every newspaper carried Shruti's exploits on its front page. Nehra walked into his office and looked at one of them with a wicked glint in his eyes as he quickly scanned the front page article. 'So this is what Shruti Ranjan has reduced herself to now!'

Lying beneath the main edition of the *Times of India* was a glossy men's magazine, the cover featuring struggling actress and model, Diya Dangi, with just a rag covering her. The caption read: *'I'm nude...will you rape me?'* This was Diya's way of getting some quick publicity by capitalizing on the grim situation and protesting against rape. Nehra's face darkened on seeing this cover. Instead of leering at the photograph as he would have in any other situation, he furiously dialled an extension from his phone. 'Send Pathak inside...fast!'

When Pathak walked in he said, 'Pathak, what the hell is this? Why is this magazine on my table?'

Pathak looked nervous: 'Sir, we want you to be aware of what all Baby has been doing...It's a matter of time before your rivals start using this against you.'

A livid Nehra pulled out his cigarette lighter and burnt the magazine. How he wished he was not related to this slut!

Half an hour later, Nehra was in a meeting with B.C. D'Souza. Nothing seemed to be going right for him that day. 'Nehraji, we tried our best but the Haryana Janata Party is tougher to crack than what we had thought. The only way they will extend support to you in Haryana is if you allow them to have two deputy CMs and all important ministries including Finance and Revenue.'

'Bloody hell! If we don't get those two ministries, it's as good as sitting in the Opposition.'

'But I can offer an alternative,' said D'Souza, giving Nehra some hope. 'We can help you form the government in Jharkhand instead by making our other ally, Jharkhand League, support you.'

'And why will they support us?'

'Don't forget that the CBI is probing the Jharkhand League patriarch, Ram Mahato on charges of murder. We can ask the CBI to go slow on the case if Mahato supports you. And if that happens, you can accomplish the same wealth in Jharkhand by dishing out mining contracts and land denotifications...'

Nehra finally smiled. 'D'Souza you're the best bastard around...that's what makes you so indispensable for Mukta Madam, isn't it?'

In no time, the smoke from Nehra's bidi was giving D'Souza some tough moments. D'Souza coped with the discomfort rather 'sportingly' until Nehra who was still thinking, came up with an idea, and snuffed it out. 'On second thoughts, you know what, it might be dicey for my party to lead the Government...it's not difficult for people to understand the motives of this kind of opportunistic alliance, that too when elections are only a year away...'

'Then...?'

'Let's replicate what we had tried doing in Haryana some years ago...'

'What?'

'Let's prop up an Independent MLA or another smaller party...we'll both support this non-entity, while the real power remains with us; that way we will hold all the key portfolios, but our reputations will be safe if something goes wrong...'

The idea brought a smile to D'Souza's face. 'Nehra Saab, you are a much bigger bastard than me – in fact the biggest that Indian politics has produced in a very long time.'

The founding members of the *Azad Bharat Party (ABP)* met at an apartment in central Delhi. The launch of the party was just 24 hours away and on their agenda was to tie up the remaining loose ends and streamline the functioning of the party.

Apart from Daivik and Catherine, the other primary members included senior Supreme Court lawyer, Pratibha Kaushal; ex-super cop M. P. Singh; Suresh Saini, marketing guru; and Faisal Khan, a journalist who ran a weekly newspaper that specialized in investigative stories and sting operations.

The members were understandably distracted by the incident of Shruti unleashing violence in a manner most unlike her. 'Hats off to Shruti! What a way she has chosen to make a comeback,' said M.P Singh,

'Comeback?' Catherine smiled dismissively. 'She is not coming back. We tried our best to convince her but she refused...'

'Besides, after what she did yesterday, I'm not sure whether she'll command the same respect,' Daivik averred. 'I mean, what she did was so unbecoming of her. At least I am a bit disappointed.'

'On the contrary, I have reports that most people supported Shruti's move. It's strange but the public identifies with her so strongly that people across the country have launched agitations demanding her release from jail,' said Faisal.

Reports had indeed begun to pour in of road blockades and protest marches across the country to demand Shruti's release, putting the Government in a rather uncomfortable position. People were justifying Shruti's behaviour by saying that the Government's frivolous attitude on the issue of women's safety had left them with no option. They were glad that at least there was someone who had set the record straight. The Government, on the other hand, was worried that Shruti's act would lead to similar acts of violence being enacted in other parts of the country; besides increasing the clamour for Shruti's comeback.

'Anyway, let's get down to what we need to discuss today,' said Daivik, trying to keep the focus upon tomorrow. He clearly felt a bit let-down by Shruti's show of bravado.

The six members of the ABP had between themselves gathered funds to the tune of Rs 1.12 crore. A large part of this amount came from personal contributions. So while Daivik had managed to obtain 25 lakhs from mortgaging his ancestral house in Ranchi, Catherine had shelled out 40 lakhs from her savings. The Supreme Court lawyer had shelled out another 30 lakhs from her pocket, whereas the rest was made up of small personal contributions from nearly a 1000 supporters of the party spread across the country.

'Will our 1.12 crore manage to give a fight to Nehra's infinite resources or the Government's unspoken authority?' M.P. Singh sounded sceptical.

'No, but that's why we have Faisal here: to break earth-shattering exposés about the Government and the Jan-Hit Party that stir up the nation! Faisal will have to use all his skills as an investigate journalist,' said Daivik.

'What about the party symbol?' enquired Pratibha.

'Since, we haven't come up with more options, I think we'll go ahead with the two fingers making a "V" i.e. a victory sign.'

'Yes, that sounds good. Maybe the victory sign will be auspicious for us,' smiled Catherine.

'So, guys, are we clear about our strategy?' Daivik asked everybody. Without waiting for an answer, he reiterated his leadership plan: 'Let's be very clear, we don't have the financial resources or the party infrastructure to take on the Government or the Opposition. What we have with us are honesty, goodwill, determination and credibility. Now the important question is – how do we offset the absence of resources? We do it in two ways: by being impartial in taking on both the Government and Opposition. We have got to convince the people that both are equal enemies and that they need a third option. We will have to do this by exposing the Government and the Opposition turn by turn. Every time Faisal does an exposé, Suresh will immediately have to exploit it further by employing his marketing skills on the internet. Let's be clear: we will have to fight this battle over the internet. Saini will help us leverage and exploit the social media to our advantage. Let other parties and people underestimate the potential of the internet. I am pretty sure that today the internet has enough users in India to influence the results of the next elections. And we will prove it. Mind you, we will fight and win the next general elections over the internet.'

Though the others heard Daivik out, none unequivocally shared his confidence. In fact half-way through his talk, even Daivik began to sound a little unsure. It was pretty obvious that the new party was a huge gamble for everybody and no one was sure what lay in store for it. Sensing everyone's anxieties, Catherine changed the topic. 'So, what sort of turnout are we expecting at tomorrow's launch rally?'

Everybody waited for the other to speak until Pratibha attempted an answer. 'Depends actually, anywhere between 1000 to 10,000…'

The vague answer irritated Daivik. *'Depends on what, Pratibhaji? The weather or the planetary position?'* he was almost tempted to ask. Instead he ended the meeting, and instructed everybody to get back to the task of promoting the next day's launch event aggressively on the internet and through their contacts.

When Daivik and Catherine were leaving the room, after the rest had left, Catherine looked at him wistfully: 'Is there no hope at all that Shruti might join us?'

Chapter 18

It was the first day of the New Year. The start of this New Year, though, was marked by a remarkable lack of enthusiasm in the people – perhaps because they knew there was little to be optimistic about. Shruti's act of aggression notwithstanding, there was nothing that gave them hope that things would be different or better in the year ahead.

The media was abuzz with two set of stories. The first concerned Shruti's detention. Home Minister S. K. Patil, has been quoted as saying that Government would press stringent charges against Shruti – a fact that the public hadn't taken kindly to. But then Patil had a reputation for being gaffe-prone; had it not been for his unflinching loyalty to Mukta Prajapati, he wouldn't have qualified as a cabinet minister. The other set of stories was focused on the launch of the *Azad Bharat Party (ABP)* at the Ram Leela Grounds, which had been scheduled for noon that day.

At ten in the morning, the Government suddenly decided to release Shruti and pack her off to Dhar in a helicopter. The reason was simple: the ABP was expected to raise the chorus for Shruti's release at its rally and push the Government further into a corner. Thus, the Government was forced to prioritize its enemies and it was clear that the Government still considered Shruti Ranjan a deadlier enemy than the ABP.

Leaving nothing to chance, the Home secretary, V.K. Mishra had been entrusted the task of escorting Shruti to the airport. In fact, the Home Ministry had charted out a special, relatively less congested route for Shruti's journey from Tihar to the airport. In order to avoid the crowds cheering for Shruti outside, she was whisked out from a rear entrance. Mishra, who was waiting in an Ambassador car, hustled Shruti and Chhavi into the back seat. At least half-a-dozen police vehicles were parked nearby. They were supposed to form a cover for Shruti, ensuring an uninterrupted drive to the airport.

As the car started, Shruti was left battling her dilemmas. She never wanted to return to Delhi but by leaving the city now, she was once again letting down the people who had begun to pin their hopes on her. The very next moment, though, she discarded these thoughts and rebuked herself for believing that she was more important than she really was.

Chhavi used her smartphone to find out the latest news. Apparently a good 20,000 people were protesting outside Tihar, demanding Shruti's release. Chhavi quietly held the cellphone in front of Shruti for her to read the story.

Shruti's copter was now about to take off. It was a comfortable *Pawan Hans* copter with two pilots, a lady attendant and four National Security Guards commandos for her security. An amiable, middle-aged, sardar air force pilot, Captain Ranjit Singh was in charge of flying her to her destination, along with a junior co-pilot. Even as they waited for the Air Traffic Control to give the signal for takeoff, Ranjit commented: 'So this is the second time that you're running away from the battlefield…'

'Excuse me...?' said Shruti disbelievingly.

Shruti was shocked when she learnt that the media had been fed stories of a 'deal' between her and the Government in which she had requested the Government not to press charges, in return for a commitment from her not to return to politics.

'Well, that's how cunning this Government is...And that's the reason why you were kept away from the media in the last two hours...' smiled Ranjit.

'This is perfidy...it's an outright disinformation campaign,' complained a livid Chhavi, even as Shruti struggled for a 'dignified' response.

After a moment's silence, Ranjit surprised her again when he asked, 'Shrutiji, do you really want to go back?'

At this point, the ATC cleared the aircraft for takeoff. Ranjit Singh though did not take off instantly. Instead, for the next one minute, none of those present in the copter spoke, each perhaps waiting for the other to do so, as they waited for Shruti to answer. When she remained silent, Ranjit Singh prepared for take-off.

At the ABP launch on Ram Leela grounds, the crowd was sparse: 3,000 was the supposed number. The first speaker, ex-cop, M.P. Singh addressed the gathering. He stressed broadly on the key point that apart from having proven itself to be corrupt, the Government had now come across as extremely insensitive and unconcerned on the issue of safety of women. By no stretch of imagination was he a great orator. And his performance was understandably inadequate in exciting the crowd.

Soon it was Daivik's turn to speak. He started by ripping the Government apart for its dictatorial acts, the latest being the manner in which Shruti had been packed off to Dhar and a false propaganda unleashed to project her as weak and compromising. Then he spoke of the unabashed corruption the Government was steeped in:

'Friends, after the East India Company, if there is an entity that has sold off the country's interests more brazenly, then it's the IDP Government. The total sum of money the country has lost in the 2G and coal allocation scam is simply scary. And to top it all, you have a PM who feigns ignorance about everything that is supposed to have happened right under his nose. Friends, how long will you allow yourself to be duped by fake arguments around secularism and let a non-performing PM and his apathetic super-boss, Mukta Prajapati get away? How much leeway will you allow a supposedly erudite PM who is intellectually dishonest?'

Even as Daivik's fervent rhetoric hit just the right notes, the crowd suddenly became conscious of the sound of a copter flying in close vicinity.

To Shruti's own surprise, Shruti's copter was hovering right above the Ram Leela Maidan, and she could actually see Daivik making his speech. She looked confused but then the captain smiled, handed over charge to the co-pilot and walked up to Shruti. Getting emotional, he bared his heart to her:

'Shrutiji, as an air force pilot, I was part of the Kargil War too, though only peripherally. I flew my injured and dead brothers away from the battlefield. I always hoped that once, during my tenure, India would carry out air strikes on Pakistan to destroy its terror camps. I don't think that will happen. Next year I am due to retire. I want to go with the satisfaction of having done a good deed…Hence, I've brought you here. This thin rally that you see below can trigger a historical change in our country, provided you join them. The decision is going to be yours. If you say no, I will fly back from here…'

Shruti had no idea how to react to the opportunity. There was something tempting about a dais with a mike and a crowd in front of it. But was she prepared for it? But then, wasn't everything destined in life, including her getting this crazy pilot to fly her copter?

The NSG commandos in the meantime had informed their seniors of the 'virtual hijack' by the pilot. In the next couple of minutes, the Home Ministry was bound to learn of the same and initiate combative action.

As Shruti looked down at the rally below, she remembered Sharad's moving speech at the Lal Chowk in Kashmir and how it became a game-changer for the Government. That's how strongly a powerful speech connected with a restive crowd. Sadly, for all the euphoria that the ABP had tried to generate, the response had been unsatisfactory, largely for the want of a more seasoned speaker who could play to the gallery better.

Even as Captain Ranjit Singh was being admonished by the ATC for deviating from his prescribed route and told to fly back to the IGI Airport, he turned to Shruti and asked one last time, 'What have you decided, Ma'am?'

'You will lose your job, Captain,' Shruti told him.

'I don't mind, Ma'am, as long as conditions in the country improve.'

Shruti looked down. By now, she was clear in her mind: 'Land the plane…' Shruti said with a straight-face.

Meanwhile there was huge commotion both outside and inside the copter. Those attending the rally were intrigued to see a copter landing so close to them; whereas the NSG commandos inside had started threatening the pilot, warning him not to land the craft.

'Kill me if you want. But today, I'll do what my conscience tells me to,' the gutsy sardar replied, deftly landing the copter a mere 100 metres away from the rally, making Daivik stop his speech mid-sentence. There was chaos all around. The fear was that this was some new ploy of the Government to arrest the ABP leaders. After all, usurping democratic rights had become a common practice for this Government.

Continuing his speech to a distracted crowd, Daivik said, 'Friends, as you see, a helicopter has just landed there. We don't know who is inside and what is the motive for the copter to land so close here...but knowing this Government, I will not be too surprised if this copter has come to arrest us and fly us directly to jail –' Daivik stopped short again; stunned to see a familiar sari-clad woman alight from the copter and walk towards him.

Shruti Ranjan!

As the crowd got a clearer view of Shruti, a triumphant chant resounded through the maidan: *Shruti Ranjan zindabad!*

Shruti looked happy and unfazed: 'When is my turn to speak?'

News channels that were beaming the rally live began reporting her presence. Thanks to the buzz generated by her presence, the crowd instantly started to swell and 20 minutes later when it was Shruti's turn to speak the crowd has trebled, with people still pouring in.

Shruti felt a tinge of nervousness when she faced the crowd. It had been three-and-a-half years since she had last spoken in public, but she plunged right in: 'As you know, the V sign made of two human fingers is going to be the election symbol of the new party, the ABP.' Shruti paused before she continued, 'It's sad that the same two fingers that make a victory sign are the fingers that cause much distress and humiliation to a raped woman. Yes, I am talking about the morbid two finger test (TFT) which most rape victims have to undergo in our country to prove they are telling the truth...'

The crowd grew more alert when it heard this unusual information.

'Lest you not be aware of what a two finger test is, let me explain it to you. The two finger test widely performed across the country, checks the elasticity of a victim's vagina. Going by the number of fingers admitted, a doctor gives his opinion on whether a woman is "habituated to sex" or not. I ask you friends, is it fair for a bruised, traumatized rape victim, lying in a semi-conscious state in a hospital, to be raped a second time, this time with the doctor's ill-intentioned fingers? That too, when time and again the TFT has proven to be unscientific, illogical and inconclusive? But sadly that's the truth! A rape victim in India is raped several times over after the first rape: first, by the doctors who perform the TFT, then she is mentally raped by the police officers, who blame it upon her "loose character" or "modern dressing" depending upon the strata of society to which she belongs. Her trauma doesn't end there. The victim is then "psychologically" raped in courts where the defence lawyer grills her insensitively by casting aspersions on her character. If she is lucky to brave these multiple rapes, then in a small minority of cases, the rapists actually get convicted...Or else at times, the court is even known to ask the culprit to marry the victim as an act of atonement…'

For Shruti it was a gamble of sorts to start her speech with a such a sensitive subject. But then she was nervous and she needed a topic that would instantly grab the audience's attention. And it worked.

People were listening to Shruti, mesmerized by the subject of her speech. Daivik, Catherine and other ABP members simply couldn't believe the change in their fortunes: the effect was instantaneous.

'Brothers and sisters, as someone who has lived the trauma of rape first-hand, I can tell you that the menace of crimes against women cannot be combated unless we go for radical, systemic changes and these systemic changes will have to include electoral reforms, police reforms and judicial reforms.

'Let me explain what I mean. As per the records that I have with me, 260 candidates facing charges such as rape, assault and outraging the modesty of a woman contested Assembly elections and parliamentary elections on tickets of various parties in the last five years. Do you expect such people to be even concerned, forget being serious about taking steps for the safety of women? Well, if they do, how would they rape and get away with it?

'Therefore, today I propose that in India there should be exclusive fast track courts to deal into criminal cases against MPs and MLAs. Unless our sitting legislators are clean, they can never clean up the filth that's growing all around us.'

Shruti's speech was telecast on all English and regional language news channels. Among those watching her was Ravi Nehra, who sat alone in his office. He looked increasingly pissed off by Shruti's speech.

'...we have been conditioned to respect and have faith in our justice system. *Satymev Jayate* is what we have been taught, isn't it? But the truth is that our judicial system is full of glaring inconsistencies and abject mediocrity. How else would you justify a judge passing a judgment on a rape case and saying that the culprit should marry the victim as his punishment? How else do you justify the *Suryanelli* rape case verdict where 35 accused were suddenly acquitted by the High Court? Why should the convicts, sentenced to death in rarest of rare cases, have the provision of filing for a mercy petition with the President? And on what basis did our esteemed ex-President Dr Pratibha Patil grant clemency to as many as thirty convicts facing death, including some of those who had carried out acts of unimaginable barbarism? Wasn't that a travesty of justice and an insult of the courts?'

Shruti was not done.

'One of the biggest impediments in fighting crime in India is the archaic functioning style of the police. If in a ghastly rape case, policemen from two different police stations spend an hour debating which police station should have a jurisdiction over the case, then I'm afraid the police really is of no use...'

Even as Shruti continued to speak, an excited Daivik whispered to Catherine: 'Do you realize Shruti has actually spelt out our broad manifesto? Both corruption and women's safety are issues that hold relevance only in specific times. But reform is a consistent process...that's going to be the key word for us. We have to press for reforms – judicial, electoral, police, educational and health. If we do this, we've got a comprehensive agenda ready to take to the people.'

As Shruti's speech neared its end, she increased her pitch like a seasoned politician, and finally shared her plans:

'For me, politics is about sacrifice...and I am ready to make any sacrifice for a better India. Hence I have decided that very soon I will sit on an indefinite fast at the Jantar Mantar until the Government bans the TFT and passes a legislation to immediately disqualify all MPs and MLAs facing criminal charges for crimes against women. I am prepared to die. I would rather not live than to witness the gruesome death of any more Nirbhayas in front of my eyes. Jai Hind!'

A thunderous applause followed...The kind of patriotic fervour that Shruti evoked in the people was reminiscent of Sharad Malviya. Daivik and Catherine were teary-eyed with joy, because they knew that with Shruti on their side, half their battle was already won.

Before the rally ended, Daivik quickly took over once again, this time to propose the formal set-up of his party. He said that while he would be the working president, Catherine the spokesperson, M.P. Singh the treasurer and Kaushal the general secretary, he humbly offered the chairmanship of the ABP to Shruti. Shruti accepted his offer – only to make way for another round of boisterous applause and patriotic sloganeering. The whole country erupted in celebration and hope as Shruti's and Daivik's speeches were played out across news channels all through the day.

As Nehra watched the event on TV, he hurled the remote hard at the screen only to see it smash into pieces. Lighting a bidi, he wracked his brain wondering how best to retrieve control of the situation.

He wondered if Shruti and he shared some sort of a karmic connection that always made her his nemesis.

Shruti and Chhavi spent the night in a room in Madhya Pradesh Bhawan. While Chhavi fell asleep, Shruti remained awake all night thinking about how her life had turned around once again. She wondered what it was about Delhi that kept bringing her back to the city and making it her home. This was her third tryst with India's capital city: the first as a college student and young journalist; the second as a greenhorn politician and protégé of Sharad Malviya; and now as a crusader aiming to clean Indian politics of the vicious mess it was in.

Shruti looked out of her window towards the rising sun. In the pristine glow of dawn, her countenance reflected a zealous determination; she was a woman with a mission.

Part 2

Chapter 19

Buoyed by the spectacular launch of the party – and thanks to Shruti's unexpected presence – the ABP was off to a flying start. Daivik, being the meticulous planner that he was, immediately got down to fixing the organizational and logistical details that would prepare the party for the long haul. Among Daivik's key priorities was to work out living arrangements in Delhi for Shruti, Catherine and himself.

Shruti was offered an apartment in Safdarjung Enclave by the ABP general secretary and lawyer, Pratibha Kaushal. This flat belonged to Kaushal's sister who had now shifted to London. Since it was lying vacant it could be used for Party work. Shruti moved in with her PA, Chhavi Gupta. Keeping her safety in mind, Shruti was provided a small police escort team. Catherine took an apartment on rent in another part of Safdarjung Enclave, not very far from where Shruti stayed; Daivik moved in with a cousin in south Delhi's Malviyanagar.

In the first few days of her third stint in Delhi, Shruti found herself more lost than she had been on the earlier two occasions. The first time round she had found companionship and then love with Abhay. The second time, she had found a mentor in Sharad. But this time she felt completely alone. Rhea was still in Gurgaon, but things had been a little awkward between them after her marriage to Nehra and Shruti hadn't bothered to take her into confidence when she had fled Delhi three years ago. Hence, Shruti spent a lot of time all by herself and with her thoughts.

Two weeks later, one morning, Shruti called Daivik early to their working office on Kasturba Gandhi Marg. Daivik had no clue about the agenda, nor did he deem it right to enquire much on the phone, but a fear lurked in his mind: was Shruti still in two minds and would she request a smaller role that would enable her to continue with her ashram work in Dhar?

These apprehensions were allayed when Daivik reached the office. Shruti was busy hammering a nail into the wall.

'Shrutiji? What are you doing?' asked Daivik, surprised.

'Putting up an inscription that has always inspired me,' replied Shruti, without turning around.

'But Shrutiji, that's not your job. Let me get a peon or a carpenter to do it.'

'Relax, it's done.'

The inscription was up. It read: *'Liberty will not descend to a people: a people must raise themselves to liberty. It is a blessing that must be earned before it can be enjoyed.'*

'These words hold a lot of nostalgia for me. Hence I wanted to put the plaque up myself,' smiled Shruti, her happiness only too evident on her countenance. Ever since morning, memories of Sharad explaining the significance of these words the first time she had gone to his North Block office, had flooded her thoughts. As she did not want Daivik to see her so emotional, she quickly changed the topic and got down to discussing some pressing issues.

Shruti said that it was very important for the ABP not to lose the momentum they had managed to generate at the launch of the party. She was of the view that every month the ABP should take up a new issue that would strike a chord with the masses and then exploit the issue to the hilt. 'Of course, we will need to do things differently in order to have a long-lasting impact,' noted Shruti.

As Shruti and Daivik discussed their immediate priorities, Shruti went on to articulate her thoughts: 'You know, the sudden focus on rape and crimes against women is only symptomatic of the larger malaise that affects Indian politics. And at the core of it lies the funding of political parties. Till black money continues to fund political parties, these parties will be accountable more to the custodians of this black money than to the general public. And since black money is invariably linked with crime, Indian politicians will continue to be soft on it.'

'I'm so glad our thoughts match,' said Daivik.

'Absolutely! We need to clean up our politics; and only a fundamental change in our thought process can ensure that.'

A few days later, the Government brought in an ordinance that introduced stricter penalties for crimes against women – including the death sentence in the rarest of rare cases. In a meeting of its national office-bearers, the ABP rejected this ordinance on the grounds that merely increasing the penalty would not act as a deterrent. It blamed Government of beating around the bush.

'So what should our stand be, Shrutiji?' asked Catherine.

Shruti thought for a moment and then replied, 'We should push for a five-point agenda. Let's push for chemical castration for all offenders of gender crimes...'

For a moment, the party-members looked a bit scandalized.

'But Shrutiji, first your thrust on TFT and now chemical castration...Don't you think a national party should focus more on policy than the details?' reasoned Daivik.

'No, in fact, that's the change of approach people are expecting from a responsible national party. We can't just draft broad policies and then shy away from detailing their execution.'

'But doesn't chemical castration sound a bit... uncivilized?' asked Daivik sounding unconvinced.

'Aren't street dogs sterilized before you take them in as pets? Then why should people with a known propensity for sexual deviance not be chemically castrated in order to help others live in peace?' Shruti asked.

A week later, Shruti went on an indefinite fast with a set of demands to clean up the political system and curb crimes against women. Apart from chemical castration for all sexual offenders, the ABP demanded that all crimes against women be tried in fast-track courts with a stipulated time frame to dispose these cases. The party also mooted a nation-wide programme called 'Shame the Rapist' in which rapists and sexual offenders across the country would be profiled on a Government website, with all their personal details. It reiterated its demand for an immediate and blanket ban on TFT.

But Shruti's thrust was really on three larger issues. One, she demanded that those facing trial for heinous offences should be banned from contesting elections. Two, that all cases against politicians be fast-tracked. Three, that all political parties be brought under the purview of the Right to Information (RTI) Act. Shruti believed that these larger issues were crucially linked with women's safety and that unless these issues were settled at the macro-level, solutions at the micro-level would be rendered inadequate.

With these demands, Shruti, Daivik, Catherine and the core team of the ABP first met Prime Minister Devender Singh. The man sat quietly through the twenty-minute meeting and as usual had nothing to add.

Shruti, then, decided to take her fight to the masses. She went on an indefinite fast with the slogan: Clean Politics to Ensure Women's Safety!

Shruti's slogan interlinking the two issues caught the imagination of the country. Her oratory helped to articulate her thoughts in the most lucid way to the man on the streets. Soon her agitation snowballed into a mass movement.

'The crux of most problems in our country is our flawed electoral system. Nothing, absolutely nothing, can justify the shameful fact that in the last nine years, more than 80% of the funds that our two national parties have received, have been from unknown or faceless donors. Unless we elect deserving people to our Parliament and State Assemblies, we cannot expect any concrete change in the system. Therefore, today, I shall propose a radical change which we believe will end most problems of our country. That solution, my friends is a system for the public funding of elections,' roared Shruti.

As the crowd heard her out in perfect silence, an impassioned Shruti went on: 'Yes, my friends, are you aware that while the maximum limit for poll expenditure for Lok Sabha constituencies is Rs 40 lakhs, many politicians spend more than ten times that amount to win a seat? Where does that money come from? Who does it belong to? My friends, unaccounted money is always the product of ulterior and unlawful acts and when the very foundation of a Lok Sabha election is laid upon something unlawful, how can you expect the legislative body to remain unaffected by the corrupt influences that hover all around it?'

The crowd waited eagerly for Shruti to spell out her plan.

'One of the main agendas of our party will be to press for public funding of elections – if not entirely than partially. We will propose a 0.5% tax on all taxpayers, known as election tax. The amount thus accumulated will be disbursed among political parties at the time of elections in a ratio proportionate to the total seats won by them in the previous election. However, this amount will not be paid in advance but as a reimbursement once all the political parties have submitted their audited poll expenses for each constituency and uploaded the same on their respective websites. We believe that this change will provide more opportunity for people with limited resources, but greater talent, to enter politics.

'The other crucial change that we will aggressively root for is to bring the functioning of political parties under the RTI Act. Isn't it strange that everytime there has been talk of doing this, our two national parties gang up to ensure it doesn't happen? That's why, friends, the future of India lies beyond its two national parties.

Chapter 20

It was the seventh day of Shruti's indefinite fast and the response had been so overwhelming that on the second day itself the venue had to be shifted from the Jantar Mantar, back to the Ram Leela Maidan in order to accommodate the huge crowds that had turned up in her support. In fact, people across the country had been observing similar fasts in their respective cities and towns to show their solidarity. Girls had been bunking schools and colleges to be with Shruti.

Daivik and Catherine felt vindicated by the response to the movement. As they witnessed the crowds swell with every passing moment, Daivik told Catherine, 'You know, Catherine, the genius of a politician can be gauged not by the issues she chooses to champion but how she manoeuvres them to give her party an obvious advantage over rival parties. By interlinking crimes against women with the quality of our polity, Shrutiji has positioned us as a better alternative to the other political parties, who often join hands to ensure that crime and shady financial deals are never weeded out of politics.'

'Hmm, she has actually hit two birds with one stone and that's incredible,' smiled Catherine.

Daivik and Catherine, though, were concerned about Shruti's health. As a result of her continued fast, Shruti's blood pressure had dropped since last night and she was running a mild fever. Given how insensitive this Government was, its procrastination was possibly a strategy to wear her down.

'Shrutiji, are you sure you want to continue the fast?' Daivik asked her in a private moment. 'I mean, your health is very important for all of us; we have to prepare ourselves for a long battle ahead.'

'We can't fight a long battle if I retreat from this one,' she replied.

Two more days went by with Shruti's condition deteriorating further. Now, apart from her BP being low, her temperature was quite high; besides one of her kidneys was showing signs of distress. This led to increased indignation among the people against the Government, with a young college student in Kolkata even trying to immolate herself. The Government's credibility stood reduced to zero, with the media questioning the silence of the IDP chairperson, Mukta Prajapati.

'Forget Devender Singh, who has anyway been an invisible PM, what is really a scary prospect for our country is that this is an invisible *Government*. In a crisis like the present one, all senior ministers and PM hopefuls just abscond,' lamented a senior journalist.

Soon, Shruti's deteriorating health put Daivik and Catherine in a fix. From brimming with optimism only two days ago, they were now in a dilemma: could they really afford to sacrifice Shruti – an eventuality she seemed hell-bent on achieving?

Another day went by.

Panic was setting in – what with the doctors strongly advising Shruti to break her fast before her body suffered irreversible damage. Even Daivik and Catherine, in as much as they knew the negative implications, wanted Shruti to call off the hunger-strike.

But Shruti remained defiant. 'I was prepared for death all through. Living in an impotent system like ours is simply futile,' she argued.

The ABP members continued to be in dilemma, while the people closely followed the developments on news channels. Anticipating law and order problems in the event of something happening to Shruti, police security had been tightened in all places. People were restive and yet nobody was quite sure how the next few hours would pan out.

That is when a surprise visitor reached the venue where Shruti fasted. It was the suave and extremely media-savvy Union Law Minister, K.P. Chinaswamy. His arrival was greeted with booing from the crowds. Unfazed, and surrounded by his security cordon, Chinaswamy went straight to meet Shruti on the stage.

For the next fifteen minutes, Chinaswamy, Shruti, Daivik, Catherine and two other ABP members could be seen locked in an animated discussion on the stage. On Chinaswamy's request, the mikes had been switched off. However, there was much speculation over what was being discussed, both among the media, as well as the crowd present at the venue. One news channel had even got a speech expert to try and lip-read the words that were being exchanged. The so-called speech expert inferred that Shruti's arrest seemed imminent yet again!

Soon, Chinaswamy was all set to make an announcement, while Shruti, Daivik and Catherine stood next to him – a clear indication that an agreement had been reached between the two parties.

'Friends, I am here to assure you all that the Government stands committed to earnestly consider all demands raised by Shrutiji. In fact I am happy to share with you that the Government has decided to ban the TFT with immediate effect. An ordinance for the same has already been drafted and will be enforced forthwith. As far as the electoral reforms demanded by Shrutiji are concerned, let me reassure you that the Government has called for an all-party meet next week to discuss the same. This meeting will also discuss the option and feasibility of chemical castration as a deterrent.'

The crowd remained wary and sceptical. The cynicism against this Government was so high that even this public reassurance by none other than the country's Law Minister was taken with a pinch of salt.

'I would like to assure Shrutiji that the Government is fully behind her in this crucial fight. I will humbly request her to have faith in the Government and end the fast immediately.'

Saying this, in a clever political gesture, Chinaswamy asked his staff to get him a glass of lemon juice that he hoped to personally offer Shruti. His staff was prompt enough to do their master's bidding but Shruti spoilt the photo-op by politely declining the drink from him. She turned to Daivik instead, who held out a glass of glucose for her. A sheepish Chinaswamy left the venue, careful to keep his fake smile plastered on till the end.

In the speech that followed, Shruti asked the masses not to be taken in by the Government's clever gestures unless the Government walked its talk. While she was ending her fast on Chinaswamy's assurance, she warned that it would not take her long to embark on another fast if the Government went back on its promise. Thus the onus this time was upon the Government to live up to its word. Of course, the moment Chinaswamy got into his car, he unleashed some of the choicest Tamil invectives upon Shruti and Daivik.

At the end of Shruti's agitation, there were two clear gainers. The first was Shruti herself. In a week's time, she seemed to have usurped the Opposition space from Ravi Nehra's Jan-Hit party. People now clearly understood why a non-performing IDP was allowed such a long run in power: this was because the Jan-Hit party was simply not serious about dethroning the Government. Business and mercenary interests held greater importance for the Jan-Hit party than its political agenda.

The other gainer was K.P. Chinaswamy. With PM Devender Singh's popularity having hit an all-time low, his exit was imminent and hence, smelling an opportunity, at least three or four leaders of the IDP had been cleverly positioning themselves to occupy the PM's post. While one of them had been brazenly playing the minority card, the other was exploiting his Dalit lineage to advantage. Chinaswamy, by comparison, appeared far more inclusive and politically adroit in his approach.

Chinaswamy, fifty-seven, had started his career as a student leader in Chennai. Inspired by the late K. Kamraj, one of the most successful national leaders in the history of Tamil Nadu, Chinaswamy was clear that he wanted to play an important part in national politics right from the start. Hence, he preferred a less popular IDP which had an all-India presence over the two regional parties that dominated Tamil Nadu's politics.

In 1984, Chinaswamy won his first Assembly elections while from 1989 onwards he was an elected MP from Tamil Nadu. Somewhere along Chinaswamy's political journey his staunch socialist ideals had given way to an entrepreneurial urge. In the late nineties, along with his younger brother, he floated a production house for producing TV software, which over the years grew into one of India's most successful software producing firms, catering to almost every entertainment channel in the four southern states of the country. In 2007, when his Wharton-educated older son took over the reins of the company, the company forayed into news programming and launched a news channel of its own. In the 2009 elections, this news channel was believed to have played a crucial role in influencing voters' perceptions in favour of the IDP, with the IDP recording its most successful performance ever in Tamil Nadu that year.

Chinaswamy lived alone in his Janpath bungalow while his two sons and wife were based out of Chennai. Nonetheless, Chinaswamy never lost an opportunity to release happy family pictures on the social media, which left people wondering as to when they were clicked.

Like all IDP stalwarts, Chinaswamy was a staunch loyalist of the IDP chairperson. What worked additionally in his favour were his deft skills as an administrator and being extremely media-savvy. For instance, most other IDP ministers would have been too egoistic to travel to the venue of Shruti's fast. Chinaswamy, on the other hand, had sensed a great opportunity in it – by elevating Shruti's status, the IDP would be playing one Opposition party against the other and a division in Opposition votes was sure to work in the IDP's favour. With his presence at the fast venue, Chinaswamy had thus hoped that he would be perceived as the brain behind his Government's move and hence emerge a stronger contender for the top job.

Chinaswamy's move provided the Government some much needed breathing space. It was no wonder then that Chinaswamy had lately emerged as Madam Prajapati's key trouble-shooter. For a Government mired in chaos and uncertainty, he at least understood the pulse of the people and was invariably successful in positioning himself on the 'politically correct' side.

Chinaswamy's was quite active on social media and his Twitter updates were aimed at impressing the youth. He'd cleverly planted several stories about how he managed to put in an 18-hour work day and managed to remain fit with just four hours of sleep.

Chinaswamy's rise in Delhi's corridors of power, had of course led to an increase in the number of his detractors, some of whom have been spreading all sorts of stories about him.

A well-known politician of his own party was recently caught on hidden camera, telling a journalist, 'Chinaswamy is the biggest chhupa-rustam you can ever come across. Just try to meet him after 8 p.m. and you'll find that even his bodyguards have no clue where he is. Wine and women are all he knows after eight, of course making an exception when he has to appear on the national media.' Even though, the politician was drunk when he said this and was later sacked from IDP's primary membership for his indiscretion, he had clearly brought Chinaswamy's personal life under the scanner.

With Chinaswamy's growing stakes in national politics, curiosity about his personal life was increasing all the time.

Chapter 21

Shruti and Rhea finally met on a calm and serene morning in late January. They met in the sprawling Lodi Gardens where they strolled together. There was more silence than words between them and yet the silence spoke more than words ever could. Rhea had filed for divorce and a hearing was scheduled next week.

'Shruti, I wish I had never met Ravi Nehra. I have wasted five years of my life,' finally confessed Rhea, barely holding back her emotions.

Shruti did not say anything for the next couple of minutes, lost perhaps in her own thoughts, and then she said, 'I wish I had not been raped. I wish I could go back fifteen years to the day before life changed so dramatically for me...'

'You really regret these fifteen years?' asked Rhea looking into her eyes.

Shruti gathered herself, aware that these past years had been both a curse and a blessing for her. She shrugged and tried changing the topic. 'So where does life go from here?' she asked Rhea.

Rhea said she wasn't sure. Right now her first priority was to get a divorce and look after her son.

'Join the ABP. Your life took a detour but you can still get back on track. We can work together once again to revive Sharad's legacy...the country needs his brand of decisive leadership more than ever today.'

Shruti was pretty sure that Rhea would respond in the affirmative but that was not to be. 'I...I need to sort myself out first. Now I want to do things that I really believe in. And I've realized that politics is not my cup of tea.'

Rhea then told her that after the next court hearing she was planning to go off to London and stay with her maternal cousin, Madhu. 'I need to be away from here for some time to mull over my priorities. I need to be away to restore my sanity.'

Shruti, being the true democrat that she was, accepted Rhea's stand gracefully.

For her part, Rhea had a piece of advice for Shruti. 'You know, Shruti, your challenges are going to be much bigger now. You now have to fight two formidable enemies: the Government *and* Nehra. Rest assured, if you need any help from me in nailing my ex I will be the first person to help. And that's not because of the bitterness of our failed marriage. That's because the country deserves to be rid of a scoundrel like him.' Rhea then assured Shruti that she could get in touch with her anytime, should she need anything.

Shruti hugged Rhea, feeling a strange assortment of emotions. 'Take care, beta,' she said.

Rhea couldn't hold back her tears at Shruti's concern.

Shruti held her hand and then hugged her in an understanding, all-forgiving, maternal sort of way as they walked out of Lodi Gardens.

Later that day, Shruti and Daivik met in office to chart out their immediate strategy for the next week.

'Shrutiji, we need to keep the momentum going and for that, apart from our sustained championing of the issues we believe in, we have decided to carry out some sting operations that will expose malpractices in both the IDP and Jan-Hit party. I have been co-ordinating closely with Faisal on this…' Daivik told her.

'So what's the progress on that front? Is Faisal ready with something?' asked Shruti.

'Well, yes, that's what he told me on the phone. He says it's something very shocking and he needs a couple of days to obtain more information.'

'Hmm… whom does it involve?'

'Rajveer Thakur. There's a huge mystery over how a man's assets can grow over 500 times in less than two decades…I have some concrete leads. Just two more days and I think I should be ready with an exposé that will shake the ruling clan of this country…'

Chapter 22

Catherine's much hyped spy-thriller movie with South superstar, Eeshwaran, was ready. In fact, the release was only four weeks away and considering that a whopping Rs 85 scrore had been spent making the film, it was all the more important to now promote it aggressively in order to recover the costs.

Catherine was required to stay on in Delhi and promote the movie for at least a week or two close to its release date. She had asked her manager, Rina Dewan, to move into her Mumbai flat and look after Nia till she was done with this extremely hectic phase of the film's release and the settling-down of her new political party. Realizing that she would need to make many public appearances, Catherine had begun working out at the Ashoka Hotel gym for an hour every day.

Interestingly, Ravi Nehra, who was also battling a tough phase – both politically and personally – had also taken to working out as a means of de-stressing himself. Ravi normally worked out late in the night but since an important court hearing of his divorce case was scheduled at noon, he had decided to hit the gym early that morning. And as fate would have it, he too landed up at the gym in Hotel Ashok.

Ravi was intrigued when, on the treadmill right next to his, he spotted a glamorous looking woman. Rubbing his groggy eyes, he looked at her more intently only to confirm that it was filmstar and ABP member, Catherine Khan.

Catherine did not notice him at first. She was surfing news channels on the small TV positioned in front of her treadmill, until she stopped at a channel that was beaming news about her forthcoming film.

'Hi, so all set for the movie's release, eh?' Ravi attempted initiating a conversation.

Catherine was surprised to find the infamous Ravi Nehra on the treadmill alongside hers. She answered with a nod and a measured smile, hoping to maintain a distance.

'So how are you going to manage a political career along with movies? Or is politics a passing fad?' Ravi asked, tongue-in cheek.

'Well, Raviji, I will manage both...can't quite afford not to be in politics considering the mess you guys have landed the country in...'

'Ha ha...well said! *Accha hai,* among other things, Indian politics always lacked a glamour quotient...at least your presence will address that!'

Catherine smiled in response. That's when she saw the news story playing out on the TV screen in front of Ravi's treadmill. It was about his divorce; Ravi and Rhea were locked in an acrimonious custody battle over their son. The court hearing later today was to decide the fate of the case.

'Hmm...it's a crucial day for you in court,' Catherine said, hoping to make him uncomfortable.

'Yes, it is. But I guess I will have my way,' he replied without being fazed.

'What makes you that confident?'

'Well, confidence is all I have...I am quite mediocre otherwise,' Ravi said matter-of-factly.

Catherine was surprised by this uncharacteristically honest confession and was going to answer him when she got a call from her manager in Mumbai. She slowed down her machine and answered the phone.

'*Whatttt?* How did this happen?' Catherine queried in shock, giving Ravi enough of an indication that something was amiss.

Nia had tripped down some stairs and was in acute pain. She was being rushed to the doctor. There were fears of a possible fracture of her left arm.

'Okay, just call me when you've shown her to the doc, okay?' instructed a panicked Catherine, winding up her gym session abruptly.

'What's happened, Catherine? Is there anything I can do to help?' asked Ravi sounding as genuine as he could.

Catherine was very distressed. She knew she'd have to rush to Mumbai on the first flight out but what added to her problems was the absence of her chauffeur on that very day. When he heard what had happened, Ravi convinced her to allow him to have her dropped in his car. Given Catherine's state of mind, she acquiesced.

Even as Ravi dialled a number on his cell, he couldn't control the familiar glint in his eye as he watched Catherine leave. '*Achcha,* listen, Pathak,' he instructed his secretary. 'I have some work for you...find out everything you can about Catherine Khan...everything, including details about her parents, her personal life and upbringing. Is that clear? And I need this information fast.'

Ravi himself was in for a rude shock later that day when the court denied him custody of his son. The efforts of Ravi's lawyers to paint Rhea as unpredictable and temperamental cut no ice with the lady judge in the family court. She ruled that at least for the first twelve years of his life, Anway would stay with his mother.

The court also ruled in favour of Ravi paying alimony to Rhea every month. However, Rhea rejected this provision. 'I can't accept money from someone I don't respect, so what if he is my ex-husband. To me it would be akin to accepting drug money,' was Rhea's radical contention – a stand that later drew massive appreciation from the media.

Ravi left the court in a great temper, pushing roughly past the large posse of media that had been waiting outside, in the hope of getting a byte from him to spice up their evening-news bulletin.

Ravi was previously scheduled that evening to go for an interview with renowned senior journalist, Harish Chawla, for his show, 'Tough Talk'. Chawla, whose weekly show was immensely popular with viewers for its no-holds-barred, unrelenting style, could also be quite rude at times – especially when he didn't get a straight answer from his guest. He was so insulting that many celebrities had stopped coming on his show.

It was after being hounded for two years that Ravi had finally consented to be a guest on his show. That Ravi's recording was to take place on the very day the court gave its unfavourable judgment was clearly a case of bad timing. However, as the interview had been fixed a month ago, Ravi chose to brave it.

Unfortunately, Chawla was at his acerbic best during the interview. 'Nehraji, do you believe in astrology?' Chawla asked pointedly.

'No, why?'

'Well, I think you are going through a horrible planetary phase. Two women – Shruti and Rhea – have ruined your happiness, one on the political front and the other on the personal front...and you don't seem to know how to respond to the situation...'

Ravi was absolutely taken aback by Chawla's provocative tone. He knew Chawla could be rude, but this rude? 'Well, that's not true. Shruti Ranjan may have had people support her during an agitation but her party simply does not have the organizational strength to fight an all-India election. The Jan-Hit party is the only Opposition party in the country.'

'But, Ravi, how did Shruti garner such a phenomenal response? Doesn't that prove that people are unhappy with your party?'

'No, it doesn't,' was Ravi's terse response.

'I think you are in denial – in the same way that you were about your personal life. If I can be brutally honest here, the people of India are worried that the Jan-Hit party might soon suffer an irreparable collapse... much like your marriage...'

At that point, Ravi lost his shirt. 'Bastard, what gives you the impression that I have come here to be insulted? Do you realize who I am? I am the f***ing president of the Jan-Hit party. Just because my chips are down today, you think you can get over my head and pee on top of me?'

From Ravi's ranting it was clear that he was drunk.

'Raviji, the camera is still on,' Chawla retorted calmly.

Ravi was so incensed that he went straight to Chawla and slapped him hard. He then rushed towards the cameraman and had the camera forcibly switched off.

Ravi walked away in a huff only to realize within minutes that he had screwed up horribly. Agreed, he was going through a terrible phase, but the onus really was on him to behave in a more dignified manner. Oh, how he wished the interview could be undone!

What followed, thus, were incessant requests, cajoling and finally even veiled threats from Ravi's men to Harish Chawla's office. In one anonymous call Chawla was even offered Rs 1 crore to drop the interview. Then Ravi personally called Chawla to apologize for his behaviour. Chawla, though remained unfazed; he went ahead and beamed the unedited interview after playing the promo extensively before its actual telecast.

As images of a provoked Ravi losing his cool and slapping Chawla were seen by viewers across the country, Ravi's popularity suffered a devastating blow. So far, people had only read of his purportedly unclean dealings; here they were witnessing live what a douche he was.

Ravi Nehra's interview was also watched keenly at the ABP office by Shruti, Daivik, Pratibha Kaushal and M.P. Singh.

'Well, this is hara-kiri...the biggest self-goal that a political leader can score,' beamed M.P. Singh.

'Poor chap...his behaviour reminds me of the famous Hindi saying "*vinaash kaale viprit buddhi*",' said Pratibha Kaushal.

Shruti, who was so far lost in her thoughts, said, 'Don't you think that after this incident Nehra will face dissent from his own party-members?'

'Well, possibly...but when such a situation arose in the past, he always bought off his detractors.'

'Hmm...but then the detractors didn't have an alternative. Now they have the ABP.'

Singh's and Kaushal's eyes lit up when they heard this. 'Are you hinting at breaking the Jan-Hit party?' Kaushal queried.

'Why not? If our democracy is indeed a mockery of numbers, why should we be closed to the idea?' Shruti sounded uncharacteristically opportunistic. Daivik was surprised – and not entirely happy – to see her in this new avatar.

'In that case you will need 41 MPs – that is, one-third of the Jan-Hit party's strength in Parliament, to defect from the Jan-Hit party in order to escape the anti-defection law,' Singh cautioned.

Before Shruti could respond to this, Daivik intervened and made his opposition to the idea known. 'No, that's not an option for us. We will not poach leaders from other parties. I know this might prolong our battles but then our idealism is what distinguishes us from other parties. There can't be any compromise on that.'

Daivik's assertion found support. For a moment, his idealism reminded Shruti of her own younger days in politics. She had been rigid in her views while Sharad invariably tried to introduce her to a more pragmatic worldview.

Shruti found the similarity ironical.

Chapter 23

When Catherine landed at the Chhatrapati Shivaji Airport in Mumbai, she was in for another shock. Before boarding her flight from Delhi, the X-ray report had confirmed a fracture in Nia's left arm. Catherine had thus landed in Mumbai thinking that she would bring Nia and her nanny to stay with her in Delhi for a few weeks.

But in Mumbai her manager instructed the driver to take the car to Juhu.

The moment Catherine heard 'Juhu' instead of 'Versova', she knew what that implied. Her manager nodded: 'When we were at the hospital, Armaan had dropped by at home to meet Nia. When the nanny informed him of what had happened, he drove straight to the hospital and took Nia with him, saying she was not safe in your house.'

'What nonsense! I mean this fall could have happened anywhere…' Catherine said.

'Yes, but he was adamant.'

The drive from the airport to Juhu was unusually long due to heavy traffic all along the route. Catherine felt an unusual helplessness. She hated being forced to go to her in-law's house and knew that her experience there would be far from pleasant.

An hour later, Catherine stood in the sprawling living room of her father-in-law's house, meaning to confront him and his timid wife. She was further infuriated upon learning that Armaan had left for the US on a 45-day shooting schedule.

'I don't understand this! I mean, if Armaan was leaving for 45 days, why did he have to bring Nia here?' an upset Catherine demanded to know.

'Because Nia's grandparents are alive and can take care of her,' replied Vikrant Kapoor suavely.

'Papa, are you trying to say I can't take care of Nia?' Catherine argued. It had taken some effort for Catherine to address Vikrant as Papa, but given the absence of a father in her life, she was instinctively unwilling to lose out on another father figure.

'Well, beta, we're not saying that…You have been an excellent mother but after what happened today and considering that you have a hectic schedule over the next few weeks, we feel that your daughter will be the safest if you leave her with us,' Vikrant reasoned calmly.

'But, Papa, I want to take Nia with me to Delhi,' Catherine pleaded.

'Leave her with us, Catherine. I am not shooting for the next couple of months and want to personally take care of my granddaughter,' Vikrant said in an affectionate, yet assertive way.

Had it been Armaan, Catherine would have reacted very differently but in the situation, she couldn't say no to Vikrant.

It was very uncomfortable for Catherine to spend the night in her ex-in-laws' house in the absence of her ex-husband. She stayed awake most of the night tending to Nia, who was restive and in pain.

Catherine woke up in the morning after sleeping for barely a couple of hours only to learn that some fundamentalist groups in Tamil Nadu had threatened to stall the release of her new film unless the whole movie was shown to them and the parts they found 'objectionable' were edited out.

Eeshwaran, who was also the producer of the movie, had refused to bow to their demands. 'Who are they to decide which parts of my film should be edited? In fact, these are the people most ignorant about religion...' Eeshwaran was quoted as having said.

Eeshwaran's provocative comment led to the fundamentalist groups retaliating with greater fervour, besides doling out a threat of violence. Suddenly, the release of the film seemed quite dicey.

Catherine wondered why problems, when they came, came all together. She was supposed to fly back to Delhi in the afternoon but the sudden setbacks of the last two days left her feeling low and demotivated.

Just then, Nia woke up and got very excited on seeing her mother next to her. Catherine hugged her little daughter tight...and instantly felt so much better. The child's innocent happiness at seeing her, and her own delight at being with her little girl, washed away all the other worries from her mind. She decided to stay back and spend another day with her baby.

Back in Delhi, the ABP members met in the afternoon. In this meeting, the spotlight was on Faisal, the sting-op expert, on whose skills the ABP was depending heavily. Faisal connected his camera cable to the LCD TV. And what the members of the party saw had them glued to their seats. It was a sting operation in which two very senior lawyers of the Supreme Court were recorded on camera talking about the gross inconsistencies in the appointment of judges to the Supreme Court and the state High Courts.

'Merit and the past record of the candidate ceased to be the criteria long ago. Nowadays what matters is the perceived political affiliation of the candidate and the likelihood of him being pro-Government. No wonder that after getting appointed, so many SC judges rush to Mukta Prajapati to seek her blessings,' one of them said.

The other Supreme Court lawyer, who had been an almost sure-shot candidate for being appointed judge before losing out, had this to say : 'The one thing that went against me was that while in college I was a member of the student wing of a party that opposed the IDP tooth and nail.'

There were other shocking revelations that raised a big question mark over Chinaswamy as most of these irrational appointments had taken place in his tenure. As the ABP members watched the remainder of the 20-minute exposé they knew they had sufficient substance with them to decimate Chinaswamy's credentials.

'Wow! Based on this evidence we can easily nail the Minister and make him quit,' Shruti averred.

'Just give me a few more days. I am working on a couple of new leads which promise to be far more explosive. I think by next Monday I should be ready with those as well,' said Faisal.

'Sounds good! By then, I should have a comprehensive case against Rajveer Thakur too,' Daivik said.

Coincidentally, just two days later, Shruti and Daivik had to meet Chinaswamy at an all-party meeting convened in Chinaswamy's office. This meeting was called to discuss the still pending Ordinance to introducing the provision of chemical castration in the judicial system.

Even though Shruti and Daivik doubted Chinaswamy's sincerity, it being an all-party meeting, they did not want to skip it. When they reached Chinaswamy's office, however, they were surprised to find that they were the only ones invited.

'I thought this was supposed to be an all-party meeting,' Shruti told Chinaswamy's secretary.

'Well, Sir wants to take your views before talking to the others,' his secretary said solicitously.

Chinaswamy walked in just then and came to the point right away. 'I have heard you are planning a sting against me,' he said abruptly.

For a moment, Shruti and Daivik were left speechless. Then Daivik said, 'Hats off to you, Chinaswamyji... You're spot on. I must say, you have an excellent network of informants.'

'What will you take to drop it?' the minister asked brazenly.

Before Shruti and Daivik could react, Chinaswamy continued: 'Trust me, these legal improprieties that you plan to charge me for, are a small thing. They have existed all the time. What if I give you a much bigger lead against our PM?'

Shruti and Daivik looked at Chinaswamy in surprise, even as he continued to explain: 'Think about it. I can give you ample evidence of the tacit involvement of the Prime Minister's Office in all the scams that have taken place in the last few years. But of course for that, you will have to abandon whatever exposé you are planning against me.'

On the face of it, his bargain made sense. It was always more productive to trap the bigger fish. But then, would taking the help of one offender in nailing the other not be unethical? 'What you say makes sense,' said Shruti, surprising Daivik.

'Of course it does, Ma'am. Think about it. How can a PM not be aware of the files lying with his own ministry? How can he absolve himself from the wrongdoing of his favourite bureaucrats?'

'Fair enough. Get us the evidence against the PMO and we will drop the sting against you,' said Shruti, much to Chinaswamy's relief and Daivik's shock. For some strange reason, Chinaswamy was supremely confident that Shruti would drop the case against him.

That night, Chinaswamy met Mukta Prajapati with an incredibly audacious proposal.

'Madam, if Devender Singh continues as PM, I can assure you, the IDP is set to lose the elections…'

'What's the way out?'

'Give him a respectable exit. Make him the President of the country. And get a new, aggressive PM.'

Needless to say, Chinaswamy was pitching himself for the PM's post, assuring Mukta Prajapati that he would undo the damage caused by Devender Singh and help the party win at least 200 seats in the Lok Sabha polls.

But that same night, when Chinaswamy was lobbying for himself with Mukta Prajapati, Shruti and Daivik had a bit of an argument.

'Shrutiji, how could you just agree to Chinaswamy's deal? I don't think it is ethical to accept evidence from one offender against another. I mean, I would much rather carry out the exposé against Chinaswamy now and wait for our turn to nail the PM,' he reasoned, persuasively.

Shruti heard Daivik out calmly and then said, 'So who is stopping you?'

'Didn't you tell Chinaswamy you are accepting his deal?'

'Does one really need to be straight and honest with someone as untrustworthy as Chinaswamy? Let Chinaswamy believe that we have accepted the deal. He will be in for a bigger shock.'

The cool, confident smile on Shruti's visage left Daivik surprised yet again. She was much more politically savvy than he had thought.

Chinaswamy's luck was bad indeed. While he had begun to believe that he was closer to 7 Race Course Road than ever before, everything was actually going against him.

Mukta Prajapati, as usual consulted her astrologer about elevating Chinaswamy to the PMO. 'Don't,' was the astrologer's strict advice. 'He will never listen to you, and will do his own thing. You will not be able to run the country by proxy.' Mukta seldom went against her astrologer's counsel. Hence, Chinaswamy's fate was sealed. He would not become the PM – not in this life, anyway.

Simultaneously, even as Chinaswamy tried his best to reach out to Shruti and Daivik, they became incommunicado.

'Daivik, can we do the Chinaswamy exposé right away? I mean, are we ready?' Shruti asked Daivik a couple of days later.

'I guess so. But is there a pressing urgency to hurry it up?'

'Well, I have a hunch that Chinaswamy being the cunning guy that he is, might suspect we've ditched him and might try to destroy the evidence.'

'Hmm… you could be right.'

Hence, instead of waiting till next week, the ABP called an impromptu press conference on that very Friday evening.

At the press conference, the ABP played out the entire video of the sting against Chinaswamy. Had it just been about the partiality in the appointment of judges, things would still perhaps have been manageable. What was inexcusable was a senior lawyer corroborating on camera that a bureaucrat from the Law Ministry had bribed a judge in order to ensure a favourable ruling for the Government. In another equally appalling revelation, a senior CBI officer was caught on camera saying how he had been forced to give a clean chit to a regional leader who was a potential ally of the IDP. This officer revealed that the Law Minster had been personally accessing the most sensitive files of the CBI and forcing the organization to toe the Government line.

Chinaswamy knew that the allegations were so damning that he would need a miracle to survive them. Though he initially retaliated rather aggressively by threatening to file a defamation case against the ABP, Mukta Prajapati eventually asked him to quit. In an election year, the IDP could not take a risk as big as being seen to be insensitive on an issue concerning manipulating something as sacrosanct as the judiciary.

Chinaswamy's resignation from the Cabinet came as a huge blow to the Government, more so as he had begun to be seen as a likely future PM candidate. Many observers believed it also marked the virtual death of an immensely ambitious career carved out by indefatigable hard work and deft image management. After getting Chinaswamy's scalp, it was expected that the ABP would allow the other political parties some breathing space.

However, that was not to be.

Just two days later, at the Monday morning meeting that followed, the ABP called another press conference. The agenda of this press conference remained a mystery till the very last.

In this press conference, Daivik alleged that the net worth of Rajveer Thakur, husband of IDP chairperson, Mukta Prajapati had multiplied 500 times in the last nine years that the IDP had been in power. He alleged that a leading builder in Maharashtra had been allotted over 10,000 acres of land in Nashik and Aurangabad by the IDP Government in Maharashtra at just 20% of the market value of that land. This builder had subsequently sold off nearly 70% of the land thus acquired to Rajveer at just 10% of its market value. Thus Rajveer acquired property whose market worth was over Rs 800 crore without any known sources of income...

The people of the country were stunned and enraged by these damning charges against Mukta Prajapati's husband. And they were as amazed by the ABP's audacity. Rumours about Rajveer's shady business deals had been floating around for a very long time. But the entire national media had decided to look the other way on this, considering that Mukta Prajapati was a stakeholder here. Now Daivik had blown the lid off the scandal. And along with Daivik, the finances of IDP had come under the scanner.

Shruti had another startling disclosure to make before ending the press conference. 'Ravi Nehra has been privy to Rajveer's financial misappropriations for well over a year now. But he consciously chose to look the other way. Twice, social activists had pleaded with Nehra to raise the issue in Parliament but on both occasions he chickened out.'

These twin assaults of the ABP on the ruling IDP shook the political scenario in the country. Moreover, by accusing Ravi Nehra of shielding Rajveer Thakur, the ABP had even put the Jan-Hit party on notice. In fact, the ABP had outsmarted the Jan-Hit party by a huge margin. And unless the Jan-Hit party came up with a counter strategy soon, it was in danger of losing the Opposition space to the ABP.

As expected, the next day's newspaper headlines were dominated by coverage of the exposé. The country's leading newspaper carried the headline, '*Resurgent Shruti Strikes off Chinaswamy & Rajveer, Puts Ravi Nehra on Notice.*'

Writing about the exposé and its fallout, another leading newspaper noted, 'The good thing that the ABP has done is it has reinfused the aggression and dynamism that had gone missing from India's politics. If the party continues this way, chances are that both the Government and the Jan-Hit party will suffer huge casualties in the run-up to the next elections.'

Shruti felt happy with the way these last few weeks had gone. Moreover, she was reassured by how nicely she and Daivik formed a productive mentor–protégé team; much like Sharad and she had done, many years ago.

Life never ceased to surprise and encourage her.

Chapter 24

Catherine, who was in Mumbai, attending to her daughter, had missed all the action taking place in Delhi. As the official spokesperson of the party, her absence was particularly noticeable. When a scribe asked Daivik about Catherine's absence, Daivik just said she was attending to a personal issue. Daivik's evasive answer had even the ABP members raise their eyebrows. They didn't want to be judgmental just yet, but certain preconceived notions about actors-turned-politicians were too strong to be rubbished.

Catherine landed in Delhi late evening on Monday. Realizing that it was too late for her to pursue any official work, she decided to go for a quick work-out session so that she could start work early the next day.

She reached the gym at 9, only to be surprised to see Ravi Nehra on the treadmill.

'Oh, hi,' Ravi greeted her. 'How's your daughter now?'

Ravi, given the astute strategist that he was, understood the importance of asking a mother about her child. For the next ten minutes, given her state of emotional anguish – and even though she knew that Ravi Nehra was from the enemy camp – Catherine nearly forgot who she was talking to as she bared her heart to him about how much she missed her daughter and how the present phase of her life was the most challenging one she had been through.

Ravi was smart enough to prolong the conversation by offering her a cup of coffee,

Half an hour later, they sat at the gym café. Out of courtesy, Catherine extended her condolences to Ravi on the court judgment disallowing him custody of his son.

'Our marriage was always doomed but it's just unthinkable to stay without my son,' Ravi said mournfully.

'You must try and meet him more often,' suggested Catherine, feeling a certain kinship with Ravi as he, like her, was struggling through a breaking marriage.

Ravi looked away as his eyes filled; his emotionally fragile look, coupled with the stubble and the hooded eyes, were the perfect foil for a sensitive woman's sympathy.

'Is there no way Rhea and you can work out your differences?'

'Nope,' he said, in a voice choked with emotion. 'When I look back, I feel had it not been for our son, the marriage would have been over long ago.'

Ravi broke down and a confused Catherine found herself comforting him.

Two days latter, the ABP team met at Shruti's house to celebrate the success of their twin exposé over dinner. The strictly vegetarian menu had been personally cooked by Chhavi. As Catherine was back in town, she too attended the dinner. Even Rhea dropped in for a bit on Shruti's personal request.

At the dinner, there was more to celebrate when M.P Singh informed the gathering that after Shruti's hunger-strike and their exposé, people from nearly 500 districts across the country had expressed their willingness to set up local cadres for the party. Among the more illustrious professionals who had offered to help the party were lawyers, advertising professionals, bloggers and journalists – all of whose services could come in handy for the party. Many of these supporters had once belonged to the IDP or the Jan-Hit party and were disillusioned by both. Singh suggested that Shruti might soon have to start touring the country in order to appoint local unit chiefs.

'Anytime. I have lots of experience of that,' Shruti joked good-humouredly and then turned to Daivik: 'So Mr Verma, are you happy with the way the exposé has gone?'

'I guess. The country is raving about the "re-invented Shruti Ranjan". I am quite surprised to see you in this new avatar…' Daivik was quite candid about his personal views of Shruti's behaviour.

Shruti smiled and turned to another guest. She marvelled at how, without even being conscious of it, she was behaving exactly like her mentor Sharad Malviya wanted her to behave. After all, re-inventing his politics according to the mood of the nation was an art that he had excelled at!

Catherine remained somewhat distracted throughout the dinner. Protests against the release of her film had escalated, with one fundamentalist group openly threatening arson and rioting if the movie was released in its present form. There were also reports that the timid and extra-pacifist Government at the centre was considering holding back the film's release till the fundamentalist groups' concerns were addressed. Actually, Eeshwaran and Catherine had in fact met the Union Information and Broadcasting Minister earlier in the day; sadly, the meeting had been unproductive with the Minister simply saying that it was a law and order issue over which his ministry did not have much control. Thus, with just two weeks to go, the future of the movie remained unclear.

Just then Catherine received a call from an unknown number. Answering it, she recognized Ravi Nehra's voice. She moved aside to talk to him, but not before her surprised 'Raviji' had left the other members looking at her askance.

Five minutes later, Catherine returned, looking a lot more relaxed. 'I got an unexpected call from Ravi Nehra,' she announced.

'And?' at least two members asked in unison.

'He is organizing a special screening of my film for the Home Minister, S.K. Patil, and if the minister finds nothing wrong with the film, he will ensure that the Government supports its release.'

While Catherine had mentioned meeting Ravi Nehra at the gym before, his unexpected largesse towards her in this politically volatile situation was viewed with considerable cynicism.

'Are you *sure* you want to take Ravi Nehra's help?' asked Pratibha Kaushal.

Before Catherine could reply, Daivik butted in: 'Why not? I think we must keep our politics away from Catherine's film career. Quite a lot is at stake for her with this film and if someone helps in its release, I don't see why she should refuse their help.' Daivik defended his friend as unflinchingly as he always had.

'But wouldn't Nehra expect something in return? He certainly isn't unselfish. Is he?' cautioned Shruti.

'Listen Catherine, trust me, Ravi Nehra is a creep. Avoid him like the plague,' Rhea warned her before leaving the party.

A slight undercurrent of potential tensions within the ABP could already be felt when Daivik ended the discussion, saying, 'Friends, I am sure Catherine is mature enough to handle this situation on her own. We ought to trust each other a bit more.'

Later that night, as Shruti flipped through some TV news channels before going to bed, she was upset by a particularly suggestive story playing out on a B-grade Hindi news channel. This news channel showed pictures of Catherine and Ravi Nehra stepping out together from the gym and suggested there was something brewing between them.

Shruti wondered what it was about a barbaric hooligan like Nehra that made him worm his way into the lives of so many accomplished and intelligent women. What did women find so attractive about him?

As an exhausted Shruti flipped to another channel before switching off the TV, she stopped short. The breaking news flashing on its scroll informed the viewer that two Indian soldiers had been beheaded by Pakistani troops along the Line of Control (LoC) in Kashmir.

Chapter 25

India and Pakistan: never have two siblings been this dissimilar and this distrusting of each other. Beneath the façade of forging friendly ties lies a history of perfidy and venom, which renders all peace efforts banal. In fact, everytime India has made a fresh effort to initiate peace, sooner than later she has been stabbed in the back.

The act of backstabbing this time around took place in the form of the beheading and the mutilation of two Indian soldiers by their rogue Pakistani counterparts along the Line of Control. What was far worse than the Pakistan army's barbaric act was the Indian Government's pusillanimous response; casually asking Pakistan to investigate the killings. The response was so weird that it seemed akin to the police asking robbers to investigate a burglary they had committed. So the country was justified in feeling more betrayed by its own Government than by Pakistan.

Shruti, along with Daivik, took off to meet one of the soldier's family in their village, some 200 km east of Delhi. On their way to the village, Shruti wondered why political leaders were expected to meet bereaved families in situations like these. Were politicians actually expected to feel the pain of the suffering family? Was it a professional obligation? Or was it a gimmick aimed at manipulating people's perceptions? Much though she would have liked to believe that it was genuine empathy that brought her to the bereaved family, her sad conclusion was that it was probably a mix of all the three.

Shruti dreaded facing the widow of the deceased – the incident reminding her of her visit to a village in Jehanabad as the Bihar CM many years ago, where sixty people, including many children, had been massacred by a gang of *zamindars*. She dreaded the thought of facing another hapless widow today.

Soon, Shruti was to relive that terrible moment. Trying to console the slain soldier's grieving wife, she felt drained of all hope; a sense of desolation that left her empty and bereft. For Daivik, on the other hand, the experience was more clinical. In preparing for this heart-wrenching journey, he had psyched himself up and told himself that he couldn't possibly allow himself to feel the pain of every Indian or else he'd be too depressed to concentrate on the important work at hand.

Two hours later, Ravi Nehra showed up at the same spot to offer his respects. Desperate to score some brownie points and frustrated that Shruti had reached there first, he played to the gallery by resorting to rhetoric and advocating another war against Pakistan. However the response to his fiery speech in the village was unusually lukewarm.

On their way back, Daivik could see how badly Shruti had been affected by what she had seen. On her return to Delhi, she went straight into a press conference at the party office.

'Our PM often says: "A prosperous Pakistan is in India's interests?" Does he know what he's saying?' she roared at the press. 'For the first time in India's history, we have a Government that is so shockingly indifferent to its own defence forces! Had it been any other country's army it would have even rebelled against the Government. You have to give due credit to the Indian Army for putting up with all the infrastructural inadequacies and now this insulting indifference by Government! The least that the Government can do in the present situation is to explain to the nation why we have to beg of friendship from our devious neighbour.'

Shruti's diatribe struck an instant chord with the masses. Bolstered by the public support she got, Shruti wrote an article for India's leading English daily where she unleashed a no-holds-barred campaign against the Government's shamelessly thoughtless approach towards Pakistan.

'Why do we love to fool ourselves by thinking that India and Pakistan can be friends? Has anything in the last 65 years given us reasons to think so? Barely a month after we attained Independence tribal armies aided by the Pakistani establishment intruded in Kashmir, occupying nearly a third of it. Instead of getting the captured land back, which we were very well capable of, our then PM committed a historical blunder by referring the matter to the U.N. That captured land came to be known as POK, the epicentre of everything sinful on this earth. We were then attacked in 1965. We beat them both in 1965 and later in 1971. Realizing that they can never match the might of the Indian troops, Pakistan then adopted more wicked means by instigating militancy first in Punjab, then in J&K and finally in the North East. From the 1990s they went a step ahead and started exploiting the communally charged atmosphere in the country by developing and aiding local terror modules. They were humiliated once again in 1998 in the Kargil War. Unashamed, they continued to carry out terror strikes at will, inflicting massive casualties

upon our country. Do we still have reasons to believe that we can be friends?'

The public support to Shruti on the issue was so huge that Shruti demanded an open and live debate between her and India's External Affairs Minister on what the right way to deal with Pakistan should be.

The ABP website designed a separate section on its site which opened onto a new webpage www.howtodealwithpak.com On this page, people were encouraged to post their thoughts on the issue. In its first couple of days, the webpage drew such phenomenal response from netizens that on two occasions, the website crashed due to heavy traffic load. At the end of the second day, the ABP members had another tedious job at hand: to delete all those responses that had used swear words and invectives to describe our neighbour. Nearly 50% of the messages thus had to be deleted. Subsequently, Faisal worked out a system in which open posts from netizens would be moderated and posted on the site only after approval by the ABP members.

Addressing a gathering, Shruti explained her tough stand against Pakistan:

'Our External Affairs Minister who seems to have made pusillanimity a state policy goes to Beijing and says he doesn't mind settling there. Now is he going to say he won't mind settling in Islamabad?'

Even as the crowd cheered her, she went on to explain her point:

'I derive no joy in spewing venom against Pakistan. My anger is more against our own Governments, both past and present, who have continued to live in denial and allowed Pakistan to take us for a ride. Hence, today

I advocate an "arm's length distance" from Pakistan. Yes, that should be our policy – "an arm's length distance" from our untrustworthy neighbour. And if at all a situation does arise when we have to re-initiate a peace process with Pakistan, the starting point of that journey should be the signing of an extradition treaty between the two nations. Let us for once stop worrying about our neighbour's prosperity and focus upon ours. Let us not fool ourselves time and again by thinking that Pakistan will ever reciprocate our niceties; for if we do that, we will be letting our neighbour walk all over us.'

Shruti's campaign was to soon escalate into nationwide protests against the Government's fresh move to initiate dialogue with Pakistan. The Government tried some hard posturing to convince people that it would not compromise on the nation's dignity. But it was too little late; once again the biggest gainer in the war of perceptions was Shruti Ranjan and the ABP, whose meteoric rise had begun to frustrate both the IDP as well as the Jan-Hit Party.

Shruti's zealous crusade, the third in less than a month, earned her many new supporters and admirers. What was particularly astonishing though was an interview that her bête noire Ratna Pandey gave to a leading TV channel. When asked why the Jan-Hit party had been continuously losing its support base under Ravi Nehra, her answer was rather surprising, 'I think we need to draw a lesson or two from Shruti Ranjan. Our leaders need to move out of their comfort zones and start slogging it out on the streets.'

Political observers knew what the remark was aimed at: to put the authoritarian Ravi Nehra under pressure and let him know that he may not have his way for too long.

Chapter 26

The tension with Pakistan delayed the screening of Catherine's movie for the Home Minister by more than a week. Even though Catherine had bumped into Ravi in the gym on two more occasions during this period, given the volatile political situation prevailing in the country, he too found it inappropriate to push the case with Patil. With just a few days left for the film's scheduled release, the producers and actors were still clueless about the film's fate. Eeshwaran had in fact visited all the famous temples in the south including the Guruvayur Temple in Kerala and the Meenakshi Temple in Madurai praying for divine help, but so far the help remained elusive.

This was when, one morning, Catherine finally got a call from Ravi Nehra.

'The Home Minister wants to watch the movie today at 5 p.m. Possible?'

'Of course, thanks so much,' was Catherine's instant answer. And then she said, 'Can I request you to please come for the screening?'

'You can't stop me. I'll be there,' responded Ravi without a second's hesitation.

Catherine found it strange but sweet of Ravi to go out of his way to help her, especially when there were more pressing issues, including a potential dissent within his party, to occupy him. But then in the situation that she was in, she was truly grateful to him.

That evening, the real-time tension with Pakistan actually worked in the film's favour. The film, a spy thriller, had some obvious Pakistan-bashing in it and the Government felt it was an opportune time for such a movie to release as its content was quite in sync with the public mood. Hence, ignoring all protests, the Home Minister assured Eeshwaran full support of his Government.

'Rest assured, if there is any law and order problem, we will deal with it firmly but I see no reason why a patriotic film like this should not be released,' Patil asserted, quite uncharacteristically.

Catherine and Eeshwaran thanked the Minister profusely before he left but Catherine knew that it was Ravi who had made it all happen. Taking him aside, Catherine thanked him from the bottom of her heart. 'Ravi, I don't how to thank you for this…had it not been for you, the movie may not have released and we'd all have suffered a huge loss.'

Ravi took her hand in his. 'You don't know this but I am one of your biggest fans. I think it was my selfishness that made me do my bit to have your movie released… having seen the promos, I wouldn't have missed the movie for anything.'

Ravi's words were calculated to win over a vulnerable person and Catherine awarded him with a grateful hug. As he watched Catherine leave, the old glint was back in Ravi's eyes. This girl would be as easy to trap as Rhea. He decided to use the same plan to reel her in. However the ringing of his cellphone brought him out of his reverie.

It was a voice that he hated. Diya Dangi!

'Bolo?'

'10 crores...You are going to finance a film for me!'

For the next few minutes, Ravi and Diya had a long and angry discussion until Diya disconnected the call.

Later that night Ravi sat with Pathak to discuss the menace that Diya had become.

'How long can this bitch blackmail me like this?' rued Ravi. 'There has to be an end to it.'

But Pathak convinced Ravi not to lose his cool and let his stepsister have her way for now. If the ten crore kept her quiet for a year, it was worth it. Ravi agreed eventually and Pathak was picked to carry the cash with him to Mumbai.

Two days later, when the ABP members met in their office for an important meeting, Catherine was conspicuous by her absence. The members of the party weren't too sure why she wasn't there. Sure, it was the day of Catherine's movie release and she was understandably busy giving interviews and visiting cinema halls, but just to be doubly sure that Catherine did not attend Shruti had specifically instructed Daivik not to inform her about it; a fact that Daivik found quite strange.

Faisal Khan and his team were investigating the dubious funding of Ravi Nehra's business empire. So, the ABP team was naturally expecting that Faisal would have cracked something there, which he wanted to share. Instead here he was telling them a completely new story, much spicier than the funding of a business empire. The meeting began with Faisal sharing some photographs that showed Ravi Nehra's PA, Pathak, giving a suitcase full of currency notes to the sultry starlet Diya Dangi and a

B-grade Bollywood producer, Sushant Mallik. From the huge volume of notes, it was evident that the sum being exchanged was in crores.

'Super! So tell us what it is?' Shruti prodded Faisal.

'That wannabe Bollywood actress Diya Dangi is Ravi Nehra's stepsister!' beamed Faisal with the confidence that the scoop could actually finish off Nehra's career.

'So? Isn't that too personal?' reasoned Daivik.

'Well, yes and no…don't forget that it's also about an exchange of unaccounted-for cash that's taking place. So there are also issues of possible money-laundering and circulating fake currency,' Pratibha Kaushal tried setting this in perspective.

'So are we ready to strike?' queried Shruti, making it amply clear that she was all for it.

'Ma'am, as you know I like to verify every detail twice over…give me four more days and I will be fully ready with both the stories.'

'By the way, how is the original story progressing?' asked Daivik.

'Pretty good…but the thing is that there's just so much round tripping of funds that we're not sure of the real source of funding of Ravi Nehra…'

'Fair enough. I'm going to work on that exposé very closely with your team. In fact, I'll come over and join you guys this afternoon,' Daivik decided.

After a pause, Faisal asked Shruti, 'Should we inform Rhea about the scoop? Maybe we can get more information from her.'

Shruti thought for a moment before she replied, 'No, I will speak to Rhea. She has already told me a lot of things about Nehra that the world doesn't know. She has also assured me that she will support us in anything that exposes the truth about him.'

Ravi Nehra's meteoric rise had always intrigued people. And almost everyone knew there were some missing links in the story that had been drafted with great finesse by him for media consumption. If Faisal was right, then this would be the first time that the truth, that was astutely hidden by Nehra from the public, would tumble out of his closet.

With the ABP thus smelling another coup, the meeting ended on a note of optimism. While the other members dispersed, Shruti and Daivik stayed back.

'Shrutiji, was there a specific reason you didn't want Catherine to know about this meeting?' Daivik asked her.

'Yes, the reason is her friendship with Ravi Nehra.'

'Oh! She just spoke to him to get her film released. Rest assured, Shrutiji. Catherine is very responsible and can be trusted blindly,' Daivik defended his friend.

'It seems you are very fond of her,' Shruti smiled.

'Well…uh…'

Seeing Daivik's discomfort Shruti decied not to pursue the line of questioning. She could tell that the fact that his love was not reciprocated, hurt him more than he let on.

That night Shruti called up Rhea – who was still away in London and informed her about the exposé they were planning against her estranged husband. Rhea heard her out, and then said:

'You know, Shruti, it's a tricky issue for me. On the one hand, I feel bad about it because at the end of the day, Nehra is the father of my son. But when I think of the way he has usurped power from people who really deserve it, and played the country to his advantage, I think he has it coming. When I think of my father's ideals, I think the country needs to be rid of negative influences like Ravi. Hence I will support you.'

'Are you sure, Rhea? I know this will impact you and Anway,' Shruti cautioned her.

'Don't worry. Do what will best serve the country's interests.'

Shruti was relieved to know that Rhea retained more than a bit of Sharad Malviya and his selfless nationalism in her.

Chapter 27

Catherine's film released to a record-opening weekend both in Tamil and Hindi, with the controversy surrounding its release only whetting people's curiosity. In fact, the response down south was so overwhelming that in most cities, the first show of the film was scheduled as early as 6 a.m.! Most multiplexes were screening almost thirty shows of the movie every day and each of the shows was running to a packed house.

The film's super success was a god-send for both Eeshwaran and Catherine. While Eeshwaran, not only managed to recover the exorbitant costs that had gone into the film's making, its success reiterated that even at sixty, his superstar status and crowd-pulling abilities were very much intact. For Catherine, too, the film's success marked a victory on many fronts. This was her first super hit after two major flops and having Nia. People had begun to write her off, with most journalists insinuating that her foray into politics signalled the end of her film career. She knew that with the film's super success, she'd given a fitting reply to her critics.

Catherine acknowledged, privately, that she owed a debt of gratitude to Ravi Nehra for becoming her knight in shining armour and turning things around for her when the movie's release had looked so unlikely. Hence, two weeks after the film was released, Catherine called Ravi late in the evening to thank him for his help.

'Hey Catherine,' Nehra's voice was warm.

'Raviji, the movie is a huge hit...it's got my best opening weekend collections ever...while information from the U.S. and London is still pouring in...'

'Wow! Hats off, Catherine...I'm so, so thrilled for you,' Ravi sounded genuinely happy for her.

'Raviji, it's all because of you. I'll remain indebted to you all my life.'

'Trust me, a night out together will help you pay off the debt,' Ravi joked.

Catherine felt a little uneasy at the suggestion, but Ravi was quick to undo the damage when he clarified that he only wanted her to take him out for a dinner. Given the context of the phone call, Nehra knew Catherine would not be able to refuse him.

Two days later, Ravi and Catherine met over dinner at an isolated roof-top restaurant in the heart of Lutyens' Delhi. It's strange how two people going through similar upheavals in their lives feel drawn to each other. Empathy becomes a huge binding factor in such cases, often making equations and relationships seem deceptively real. When Ravi and Catherine chatted late into the night, something similar seemed to happen between them.

'How's your daughter now?' asked Ravi, solicitously.

'Ah, well, she's okay...though I'm not that okay being away from her,' she replied, trying to contain her emotions.

Catherine opened up more than she really ought to have, after downing two glasses of wine. Somehow she ended up revealing to Ravi that she had been a victim of physical abuse in her marriage. Yes, Armaan the frustrated and failed star, had been abusing her physically for a whole year, until she decided that she would not take it anymore.

The information surprised Ravi, in as much as it made him sense more opportunities. 'Gosh! I don't believe it! How could someone like you put up with physical torture? You should have walked out of such a marriage much before,' Ravi said, oozing concern and sympathy.

It was of course quite ironical that of all people, Ravi, who had made life miserable for his wife, was offering his sympathies to another woman for the same offence that he committed on his wife all the time. But then, a lonely, insecure heart like Catherine's was infinitely vulnerable to manoeuvre. Ravi, for his part, tried to win her trust by projecting himself as a dignified sufferer. And for the next hour-and-a-half, Ravi and Catherine talked their hearts out, swapping tales of sorrow like they were the closest of friends and had known each other for years.

Strangely, just when they were ready to leave, Catherine's driver came rushing into the restaurant searching for her, along with a hotel security guard.

'What's happened, Ram?' Catherine asked him, surprised to see him there.

'Ma'am, two men came looking for you, saying they had travelled all the way from Junagarh to meet you. They gave me this letter saying it was from your father and wanted me to hand it over personally to you.'

Catherine could not believe her ears. 'My...my dad?'

The driver nodded, giving her an envelope, which had a paper with something scribbled in Urdu on it. Ravi called up his driver, Anwar, who was proficient in the language and then asked him to read it out.

'Dear Catherine beti, I am the world's most unfortunate father to have not been able to give anything to my children. But today I regret all that I was and Allah has rightly punished me by giving me a lonely death. Everybody close to me has abandoned me. I know I have been unfair to you and to your mother, yet today I beg a favour from you. If I meet you before my death, I will die a redeemed man...Please, beti, come and see me, Your abba, Nawab Khan...'

'Who gave you this letter?' Catherine questioned her driver, virtually trembling in shock and disbelief.

'Madam, two men had come...one of them wore a tagiyah and had a thick beard. They came to the parking lot and told me that your father was critically ill.'

'Where are they?'

'They are waiting by the car.'

Catherine rushed down with Ravi who insisted on accompanying her. There was nobody near the car. The watchmen and the driver tried looking for the two men but they had disappeared. Sensing the anguish Catherine was in, Ravi took her aside. 'Catherine, what's the matter?'

'It's my father who left us when I was just a few months old...When I came to India, I wanted to look for him but I also feared that finding him would only upset me more...And today, he comes back into my life in this bizarre way...'

Catherine was in tears. Ravi put his hand around her shoulder in a supportive way and then hugged her, caressing her back lightly. Catherine rested her head on his shoulder as she blurted out everything about her early years and the absence of her father. Ravi took the letter from her and turned it around. It had the sender's address scribbled on it.

'Do you want to go and meet him?' he asked.

Even as she remained undecided, Ravi – like a spouse in such a situation would – offered to take her to the address mentioned on the envelope right away.

'Right now?' Catherine queried.

'Yes, in my private aircraft...besides, if your father is on his death-bed every moment is crucial, isn't it?'

An hour later, at nearly three in the morning, Catherine and Ravi took off from the VIP terminus at the Indira Gandhi International airport in Ravi's private jet. They were off to Keshod, the nearest airport to Junagarh from where Catherine's destination was at the end of another 40 km drive.

Catherine sat in the aircraft, dazed and clueless about what was happening, her mind in a whirl. Did she really want to meet her estranged father? She didn't really know. Somewhere, in her subconscious mind, it was perhaps the hope of reconnecting with her roots that had held her back in India. At the same time if she had really wanted to meet her dad, she wouldn't have sat on it for this long without making an effort. The conflict kept her wide awake all through the journey.

At some point during the flight, Ravi even held her hand like a more intimate partner would; she was so preoccupied that she barely noticed when it became a tight clasp. Ravi's expression though was as cool and unfazed as ever, giving ample indication that the reasons for him making this trip were pretty well thought out in his head.

At six in the morning, just as dawn was breaking, Catherine reached her destination. She was shocked at the state of her father's abode – a large dilapidated structure in the corner of a village on the outskirts of Junagarh. What was more emotionally traumatic, however, was the fact that he had passed away the day before.

Champu, a sixty-five-year-old family retainer, who had worked for Nawab Khan's family all his life, had been by his side when the end had come. He informed Catherine that the Nawab had died just the last evening and had been buried late in the night.

'Nawab Khan's own family had gone bankrupt many years ago when they lost everything in the stock market. Thanks to his second marriage into a rich family, he had enough wealth from his wife's side to see him through. But fifteen years ago, his wife left him and took their two daughters with her. She had fallen in love with another man and dumped the Nawab. The Nawab became an alcoholic. He died a painful, lonely, death, the worst that any man could have...'

'But why didn't my father try to reach out to me before, if he knew I was his daughter?' queried Catherine, still hunting for answers.

'Nawab Sahib was too proud. Even three days ago, when he decided to get in touch with you, it was because the doctors had told him that he could die anytime.'

Catherine heard Champu's story with a sense of detachment. She felt bad for the man who had brought her into the world. She felt worse to learn how the man had left it. She figured that her father must have been horribly unfair to people close to him to deserve this fate.

Catherine requested Champu for any photographs he had of the Nawab. Champu gave her two, which had been taken in Nawab Khan's last few days. The pictures were of a frail thin man with a beard. Catherine compared these with an earlier picture taken with her mother soon after they were married. Though the Nawab looked very different in his old age, his eyes and the nose were same.

The emotional highs and lows of the last few days were proving too much for an already fragile Catherine, and she broke down, burying her head in her hands, crying her heart out.

Ravi drew her to his chest and held her close till the storm of tears subsided. Then he took her to her father's resting place and asked a local maulvi to say some prayers for the departed soul. Catherine stared at the fresh mound of mud under which her father was forever concealed from her. Now even the hope that she might someday meet her dad had been taken from her. She felt completely drained; completely bereft.

Ravi was in the middle of quick call he was making to Pathak when Catherine put her hand on his arm from behind, startling him. But one look at her face and he cut the call and put his arm on her shoulder. She leaned against him like a small child.

'Shall we leave?' he asked Catherine, his voice full of concern.

Catherine nodded faintly.

'Catherine, are you okay?' he asked, steadying her limp body.

'No, Ravi, I don't think I am...'

Instead of driving her back to the airport, Ravi took her to a beautiful guest-house located on top of a hilltop.

'Catherine, your face looks a bit flushed. I think you might have a touch of fever. I suggest you have a shower, have something to eat, maybe take a nap for a few hours and then we will fly back in the evening, okay?'

Catherine would have declined in any other situation. But in the present one, she felt just too emotionally exhausted to put up any resistance.

'There are two rooms here; luckily both are vacant… so you'll get your privacy,' Ravi added, conscious enough to mask his intentions.

So Catherine and Ravi checked into the guest-house. All along, Daivik kept trying Catherine's number only to get the message that it was switched off. Daivik was now getting worried for her.

It was noon by the time Ravi and Catherine managed to grab their first bite of the day. Catherine looked tired; her eyes red from exhaustion and lack of sleep. She and Ravi were both on their computers checking their mail when Ravi got a call from Pathak. He moved aside to take the call.

'There are very strong rumours that this time you are the target of the ABP's latest exposé,' Pathak informed him.

'What? And what would the exposé be about?' Ravi's face turned pale.

'That is still speculative. Maybe it's your nexus with the ruling party and certain illegal land deals in Haryana…'

'Bloody hell! What time is this press conference?'

'1 p.m.'

Ravi looked at the watch. It was already 12:30. What could he do in the next half hour to stop himself from getting ruined? He seemed to have run out of options.

'What's the matter Ravi, are you okay?' Catherine called from behind.

Ravi looked disoriented even as he told her what Pathak had just told him on the phone.

'Oh my God! I didn't know anything about this exposé!' Catherine was as shocked and clueless as he was.

Initially, Ravi did not quite believe that Catherine could not know of the exposé. But when he saw the state she was in, he knew she was telling the truth. In her weak and chaotic frame of mind, Catherine however confessed that she was aware of another exposé – one that involved the Jharkhand government.

'Catherine can you just call up Daivik and stop him from ruining my career?' Ravi asked her helplessly.

This request left Catherine torn between her professional duties on the one hand and gratitude towards the man who had stood by her in one of her most vulnerable moments, on the other. She had a difficult decision to make and mulled over it for a good five minutes before she replied: 'Ravi, I am really, really sorry but I can't stop them.'

Half an hour later, the ABP team in Delhi was ready for its press conference, which Ravi and Catherine watched rather helplessly on TV, many hundred kilometres away from the centre of activity.

Shruti, Daivik, M.P. Singh, Pratibha Kaushal and Faisal Khan were all ready to carry out what had been touted as the biggest exposé against any political leader in India's history. While there was huge excitement and even elation in large sections of the media and the people at the prospect of Ravi Nehra finally getting nailed, the ABP members were as aware that if the exposé backfired, then their credibility could take an irreversible beating.

Given how important this exposé was, Shruti took control of the proceedings from the start.

'Friends, today will hopefully be remembered as a very crucial day in India's political history. We all know that the cause and origin of all the ills that plague our politics lies in the uninhibited use of illegal, unaccounted money, whose parent source remains unknown. Hence, it is quite likely that some of the sources that fund our politics, also fund some of the worst illegal activities like drug-trafficking and terrorism…As an elected member of parliament, it's a duty of all MPs to safeguard India's national interests. However, most politicians are hand-in-glove when it comes to exploiting illegal money for furthering their short-term gains…' she paused significantly before she asked Faisal to give her some of the pictures he was carrying.

Faisal passed around photographs in which Ravi's PA, Pathak was seen handing over a large suitcase of currency notes to porn star Diya Dangi and B-grade producer, Sushant Mallik.

'Take a good look at these pictures. That gentleman on the right whom you can see in the picture is Ravi Nehra's, PA, Shridhar Pathak, while the people to whom he is paying the cash are porn star Diya Dangi and film producer Sushant Mallik.'

News watchers were abuzz with excitement. On the other hand, Nehra's face grew whiter as he realized that another dark chapter of his life looked set to be exposed to the public.

'Diya Dangi is Ravi Nehra's stepsister and the money that is exchanging hands is to prevent Diya from releasing a video of Nehra negotiating a deal for spending a night with a Bollywood starlet for Rs 1 crore…'

'Bloody hell,' Nehra exclaimed in anger, banging his plate on the floor.

For the next five minutes, the ABP team explained how Diya Dangi was related to Ravi Nehra, digging out embarrassing details from the life of Ravi's father. Shruti would have preferred not to dwell upon the life of someone who was not alive anymore but then they couldn't talk about this exposé without explaining the background. Having explained the back story, Shruti then began to explain the pictures exposing the exchange of currency notes.

'Friends, our investigations have revealed that Ravi Nehra is a depraved man who patronizes paid sex and covert prostitution. In fact, depending upon the quality, status and demand for the girl he wants to engage with, he is reported to have shelled out anywhere between Rs 50,000 to Rs 1,00,00,000 to fulfil his desire. Now it is anybody's guess as to whether he has set aside funds in his business for his lascivious pleasures or if these acts are funded by the Jan-Hit party. But yes, Bollywood actresses hold a special charm for him, with him having shelled out a whopping one crore to spend a night with a lead actress in Dubai, only last year...

'Ravi Nehra operated in Bollywood through a small-time casting director, Peter. About a year ago when Ravi was in Mumbai for a day, he had called up Peter and asked him to fix up the newest sex symbol, Aliya for him. Ravi had a huge crush on the 5ft 9 inch beauty and was desperate to bed her. Unknown to him, Aliya and his stepsister Diya were shooting together for a film, which ultimately got shelved half way through. Even though Diya had only a very small role, she had befriended Aliya and the two of them would often end up spending time together in between shots. They were in fact, seated together when

Aliya got a call from Peter. She reacted rather angrily to Peter's proposition and even banged down the phone.

'"What happened?" Diya had asked her unsuspectingly.

'"Bastards...they think all women can be bought for money! Ravi Nehra is in Mumbai and wants to spend a night with me! He is ready to pay whatever I ask. I asked Peter to tell the bastard to go and sleep with his sister."

'Till then, Aliya had no idea that Diya was Ravi's estranged stepsister, seething for revenge. Diya, after all, hated to talk about her Nehra connection just as much as he did. But sensing an opportunity to get even with him, she convinced Aliya to help her in her plan. Aliya, though reluctant initially, finally agreed to execute it. She too had a crazy, spunky side to her which was perhaps also the reason she bonded so well with Diya – despite the obvious difference in their status in Bollywood.

'That night, Aliya had arrived at Ravi Nehra's suite at the Four Seasons Hotel in a burqa, which she soon cast off to reveal a tiny black dress barely long enough to keep her modesty intact. Ravi couldn't believe that the latest new starlet of Bollywood was actually in his room! But within minutes, Ravi's excitement was replaced with irritation as Aliya seemed to be on her own trip. When Ravi was about to plant a kiss on her lips, she pushed him back saying, "So you think I'm like the other women who you bed at will?" This was a weird sort of comment from someone who was being paid a whopping sum of Rs 50 lakhs for the act. Aliya nonetheless was unrelenting.

'"So what are we supposed to do? Just stare at each other's faces?" a miffed Ravi Nehra asked her.

'She sat on a chair and raised her leg rather scandalously on the table. 'Will you do what I tell you to? If yes, then

I'm all yours,' she said seductively, looking towards the muted TV screen that was playing a Bollywood music channel.

'Even though Ravi knew the girl had mischief on her mind, nothing had quite prepared him for what she actually demanded. "Will you take off your shirt, get on top of the bed and dance to whichever song is played next on the channel?" Aliya asked him teasingly.

'By now Nehra had become so lustful for this girl that he gave in. He was two pegs down. So he stripped and danced his heart out to *Yamla Pagla Deewana*, hoping his performance would finally help him seduce the girl. Aliya, on the other hand, took out the bundle of notes that Peter had given to her as advance and showered the notes on Nehra, applauding his performance in the cheap manner of Indian men, before quickly rushing out of the door. Ravi couldn't chase her beyond his door in the state of undress that he was in. What he did do was unleash the choicest invectives upon her.

'The next morning, before Nehra left for Delhi, a waiter came to his room with a DVD. Nehra had a bad feeling the moment he saw it. Even as he watched himself making a complete ass of himself, his phone rang. It was Diya calling from an unknown number.

'"You dance quite well without your clothes," she said.

'"Bloody whore...Why did you have to do this?"'

'"Don't tell me you don't know why, you bastard. Your father killed my mother, leaving me to die many deaths of humiliation and despair. I grew up determined to destroy the Nehra lineage. And this DVD will now help me achieve my purpose."

'"Listen I will pay you whatever you want but I need this video."

'"You will anyway have to pay me whatever I demand and whenever I demand because I will never give this DVD to you...In fact, if you kill me, rest assured that I have already shared it with five other people, one of whom will release it. So the only way you can ensure that this footage never gets released is by meeting my demands."

'Twice in the last two years thus, Ravi had to shell out hefty amounts to keep Diya in check. And this was the third time that Diya had suddenly demanded money. Of course, this time the money demanded had been simply astronomical. She had demanded 10 crores, which was supposed to the entire budget of a movie that was supposed to be one last launch-pad for her in Bollywood.'

The exposé of Ravi's depraved personal life shook the media and the nation. But lest the focus shifted elsewhere, Shruti once again took over to set things in perspective.

'Friends, the purpose of this exposé was by no means to expose Ravi Nehra's philandering ways. The purpose here was to make him accountable for the vast amount of public money that was squandered to cover up his personal misadventures."

At this point, Daivik, who had been feeling uneasy about the exposé seeming like a personal attack, took over the mike.

'While Mr Nehra owes an explanation to the nation on the exact source of money which we just saw his PA, Pathak, shell out to finance a C-grade Bollywood film, for now, we will share with you our findings about Nehra's spurious funding. With our extensive research we are going to expose the gargantuan fraud that has gone into the setting up of his business empire…'

As Daivik took over to get into the details, Nehra wiped the sweat off his face, while Catherine sat nearby, clueless and confused.

'As you know, Ravi Nehra today has an empire worth Rs 400 crores with interests in real estate, hospitality, infrastructure and irrigation. Today, we will tell you how the company manipulated its capital and deceived its investors at will.

'Friends, you will be shocked to know that more than 80% of the shares of the Nehra group are held in the name of shell companies, which exist only on paper. Another 7.5% is held by Nehra's close relatives, some of whom are again fictitious characters.

'Moreover, our investigation has revealed that the capital invested by shell companies reached the Nehra group through five different layers. The total amount invested into the company has been pegged at around Rs 90 to 100 crore. Certain transactions show that a big part of the capital was merely fudged through book entries with funds not actually being there. The funds that reached the Nehra group have questionable sources. Before reaching the Nehra group, they were routed through five different entities. We have found a maze of transactions with the Nehra group's shares changing hands multiple times before reaching the last set of investors…'

Ravi couldn't believe his ears. The ABP's attack was aimed at deflating the very foundation on which his political and business careers were formed! An awkward silence loomed between Catherine and him, with neither knowing what to say.

'Friends, as you can see, there was a maze of illegal transactions and round tripping of funds. This is normally done when there is black money and when there is a critical need to shield the source of funds. In our investigations, we followed one source who suggested that one of the actual investors in the Nehra group is a Dubai based businessman of Pakistan origin – Rameez Owaisi. But since we can't corroborate this information at this point, we leave it at that. Instead we demand that Ravi Nehra come forward and disclose the real share-holders and investors in his business empire...'

By the time the ABP's press conference ended, almost all news channels had sensationalized the Ravi Nehra scoop to the extent that it seemed that the country was prepared to lynch him that very moment!

There was no official reaction from any leader of the Jan-Hit party, what with Ravi Nehra himself being incommunicado. On being contacted, his staff told the media that Nehra was abroad on a personal visit. On the other hand, the scoop gave the ruling IDP a reason to smile. The IDP leaders were glad that for once the public angst against Nehra was much higher than it had ever been against PM, Devender Singh.

Even as New Delhi witnessed intense political activity, the man who was the cause of the storm, stood many hundred kilometres away from it, tense and shaken, but already thinking of how best to use Catherine to get back at Shruti and the other members of the ABP

'You could have *at least* informed me about the exposé, Catherine…that's the least I expected from you when we've been together for the last sixteen hours,' Nehra looked suitably devastated.

'Ravi, trust me, I didn't know about this scoop at all. I swear I didn't know a thing,' Catherine said.

Ravi did believe her. Catherine's hands shook as she tried to light herself a cigarette. She was feeling dizzy and could feel a migraine coming on.

It made sense for Ravi to be good to her in this situation. Ravi convinced her to have a stress-reliever pill that would soothe her nerves and make her feel calmer. Catherine had it reluctantly, only to doze off. Ravi utilized the time to connect her cell to his laptop in order to charge it and to subsequently transfer all important files from her cell to his laptop via Bluetooth. He desperately scanned close to a 100 files looking out for familiar names or initial alphabets such as those similar to his name or the name of his party. He finally came across a file called, 'Op Last Straw'. He opened the file and was shocked to find that the file contained extensive information about the underhand dealings of the Jharkhand government which was helmed by an Independent CM, supported by both the IDP and the Jan-Hit party.

'What does"Op Last Straw" denote?' Ravi wondered hard. As he scrolled down the 3 page file, which mostly had only coded words and sentences in it, a note at the end provided some clarity as to why the file may have been named thus:

'This will be the biggest exposé as it will conclusively prove the collusion of both the IDP and the Jan-Hit party in trading

off the country's interests. If it is carried out closer to the polls, it gives us a clear advantage over both parties – S.R'.

Ravi Nehra knew that S.R. stood for his bête noire, that prize bitch, Shruti Ranjan. Seething with intense rage, Nehra shut down the laptop and went out and made a series of calls. Most of them were to his trusted staff and stooges within the party. He took a vow in the name of his ancestors that if he was indeed their true descendant, he would eliminate all his enemies.

Three hours later, Catherine woke feeling guilty for having dozed off this way. She was surprised to find her cellphone fully charged.

'I did it. Someone could be calling you,' said Nehra trying to act normal.

In fact there were three missed calls from Daivik. Catherine called Daivik and briefly told him that she was in Junagarh and would be back in Delhi in the next few hours. Daivik, worried for her, kept asking her, what had led her to Junagarh and if all was well. She promised to tell him everything once she was back in Delhi, requesting him not to tell anyone about her trip.

In the evening, Catherine and Ravi finally took the flight back to Delhi. All along the journey, Ravi held her hand protectively, as if to prove his concern. There was however a deep-seated anger in him which was apparent in the rough grasp of his hand. Catherine did not protest; she wasn't even sure if she liked it that way. What she knew was that she had never been this confused before. She didn't know from where her father from whom she had been estranged for ages, had suddenly sprung back into her life. She was equally clueless about who the real Ravi Nehra was: the one she had seen being ripped apart in the ABP exposé or the one who had been her rock-solid pillar of support these last 24 hours? Why had the ABP members, including Daivik, keep her in the dark about this exposé? Did they already have doubts about her sincerity merely on account of the fact that she considered Nehra a friend?

This wasn't the first time Catherine felt she had little control over what seemed destined to happen in her life; she felt inadequate and depressed.

At around 9 in the evening, the aircraft touched down at the airport. Ten minutes later, when Catherine and Ravi stepped out of the VIP exit, Catherine was surprised to find her best friend waiting for her. Wordlessly, and with tears in her eyes, Catherine hugged Daivik. Even as they stood locked together, Daivik exchanged an uncomfortable stare with Ravi Nehra, who looked at him sardonically. Daivik was quite shaken when he realized that Catherine and Nehra had actually flown in together.

'How long have you been waiting?' Catherine asked Daivik.

'Two-and-a-half hours.'

'What?'

'Well, you mentioned you'd land in the evening...I didn't know the time and your cell was unreachable after we spoke. All I knew was that there's no regular flight from Junagarh and that you'd probably leave from this special exit.'

Catherine asked Ravi if the three of them could travel in the same car – a proposition that neither Nehra nor Daivik were game for. Nehra excused himself on the pretext of work. Once he had left, Daivik hugged Catherine hard once again.

Catherine and Daivik chatted almost all through the night at her place.

'I'm glad you've found a closure or else the mystery about your Dad would never cease to haunt you,' said Daivik.

'Yeah...even though I am not sure this was the way I wanted it to happen.'

Daivik was very keen to know more about Ravi Nehra's involvement in Catherine's life; his jealousy was quite apparent in the way he asked her about him.

'I don't know if he has agenda, but I can't deny he has been extremely helpful...it would be unfair not to consider him a friend,' admitted Catherine, summing up her trip with Ravi.

Daivik knew it wasn't wise to probe Catherine further on the issue. He knew how fiercely independent she was and that she would not appreciate intrusion in her personal space – not even from her best friend.

'But Daivik I need to ask you something,' said Catherine, changing the topic. 'Why was I kept in the dark about Ravi Nehra's exposé? Does the team doubt my integrity?'

Daivik tried to hedge her question but when probed further, had to concede that it was Shruti Ranjan's decision and in all likelihood, yes, it was because of Catherine's perceived proximity to Ravi Nehra. He tried to explain the way Shruti looked at things. 'This is a different Shruti Ranjan altogether, perhaps as ruthless and manipulative as any other politician,' he confessed to Catherine.

Catherine felt hurt to think that her integrity had been put under the scanner by the woman she idolized the most, but was nonetheless ready to see things in a more holistic way: ‘Maybe you’re right, Daivik, but if her ruthlessness helps us grow as a party, I think we can put up with it.’

‘Well, let’s hope so. I just hope she is not a closet dictator like many of our leaders have shown themselves to be…’

In his bed that night Daivik wondered at his inability to understand women. What was Shruti’s reason for coming back to politics? Was it idealism or power that propelled her? And Catherine? Sweet, beautiful, smart, Catherine. What could she possibly see in a bastard like Nehra? What was it that drew intelligent, attractive women to all the wrong men in the world? Besides, what was it about ‘good guys’ like himself who more often than not, found themselves coming a distant second in a woman’s affections?

Didn’t Catherine ever feel bad about snubbing him?

Chapter 28

The ABP's double whammy on Ravi Nehra was to have far-reaching consequences. For one, Shruti Ranjan became the new crusader of the nation. While the regional media raved about her new avatar – with one magazine carrying a cover story on 'Shruti Ranjan 2.0' – the English media was increasingly critical of Shruti's 'witch-hunting' brand of politics.

Thanks to the momentum generated by her latest exposé, the ABP's popularity touched an incredible high. There were already at least fifty fan pages on the social media about the ABP – each voluntarily started by a party activist and each with a different demographic reach. Purely through the social media, thus, almost five million people were connected to the ABP pages and were receiving the latest updates; many voiced their opinion on how the movement could be made even more impactful.

'I have the figures with me. India has eight crore active internet users as of today and 6.6 crores of them are pretty active on the social media, with the number only increasing every day. Facebook has the maximum users with Twitter being in the second position. Thus, if we build up a dedicated audience of say six crore people across the country via the internet, we may actually not need a party cadre at all in many of the constituencies,' Daivik said excitedly to her.

Shruti absorbed the information with a smile. 'To win an election or to come near to it, I think we will need a vote share of 25%. And to achieve that via the internet would mean a social media support base of 25 crore people. So that's still a few years away. Until then, there's no real substitute to having local cadres...'

'But it is funds which are holding us back.'

'The social media can substitute for the funds. Both IDP and Jan-Hit party spend heavily on advertising. What if we do not spend a penny on advertising and instead have our dedicated supporters publicize the party for free over the internet? With the money that we save by not spending on print ads and TVCs, we can set up dedicated cadres across the country. Besides, when we start our nation-wide tours, let's all of us travel by road instead of by air. That will save costs and increase our reach.'

Shruti's thoughts carried a huge amount of conviction and clarity in them. It seemed like she had every little detail planned out in her mind. Daivik wondered why she acted so reluctant to return to politics just a few weeks ago. Had she already made up her mind to re-enter the fray and was waiting for an opportunity as apt as the one the ABP had provided her?

Not for the first time, Daivik had some misgivings about Shruti. She certainly wasn't the saint people made her out to be. He felt a bit unhappy playing second fiddle to Shruti and he could feel that there were going to be major differences of opinion in the days ahead. Left on his own, he would not have carried out the exposé on Nehra's personal life; nor would he have kept Catherine in the dark about it. He would have instead initiated a debate series in college campuses called – '*Soch jo desh badal de...*' or '*Ideas that can transform the nation.*'

Interestingly, the ABP's exposé of Ravi Nehra rejuvenated the incumbent Government as it realized that with the IDP decimated and the ABP still young and inexperienced, it actually had a chance to put its house in order. However, the agenda-less Government was to soon realize that doing so was probably tougher than pulling down the ABP.

Hence, the Government engaged one of India's top-most PR agencies for a whopping sum to carry out negative propaganda against the ABP and to besmirch the reputation of its key members in all possible ways. Soon enough, Shruti was accused of getting funds for her ashram in Dhar from dubious sources including a Russian philanthropist who had been accused of being a paedophile; Daivik was accused of tax evasion; M.P. Singh was accused of fudging his birth certificate to add years to his government job; while Pratibha Kaushal was accused of getting a 40-acre plot in Himachal for free in an underhand deal with the state government. Only Catherine's character assassination was held back; probably because the IDP wanted it to be the most explosive of all.

The levelling of accusations against the ABP members only vindicated Daivik's stand that digging skeletons from their rivals' cupboards, especially where it involved their personal lives, would incur retaliation.

Daivik was upset that he was party to this approach and decided to talk to Shruti about it.

'Shrutiji, are you sure we should follow this approach of dragging skeletons out of closets? Why can't our politics be more about ideas than people? Ultimately, this approach will diminish everything we stand for and reduce us to being brazen mud-slingers,' he said to her one evening when the two of them were alone.

'Daivik, sadly, the majority of our population is too unevolved to understand ideas. Second, I don't think we're nailing people. We are simply exposing unlawful practices that ought to be reported,' Shruti said, quite smugly.

'But Shrutiji, shouldn't we focus on the core issues which we had decided at the time of the party's launch – you know: security of women and children; corruption; unemployment; besides the need for comprehensive reforms – police, judicial, electoral, education, health?'

Shruti Ranjan sighed. 'Daivik, the issues that you just mentioned will be our governance agenda if and when we come to power...but trust me, the man on the streets finds these issues too intellectual and alienating. You need emotive issues to win an Indian election; and since most emotive issues have been done to death, we're using these sensational exposés...and it's working for us, isn't it?'

'But, Shrutiji, what of ethics?' Daivik questioned her somewhat exasperatedly.

'Are you trying to say my approach is unethical?'

Daivik was pointedly quiet.

'Get this clear, Daivik, we were not ripping apart Nehra's personal life. We would not have carried out the exposé, had there been no legal implications in the case. You tell me, is it normal for a politician to shell out Rs 10 crore in one shot to finance a film? And when we are probing the transaction of such a big amount of black money, I am sure that apart from tracing the source of money, we are entitled to investigate the cause that compelled Nehra to resort to this illegal act. What wrong have we done?'

Before Daivik could say anything, Shruti added, 'Moreover, since we have nothing to hide, we should be more than happy to let investigative agencies probe us. That will only expose the IDP further.'

Daivik accepted Shruti's contention, partly because of her seniority and partly because the other ABP members were supporting her aggressive posturing, but not for the first time, he felt a major disconnect with Shruti's way of going about things.

Shruti, on the other hand, could sense that Daivik was battling the same dilemmas that she had faced at one point of time, back when she had first entered politics. After all, it took ordinary mortals some time to embrace the omnipresent guile that suffused the crooked world of politics. Then, it had been Sharad who had mentored her to draw a distinction between her personal sensibilities and her political needs. Now she'd have to mentor Daivik and help him shed his naiveté. Politics, after all, demanded ruthlessness against rivals, a fact that Shruti had learned the hard way.

Chapter 29

Ravi Nehra's credibility had taken a giant beating. From being in firm control of his party until only a couple of months ago, murmurs of dissent were now rampant within the ranks. And if the rebels had not yet drawn out their daggers it was only because of the fear psychosis that Nehra had crippled his party with.

'Nehra sits in Delhi, engages in shady business deals, slugs alcohol, screws women and only occasionally makes public appearances, while we have to go door-to-door begging for votes. How do we explain his conduct to the voters?' a party-worker lamented on a TV camera, with his face pixellated in order to hide his identity; making it clear that the party cadres felt highly de-motivated under him.

With Ravi Nehra clearly facing the heat, Shridhar Pathak, Ankur Yadav and two other members of his core team, quickly drew up a plan of action for Nehra to strike back.

The first part of the plan was to hold a press conference and clarify his stand to the media. When Ravi Nehra addressed the press conference that evening there was considerable curiosity about whether he would quit as President of the party. However, his brazenness was even more shocking than the wrongdoings he was accused of:

'I will not stoop to the level of the ABP and hence I will not answer the charges they have made about my personal life. I strongly deny *all* allegations of financial irregularities in my business. I have never raised capital through illegal means nor do I need to hide who my investors are.'

'So that means you are not quitting your post?' a lady journalist asked.

'Why should I quit? I have done no wrong... I am open to any probe by a government agency as I have absolutely nothing to hide. Let a government agency indict me and I will quit public life.'

After his bombastic claim, Nehra released a video of himself driving Shruti and his ex-wife Rhea around his constituency in 2007 to acquaint them with his development initiatives.

'As you can see, Madam Shruti Ranjan looks very impressed in this video. She had even congratulated me for my employment generation initiatives for the people of Rohtak. After that, we had lunch together. And today, just because we are political opponents, she is stooping to such lies? I request my friends in the media not to be swayed by false allegations. The ABP cannot replace the investigative agencies of this country. I stand for the truth and will request the Government to initiate a thorough probe into my business dealings. I will quit if I am found guilty.'

The press conference was aimed at fooling both the Government and the public. Ravi knew he had shielded the Government enough times to now extract a return favour; at the same time he hoped to win some public sympathy with his righteous posturing. However, his drama cut little ice with both. Everybody knew that the Government stood to gain more if the Jan-Hit party continued to carry Nehra's venal baggage on its shoulders. In that situation, Nehra's party would be forced to be on the defensive and would simply not have the moral authority to attack the IDP.

Far from his press conference reaping any dividends, within minutes of it ending, his party had to confront another crisis. The first major sign of revolt came to the fore when veteran leader Ratnesh Prasad quit his Rajya Sabha membership of the party, saying he would not be associated with the party until Nehra resigned as president.

'In politics, it is as important to be perceived as honest as it is to be honest. Hence, I feel Ravi Nehra should quit on moral grounds until all charges of financial irregularities against his company have been disproved,' Pandey said in his press release.

Frustrated by this revolt and because nothing was going right for him, an agitated Nehra ended up yelling at Pathak, abusing his cook, and throwing things around in his office – stuff which his staff had got used to expecting every once in a while. When Nehra finally cooled down he knew who exactly could bail him out from this sticky situation.

He called up B.C. D'Souza.

Late that night, Nehra and B.C. D'Souza met the Home Minister, S.K. Patil over a drink in his large farmhouse. He handed Patil a list of seventeen people. Patil put on his glasses and read the names carefully. 'This includes seven senior leaders from your party as well.'

'Yes. I want all their phones tapped. Trust me, if you do as I say, both our parties will stand to gain. Else the ABP will finish us off.'

'And what if it gets exposed? This kind of illegal phone tapping could even make Government fall.'

'Don't worry; we'll organize it through a private detective who is connected to one of the country's top-most criminal lawyers.'

'Hmm...well, okay, we can't say no to you, Nehra Saab.'

The illustrious list of politicians whose phones were to be tapped included Shruti, Daivik, Catherine, Faisal and all members of the ABP; it also included Ratnesh Prasad, Ratna Pandey and Ankur Yadav from his own party. The surprise inclusion was Pathak – his trusted PA of the last seven years. Nehra was clearly going through his most insecure phase and didn't trust anybody.

Even as Nehra went about trying to contain the damage, he was told that a group of MPs owing allegiance to Ratnesh Prasad had secretly initiated a signature campaign demanding that Nehra step down as party president. Sensing the ground beneath his feet crumbling, Nehra immediately drove to Ratna Pandey's residence and offered her a deal: if she issued a strong statement supporting him now, he would push her as a consensus candidate for the party president's post three months later.

And so it happened.

'Ravi Nehra is innocent. There's no question of him stepping down as we all stand by him,' Ratna Tweeted just 20 minutes after meeting him. To an extent, thus, the wily Nehra managed to quell the dissidence.

Two days later, a combative Nehra unleashed the third part of his counter-attack.

He leaked pictures of himself and Catherine taken at the Junagarh resort to the media. His intention in doing so was pretty clear: to shift focus from the even murkier things he was accused of; moreover he knew that these pictures would drive a wedge in the ABP team and possibly break it. In Nehra's assessment, the Indian political scene had space for only one main Opposition party; orchestrating a possible collapse of the ABP was his last hope of resurrecting the Jan-Hit party.

These pictures, quite expectedly, created a furore and even boomeranged on Ravi Nehra. For once, the IDP got a chance to rip apart both the Jan-Hit party and the ABP in one shot.

'We always knew that the ABP is a decoy offshoot of the Jan-Hit party. Since the Jan-Hit party today is left with no credibility, it thought it could spring up a new party with people who had relatively clean reputations and dupe the public! But these pictures of Nehra and Catherine's escapades at the Junagarh resort have exposed their vicious plan – besides revealing the intimacy between Nehra and Catherine.'

Shruti was livid when she saw the photographs. She immediately called Catherine and Daivik to meet her at her place. Since Catherine was away in Mumbai, she could only reach Shruti's house around midnight.

'What is all this, Catherine? I thought you had been busy promoting your film. But instead it seems you were on a personal romantic sojourn – with the enemy!'

As a devastated Catherine fumbled for words, a protective Daivik said, 'I'll tell you everything.' He then explained the chain of events surrounding Catherine's journey to Junagarh with Ravi Nehra.

'It was entirely a co-incidence that all this happened on the very day we carried out the exposé,' Daivik said.

Shruti heard him out but her expression was sceptical. 'It wasn't entirely a co-incidence. It can't be,' said Shruti, rejecting the defence.

'What do you mean, Shrutiji? Do you have doubts about my honesty?' Catherine confronted her.

'Did I say that?'

'No, you didn't but you implied just that.'

'Oh come on, Catherine. You can't be so naïve as to not understand the implications of travelling to Junagarh with Ravi Nehra; I'm sure you are aware what the IDP is alleging.'

'Ma'am, I didn't go on a picnic. I'd gone to meet my father who was on his deathbed and who unfortunately died before I could meet him,' Catherine defended herself, her eyes glistening with tears.

'There's really not much that can be done about it now,' Shruti said, dismissing her explanation.

'Shrutiji, what if Ravi Nehra and I issue a joint press statement and explain the whole trip? I'm sure that will deflate the IDP allegation,' Catherine said.

'You think Ravi Nehra will agree to issue a joint press statement?'

'Why shouldn't he? It will only help his image.' And Catherine picked up her phone then and there and tried to call Ravi. But he didn't take her call.

The disgusted look Shruti gave her as she frantically called Ravi was missed by Catherine, but Daivik saw it and was deeply angered by it. When Catherine finally got through to Ravi an hour had passed. To her shock, Ravi flatly refused to issue any press statement with her.

'Catherine, let's just ignore those pictures. The issue will die a natural death. If we issue clarifications, we will only be dragging the issue and it will give more cause for the IDP to run us down,' argued Nehra.

Catherine tried to convince him otherwise but Nehra didn't budge. His rigidity surprised her. Even as Catherine cut a sorry figure in front of Shruti, Shruti posed a question that left her struggling for a clear answer: 'Can you prove that the person who died in Junagarh was your father?'

Though Catherine wanted to believe so, she realized that she could not prove what Shruti had asked. Daivik was about to say something when Shruti cut him short.

'Stop defending your friend, Daivik. Politics is no child's play. I'm sure Ravi Nehra is not the only friend Catherine has in Delhi. If you guys can't exercise discretion in your personal life, there's no point going ahead with our agenda.'

Daivik's response was as sharp: 'Shrutiji, we all know and accept that you have greater experience than us. And that's why you are leading us. But aren't you being high-handed in presuming to tell us how to live our lives? Everyone is an adult here.'

Saying this, Daivik stormed out of the room. Catherine followed him, upset that she had become the bone of contention between Shruti and Daivik.

Much after Daivik had left, his words – *'aren't you being high-handed in presuming to tell us how to live our lives? Everyone is an adult here,'* kept ringing in Shruti's ears.

Strangely, it reminded her of her own run-in with Sharad Malviya against the Maulana's politically-motivated arrest, back when she was still finding her feet in Delhi politics. In many ways, Daivik actually reminded her of her younger self – the same idealism, honesty, the undercurrent of rebellion and aversion towards anything that wasn't straight or ethical.

That night, Shruti got an unexpected call from Abhay who was now settled in New York and worked with *The New York Times*. He called to congratulate her on the successful start of her second innings in Delhi.

'I must tell you that the U.S. media has been following you very closely. In fact, we are all surprised at how you've managed to shake up a comatose system in less than two months.'

'Well, anything that doesn't have answers, is destiny,' was all Shruti had to say.

Chapter 30

A month went by without any significant change in the political scenario. Ravi Nehra continued to cling to his position by dangling the position of president to Ratna Pandey as bait. Those who knew him also knew that he was merely buying time; there was no way he would let go of the post of party president.

What was equally interesting was that the IDP was just as keen that the beleaguered Nehra continue as the Jan-Hit party president. Therefore, investigations into the money laundering charges moved only at a snail's pace, with the Government seeming disinterested in nailing Nehra.

Shruti, on the other hand, had got down to setting up her party organization in different states. Party presidents for seven of the crucial states where Assembly elections were due in the next two years and which contributed to over 200 Lok Sabha seats, had been appointed. At the same time, the itinerary for her nationwide *Jan Jagran Yatra* was being worked out. There were some cold vibes with Daivik, which both chose to ignore, and instead concentrated on the work ahead.

Catherine had been spending more time in Mumbai – playing with her daughter, taking a call on her future as an actress, and setting up the party's base in Mumbai. Ravi Nehra had called a few times but Catherine's response – especially after the censure from Shruti Ranjan – was cool.

She did not want to encourage the kind of bonding that Ravi Nehra was perhaps looking for, but her gratitude to him forced her to be polite and gracious.

Then, one fine day, one of the key allies of the IDP, the U.P. Jan Morcha suddenly decided to withdraw support from Government, citing flagrant corruption as the reason for its move. It wasn't too difficult to guess the real reason: the regional party's own government in U.P. was unable to contain crime and feared that if Lok Sabha elections were not held early, disillusionment with the state government would only grow, leading to it getting far fewer seats in the Lok Sabha. In the changed political scenario, it seemed that the country might indeed go to the polls sooner. Hence, the ABP's most crucial exposé which they had codenamed 'the Big Bang exposé' and had reserved for closer to the polls, had to be advanced.

The ABP leaders thus met in Delhi to review their preparation for the Big Bang exposé. This was the first formal meeting of the party after Shruti had given Catherine a piece of her mind, only to invite an unpleasant retaliation from Daivik. Thus, there was still some lingering awkwardness between her and the younger members, but she hoped this would soon resolve.

Faisal started by briefing the ABP members on his investigation of wrongdoing by the Jharkhand government.

'As you know, only on one previous occasion has an Independent MLA become the state's CM. Besides, given the Indian system which is entirely number-centric, the possibility of an Independent heading the Government is next to impossible. Hence, a few months ago, when both the rival national parties, IDP and the Jan-Hit party, decided to support an Independent MLA and have him head the government in Jharkhand, we knew there was something fishy. I guess we had underestimated the magnitude of the scam that was to reveal itself. If the figures that we have at present and which we are still investigating are true, then the Jharkhand CM, Debjit Pal is involved in an unprecedented money-laundering cum illegal mining cum land de-notification scam worth over Rs 8,000 crore.'

'Rs 8,000 crore in just two months? And nobody in Government even got wind of it?' Daivik asked disbelievingly, to which Faisal only smiled wryly.

'Forget getting wind of it, on the contrary, I get the sense that this was the sole motive behind getting an Independent to lead Government. In fact, if my preliminary findings are correct, then the IDP and the Jan-Hit party are meant to be equal partners in this loot! Just look at the exhaustive planning that has gone into the formation of the Government: for a year-and-a-half, instability was created in order to convince the public that supporting the Independent was the only way to prevent a mid-term poll that would have drained the Government's exchequer further. Now the funny part is that this Independent CM has in the past been a member of both the IDP and the Jan-Hit party. He has an excellent equation with leaders of both parties and can sell his loyalty at the drop of a hat.'

'So what you are trying to say is that this scam is actually the brainchild of the IDP and the Jan-Hit party, and the CM is just the front-man executing it?'

'Exactly! Ravi Nehra, and Mukta Prajapati's secretary, B. C. D'Souza are the brains behind it. This Government was formed with the clear objective of looting funds that would help both parties before the next general elections! Moreover, the idea of projecting an Independent as their front-man was to shield both the national parties, in case the scam was exposed.'

The ABP members were shocked to learn about the magnitude of the scam.

'Great! I think this is awesome. What we need at this stage is conclusive evidence of the connivance of the IDP and the Jan-Hit party. If we manage that, then both parties will be exposed and we'd have achieved what we set out for,' said Shruti.

'Just give me a week to make the case foolproof.'

The Jharkhand exposé had naturally filled the ABP with an air of optimism. If the ABP was able to pull this one off, then there would be no stopping it.

Shruti, realizing she had to address the cold vibes between her and the youngsters, turned her attention to them.

'So, Daivik, what do you feel about this exposé?'

'It sounds like it will shake things up big time.'

'So we must go ahead with it, right?'

'Of course. In any case, you're the leader and don't need my approval.'

'I see. Catherine?'

'Yes, Shrutiji?'

'Do you realize that this exposé can finish off Ravi Nehra's career?'

She nodded.

'Are you okay with it?'

'Of course. I have clarified that Ravi Nehra is just a friend.'

There was an awkward, ominous silence in the room before Shruti spoke again. ‘Catherine Khan will be in charge of this exposé. Along with Faisal, she will go through all the evidence and decide how much of it is legally valid. She will work out the logistics of when and how we break this exposé to the media.’ Looking Catherine straight in the eye, she asked her again, ‘Think well about it, Catherine. Are you up for it?’

Catherine nodded – with a determined look on her face and with a sense of hurt in her heart.

Chapter 31

For Catherine, the Jharkhand exposé was to be one of the biggest tests of her life. She started working on it diligently – almost locking herself away from the world. She started to spend entire days in Faisal's office, scanning tonnes of files from which evidence had to be derived.

Interestingly, ever since she had been assigned this responsibility, Ravi Nehra had been calling her and wanting to meet. This hinted at one of two possibilities: either Nehra was exceptionally intuitive, or he had an amazing informer network. On one occasion, when Catherine asked him if there was something specific he wanted to discuss, Nehra had replied somewhat possessively – *'Do I need a reason to meet you?'*

Catherine was not sure if she had accepted Nehra as part of her inner circle of friends but the gratitude that she owed him made her feel bad. She sensed that Nehra was perhaps lonely and depressed. But she avoided meeting him on the pretext of being overworked. Catherine wondered if Nehra knew what she was involved in and found herself battling an acute dilemma. It was so very difficult for her to level allegations against the man who had led her to her father. And that only made her wonder how could a man, so warm and compassionate in his personal life, be such a schemer in politics? Did politics breed an evil side in one? She hoped not, for it made her feel a lot more pessimistic about her own future in politics. She wondered if it would be a good idea to chat with Rhea, Nehra's ex-wife, about her tryst with Nehra. However, the very next moment, she dispelled the thought, realizing that Rhea may not have the most objective view; besides involving Rhea would also be unfair to Nehra.

Daivik felt bad for Catherine. By now he had begun to feel stifled by Shruti's overbearing approach. Of all people, why did she suddenly have to put Catherine in this position? In fact, he had a chat with M.P Singh about the same, but found no favour from the ex-cop.

Two days before the exposé, when Catherine returned home from work around midnight, she got a call from Ravi Nehra. Since Nehra had already called her thrice during the day and she had not taken his calls she decided to speak to him. Nehra clearly seemed very disturbed, and deep in some kind of emotional turmoil.

'Catherine, why are you doing this to me? I mean we have hardly met after Junagarh...what wrong have I done to you?'

Catherine did not quite know how to react.

'Listen, I am at the Hyatt, which is a stone's throw from your place. Please let me come and meet you for just ten minutes.'

Catherine couldn't say no; perhaps she didn't want to. Damn Shruti Ranjan. Catherine did not need her permission to meet a friend.

Half an hour later, Catherine and Nehra sat over coffee. That Nehra was slightly drunk was apparent from his drooping eyes and the smell of liquor on his breath. He sounded unusually dejected.

'I just feel like running away from this madness sometimes. Just twenty years ago, all we had was a small plot of farmland in Gurgaon. Life was tough but it was also happier. Today, after all that I have achieved, I really miss that small plot of land. I think life would have been happier if I'd spent the rest of my life farming.'

As Nehra reminisced about his humble origins, he showed Catherine some pictures from his childhood on his iPad. For a moment, Catherine wondered if there was a motive in him doing so, but soon abandoned the thought blaming herself for being too cynical.

Nehra's words were laden with regret and remorse, making him sound so unlike himself. Catherine felt bad for him. She found herself more inclined to be his friend in this grim hour. She was convinced that Shruti Ranjan did not understand friendship.

For the next one hour, Nehra and Catherine talked their hearts out. Even though they were not the best of friends, they were definitely two lonely and misunderstood souls who took comfort in each other. While Nehra spoke about his ruthlessly isolated life despite being in an 'apparently enviable position', Catherine for the first time confided that she was not sure if she was cut out for politics.

As she spoke, Nehra's eyes were checking out Catherine's home – as though he was searching for something. In a lighter vein, he even asked her who was next on the ABP's 'hitlist'; a query Catherine warded off with a smile. And then at one point, Catherine stunned him with a pointed question which he was not prepared for.

'So who is the real Ravi Nehra? The gentle soul I know, or the one who is a money-launderer and a womanizer?'

Nehra was too taken aback to respond immediately. He finally answered her with a question: 'Do you trust your instincts?'

'Of course I do.'

'Then let them decide which one I am.'

'Aren't you dodging my question?'

'No. I am just too tired of answering the same question again and again. I mean, you almost sound like one of those journalists who have nothing better to ask.'

Catherine felt very uncomfortable as she knew it was deceptive and sly of her to keep Nehra entirely in the dark about the exposé she was going to carry out two days later. And yet she knew it would be even more unethical to not be able to maintain her professional integrity. It was a tough choice for her to make and she didn't like being in this position. She felt from Nehra's reaction that he was both these men – he no doubt possessed all the vices that he was accused of, but he had some goodness in him as well.

Nehra finally took her leave, thanking Catherine for spending some time with him. 'I can't thank you enough for not shunning me like most people close to me have. Good night,' he said in parting.

After he had left, some of Nehra's carefully played out words kept ringing in her ears. Was he really so hopelessly lonely to virtually beg her friendship? And was she being unfair by shutting him out? After all, he didn't seem to demand much beyond some innocuous conversation!

Catherine decided to take a quick shower before going to bed. In the middle of it, her bell rang. She answered the door dressed in a bathrobe. It was Nehra, who had come to return her iPad which he had taken with him by mistake. Catherine gave him his iPad. She could sense he was entranced by the sight of her in a bathing robe and with damp hair. She didn't mean to entertain him in this state and made him leave.

Chapter 32

Ten days later – after a slight setback of a few days due to a terror strike in Hyderabad – it was finally time for the ABP to execute 'the mother of all exposés'.

Catherine reached the office as early as 9:30 a.m., finding the confines of her home too stifling on this crucial day. She felt less guilty about what she was doing when she was in office and going through the relevant files, but today even here, thoughts of the exposé's repercussions constantly plagued her mind.

That was when Daivik walked in. From the expression on her face, he knew what was bothering her. 'It's a very important day for you, Catherine. Are you ready for it?' Daivik asked, putting his hand on her shoulder.

Catherine smiled ruefully, 'I do feel that I might be betraying Ravi Nehra with this exposé. But I guess Shrutiji is testing my commitment to the ABP and there's no way I can fail this test. Besides, life has always forced me to make tough choices.'

Around the same time that Catherine and Daivik were chatting in office, Shruti received a call from Abhay.

'Hey Shruti, I have some very important information to share…' he said with a sense of urgency that seemed ominous. When Shruti heard what he had to say a large frown clouded her forehead.

Two hours later, the ABP was ready to break 'the Big Bang exposé'. Catherine entered the hall. There was so much hype attached to this particular exposé that the media turnout was simply unbelievable. Nervously, Catherine started to speak:

'In just three months' time, the Jharkhand CM, Debjit Pal has swindled or embezzled away public money to the tune of nearly 20% of the state's annual budget! This money has been used to buy mines in Liberia, Indonesia and Philippines. Another portion of this money has been used to buy at least five resorts in Cambodia, Vietnam and Thailand while some of it has been used to buy a manufacturing unit in Kenya. All these were bought in proxy names of three of Pal's oldest confidants, who also doubled as hawala dealers and played pivotal roles in the execution of this gargantuan scam...'

The press listened in pin-drop silence. Catherine took a deep breath and continued:

'...There are two aspects here which are particularly baffling. The first is how can an Independent, first-time CM be this adept at siphoning away Government money? Our preliminary investigations have revealed that Pal was into this practice for the last three years. It is interesting that in the three years preceding his becoming CM, Pal was both the Revenue Minister as well as the Irrigation Minister and in both the ministries he made huge sums of underhand money.

'Indeed, funds worth Rs 300 crore sanctioned by him as Irrigation Minister were never used and nobody knows where the money has gone. What is most startling is that both the IDP and the Jan-Hit party were privy to his venal acts. In fact, it was his ability to carry out this fraud so effortlessly that made them promote him to the post of CM. Both the IDP and the Jan-Hit party wanted a major share of Debjit Pal's booty while using Pal as their frontman...

'The second crucial aspect is where did such massive black funds come from? Our investigations have revealed that they came from three sources: the first was money-laundering. So as a matter of course, the revenues and profits made from these mines and resorts acquired in foreign country are ploughed back into our economy as white money and the vicious cycle repeats itself. The second source of these illegal investments abroad is embezzlement of Government funds. You will be shocked to know that more than 50% funds allotted for various schemes by the State Government ministries of Irrigation, Animal Husbandry and Rural Housing are missing and can't be traced. Our investigations suggest these "missing funds" were illegally invested abroad and since the Animal Husbandry and Rural Housing ministries are currently held by the IDP and the Jan-Hit Party, it clearly points to a deeper collusion between the two parties in engineering this scam. The third source of these illegal funds are certain Maoist groups who are supposedly very close to Pal – particularly one headed by their veteran extremist leader, Hemnathji.

'It is alleged that the money which came from the Maoist groups was accumulated through extortion and killings. In return, these Maoist groups were given 30% of the share of profits made by from their investments. Furthermore, the Maoist groups were expected to throw their might behind Pal in the elections – whether by violence or otherwise. As a quid pro quo deal, Pal was supposed to go soft on the Maoists.'

The allegations that Catherine had just levelled were of such a serious nature that the entire press team heard her out without interruption; until one senior journalist demanded proof of the complicity of IDP and the Jan-Hit party.

'And for proof, the ABP staged a sting of the ex-CM from the Jan-Hit party who was forced to step down as CM of Jharkhand two years ago due to rebellion from his own party-members.

'A sting reporter from Faisal's team pretending to be an entrepreneur who wanted to invest in the state, met the ex-CM and complained about Pal being inaccessible. The reporter after winning the ex-CM's trust, offered to meet Nehra and request him to get the ex-CM re-installed. The miffed ex-CM, still upset about being replaced, ended up blurting out, "*Arre bhai*, all this is Nehra's plan only. Can you imagine the Jan-Hit party's MLAs rebelling against me without Nehra's backing? Nehra never liked me because I couldn't cough up enough money for the party funds…I have my morals and couldn't cheat my state…"

'"But how do you know it is Nehra's plan?" the sting reporter asked him.

'"That's what the IDP state president told me. The decision to make Debjit Pal the CM was taken at the highest level between Nehra and Mukta Prajapati."'

'"Oh my God! So that means there *is* a direct collusion between the IDP and Jan-Hit Party?"

'"*Arre haan bhai*…what is more shocking is that I have heard that if the Jharkhand model is successful, the IDP and Jan-Hit party might replicate this model is another small state: Uttarakhand."'

As this recorded video was played out for the media, a deafening silence descended upon the venue. With this exposé it was now official:

India faced a far graver threat internally than from external enemies. As the ABP wound up its press conference, the media posse present at the venue stood up to give a standing ovation to the team. Shruti looked at Catherine with a small smile on her face and gave her a thumbs-up sign, clearly signalling that she felt proud of Catherine for pulling this one off.

Shruti also looked just a wee bit hassled, as though she had something on her mind which she meant to talk to Catherine about.

Two hours later, even as the country was coming to terms with the earth-shattering exposé and all the news channels played out the exposé on a loop, there was 'breaking news' of a rather unusual press conference taking place in the next half hour.

This press conference was convened by the spokespersons of both IDP and the Jan-Hit party, along with the CM of Jharkhand – Debjit Pal. From the very composition of the speakers at this press conference, one could easily surmise that the conference would be aimed at rebutting the ABP's claims.

And so it was.

'The ABP is a team of thugs and liars,' roared Debjit aggressively, 'And I will prove it.'

One by one, Pal rebutted all the claims of the ABP. He asserted that the associates mentioned by the ABP had absolutely no ownership rights in either the mines or the resorts mentioned by the ABP in its exposé. Pal, in fact, demanded that a CBI team be dispatched to the concerned nations immediately to prove the same. Money had not been swindled out of any of the Government schemes alleged by the ABP. In fact, in the next few hours, the concerned bureaucrats would give a detailed report of how the funds had been spent.

'As for the accusation that I have a tie-up with extremist leader Hemnathji – nothing can be further removed from the truth. In fact, if the ABP does not withdraw this accusation in the next 24 hours and render a public apology to me for the same, I will be filing a defamation suit against them.'

Simultaneously, Ravi Nehra sacked the ex-CM from the party, besides filing a defamation case against him, while the IDP spokesperson threatened to move the Election Commission to derecognize the ABP, calling it a professional vendor of lies and disinformation.

Soon after this, one news channel got the MD of one of the hotels mentioned by the ABP in its exposé, on the phone line from Phuket. This MD flatly denied that any Indian was a stakeholder in the hotel.

Strangely, in just a matter of hours, the entire situation had turned around.

From virtually crucifying both the IDP and the Jan-Hit party, the national media was now questioning the motives of the ABP in carrying out this 'hasty, ill-researched exposé'.

'In their greed to usurp power, they have spun a web of half-truths and lies which has killed whatever credibility they enjoyed,' rued a top journalist on a national TV channel.

Catherine, as the spokesperson of the party, was on almost all news channels for their evening news-hour debate. But instead of being applauded, she was grilled ruthlessly and, indeed, didn't seem to have an answer to many of the queries.

This turnaround in media perception was further compounded by a lavish social media campaign commissioned by the ruling party. So strong was its impact that by the end of the day it had begun to seem that ABP's claims were hollow propaganda and that the party was misleading the public for its petty gains.

A shattered Catherine was in a state of shock. How had this project backfired? Was the information that she had shared with the media indeed a lie? How could that be? After all, she had personally scanned all the documents umpteen times. As she thought hard about how she could have messed up this one, she remembered the night, ten days ago, when Nehra had suddenly dropped in and after leaving had come back once again on the pretext of taking away the wrong iPad. Had Ravi Nehra tipped off all the people involved? Was he the reason for her failure? She shuddered at the thought.

That night, Shruti, jolted by the unexpected volte-face, sat in her office to take stock of the situation. Faisal was supposed to give her an account of how his investigations had gone wrong and was on his way to meet her.

'Ma'am, I have reviewed the investigations and can tell you for sure that we were absolutely right in our findings,' he said when he arrived.

'How can that be? The bureaucrats have presented exhaustive reports on the usage of funds. Moreover, the management of the concerned resort in Phuket and the mine in Liberia have issued statements denying that the persons we mentioned in our exposé held controlling interests in their business. How can we be so off target? There is something wrong with our findings.'

'There isn't, Ma'am. All our facts and figures were correct. Sadly, all these changes, including the selling-off of bulk shares, took place in just the last ten days.'

'What? What does that imply?' Shruti asked, shocked.

'Apparently, associates of Debjit Pal knew about our exposé. And hence, before we broke it, they had sold off their interests in the resort and the mine. Besides, their hawala network is so strong that they immediately pooled the money back into Government funds.'

'Oh my God! This is horrible news. How did they find out? Does this mean that our phones are being tapped?'

'Possibly.'

Faisal took a pause before he uttered his next sentence. 'Shrutiji, I have some other information which will disturb you.'

'What?'

'Ten days ago, Ravi Nehra dropped in at Catherine's house around midnight. He stayed for an hour before leaving, and then came back for a few minutes.'

'How do you know this?'

'Well, we were concerned for Catherine's safety and hence on the three days when she stayed late in office, one of us followed her home. Nehra's visit that night had been a complete surprise to us. We didn't tell you this before because we trusted Catherine's professional integrity – but not anymore.'

Shruti was furious with Catherine. How could she just allow herself to be used by Nehra like this? Or did she willingly divulge information to him? 'Faisal, I need more information from you about Catherine's Junagarh trip... Can you help with that?'

'Yes, sure...but what precisely are you looking at?'

Shruti quickly opened an email that Abhay had sent her just that morning.

The next morning, a chastized looking Catherine stood in front of Shruti with Daivik by her side. Shruti was livid as she repeated her pointed query; a query that had put Catherine in a spot. 'Is my information correct? Did Nehra visit you twice one night ten days ago?'

Catherine nodded and narrated the chain of events.

'Great! So you goofed up your most important assignment! Do you think you still have the right to continue with the ABP?' Shruti railed at her.

Shruti's tone hurt Daivik who answered her with the same passion: 'Shrutiji, I think you're being too harsh on Catherine. I have known Catherine for the last ten years and she knows her responsibilities well. I don't think knowing or being friends with a political rival is a sin.'

'No, it's not. But being taken for a ride, is. How could Catherine not stop herself from meeting the man despite being cautioned; at least till the exposé was over? Do you realize that we have lost all our credibility due to this one lapse on her part?'

'Shrutiji, I understand all that you are saying. But please try to understand Catherine's position. Catherine did not want to meet Nehra. It was Nehra who had virtually forced the meeting by landing up at her place. And given the gratitude that Catherine owes him, she couldn't say no.'

'What gratitude are you talking of, Daivik?'

'Nehra took her to her father. It's just sad that he'd died before she could reach him.'

Shruti gave a wry smile before she confronted Daivik's claim. 'Are you both really that naïve?'

'What do you mean?' Catherine asked her.

'Your father isn't dead. He is very much alive – a rich businessman, and lives in Pennsylvania, USA.'

'What?'

Shruti showed her a video message from her father where he regretted having left his first wife, that is, Catherine's mother. In this video taken on board a flight, Nawab Khan talked fondly about Catherine, whom he last saw when she was just a year old. Nawab Khan says he always wanted to come and meet Catherine but didn't, as he had nothing to give her except emotional turmoil. But yes, the pain of his daughter's separation continued to haunt him till this day, when he had two grown up children from his other wife. He hoped that Catherine would forgive him someday.

Catherine took out the picture she had always carried of him. Yes, the resemblance was striking.

Wiping her tears, Catherine asked Shruti, 'How are you sure he is my father?'

'Last week, my friend, Abhay happened to be his co-passenger on a long flight from London to New York. That's when they got talking and Nawab Khan who was in an emotional mood, ended up talking about you.'

Catherine was happy to know that her father was still alive. Nonetheless, yet another unanticipated twist in her life had left her with more questions than answers. 'Then who was that man whom Nehra presented as my father?'

'Well, I asked Faisal to find out.'

Catherine and Daivik looked on in anticipation.

'Faisal says in all likelihood the man was a small-time activist of the Jan-Hit party in Junagarh whose job was to put up posters before a rally. He had died nearly a year ago.'

Catherine felt a deep sense of betrayal and hurt when she heard this.

'And why did Nehra have to do this?' said Daivik.

'Well, I spoke to Rhea. She says he has employed even more bizarre ways to win a girl. Either he was smitten with Catherine or he saw her as a soft target to steal all the information about our investigation. Besides, of course Catherine served him a potential dual purpose – that of creating a wedge between the ABP members and sabotaging our party.'

Catherine sank down on her knees and sobbed in grief, as Daivik and Shruti looked on helplessly. An hour later, Daivik dropped her home. Daivik wanted to stay with her for a few hours, but Catherine insisted she wanted to be alone.

By evening, an upset, unstable and very agitated Catherine decided to confront Nehra. She hated the man now, with all her heart. But she just had to know why he had done what he did. Why on earth did he have to play her on her most vulnerable, her most fragile, emotion? The thought and realization that she had allowed herself to be used and exploited yet again, filled her with self-loathing.

Chapter 33

Catherine dialled Nehra several times with shaking fingers. But his phone was not reachable. She turned on the TV and nervously flipped news channels. Most of them were telecasting Nehra's speech at a leadership conclave organized by a leading fortnightly magazine. Buoyed by the failure of the ABP's latest scoop, Nehra was back to his arrogant self.

'A democracy doesn't run by hidden cameras or gimmicky hunger strikes. As you can all see, the blatant lies in the ABP's latest exposé stand exposed – and it has proved that there is no alternative to the main Opposition party. The Jan-Hit party was and is the main Opposition party as well as the future ruling party of this country!' Nehra proclaimed, pumping his fist in the air.

'Mr Nehra, does that mean your resignation from the post of the party president is ruled out?' a journalist asked him.

'Why should I resign? Not a single case has been filed against me by any Government agency. Why should I resign just because the ABP wants me to? I will not resign – because I have done no wrong,' he asserted brazenly.

Just when Nehra was done with his session and was taking leave with folded hands, something astounding happened. A piece of footwear – a lady's sandal to be precise – caught him smack in the face, shocking him and the entire crowd present. A middle-aged lady, apparently a journalist from a vernacular daily, had thrown the slipper and looked completely unfazed about her action. Since there were no policewomen present on the spot, the lady had all the time to launch into a verbal attack as well.

'You have sold off the country, Ravi Nehra. Till the time a Raavan like you is killed, this footwear attack is the only thing that can give me solace,' she asserted.

The incident left Nehra disoriented. At first he gave a mouthful to the organizers for inviting 'goonda elements' and then, realizing that most of the crowd had thoroughly enjoyed the footwear attack, he beat a hasty exit.

Catherine felt somewhat cheered by the sight of Nehra being hit by a slipper. For a moment, she almost felt that it was she who was punishing him for his perfidy. She found it strange that she hated him so much, considering she had cared for him so deeply until just a few hours ago.

Catherine's animosity for Nehra notwithstanding, she wanted an answer from him. Nehra's phone remained unreachable even two hours later, making Catherine even more upset.

That night Catherine landed up at Nehra's place unannounced. Nehra was locked in a secret discussion with his trusted confidant, Ankur Yadav, when his peon came and informed him that Catherine had come to meet him. Nehra kept her waiting for an hour before he finally met her.

No sooner did he appear in front of her that Catherine burst out in wild rage: 'You have been cheating me, Ravi! Why on earth did you have to do this to me?' she yelled at him.

Nehra for his part remained cool and unperturbed and even pretended that he didn't know what Catherine was talking about. When Catherine accused him of stealing files from her laptop, he changed his tone and hit back at her with viciously: 'What was wrong with what? I took you to meet your dying father. Forget gratitude for that – you repaid me by plotting to destroy my career and then you expect that I would take it all quietly? Do I look like such a moron to you?'

'You didn't do anything for me, Nehra. A beast like you can never help anybody. The man whom you took me to meet, claiming that he was my father, was your party-worker, who had died long ago,' Catherine shot back, leaving Nehra unnerved for a moment.

Nehra's split personality immediately came to the fore; he broke down in front of Catherine and started telling her how much he loved her. 'Just think of it, Catherine. Why would I do all that, to take you to Junagarh? It's because I had begun to care for you and love you. I knew the thoughts of your father would never let you rest in peace and in any case it was unlikely that you would meet your father. I wanted to give you a sense of closure so that you could be happy in life.'

Despite Nehra's award-winning performance, Catherine did not buy his story, so he continued: 'When I discovered that you were still going ahead with your exposé, I felt betrayed and hence stole the relevant files.'

'That's just not done, Ravi! You have been spying on me! Or else how would you know what I was doing? In fact, even in Junagarh you copied a lot of data from my phone on the pretext of charging it,' Catherine was screaming and trembling as tears coursed down her cheeks.

Nehra begged for forgiveness, pleading repeatedly that he truly and deeply loved Catherine and that he was prepared to make amends for his mistake. He said that he did what he did to save his political career. But if she reciprocated his feelings, he was prepared to even quit politics for her. He loved her and wanted to be with her.

Catherine was simply stunned by this new angle that Nehra had sprung out of nowhere. 'Listen, Ravi, you are mad. Just leave me alone. I will not bother you in future and let's simply not cross each other's paths ever. Is that understood?'

Catherine had begun to make her way out of the house when a sobbing Nehra grabbed her hand and once again pleaded for forgiveness. A confused Catherine eventually relented. Nehra then persuaded her to at least allow him to drop her home, insisting that it wasn't safe for her to travel alone at that hour – more so when she didn't have her own vehicle.

That night Nehra had her dropped home not in his Audi, Porsche or BMW but in a nondescript Maruti Swift, driven by a driver whom Catherine was seeing for the first time.

After a silent twelve-minute drive in which Catherine and Nehra did not exchange a single word, Catherine reached home at around a quarter to one.

Nine hours later, pictures of Catherine's ransacked and plundered apartment were all over the news. A crowd of media people was assembled outside waiting for news from inside. A team of policemen were scanning the flat for clues. Catherine had been found dead in her bedroom. She had been sexually assaulted before being strangled to death.

Chapter 34

Catherine's brutal and macabre death sent shock-waves across the country, leaving Daivik the most devastated of all. Daivik went about in complete disbelief – so numbed by the death of his beautiful friend that he registered nothing around him, and behaved almost surreally calm. Only the dazed empty look in his eyes gave away how bereft he felt. How could Catherine have been so helpless and unprotected even with him around? As Daivik sat next to Catherine's body, a flood of thoughts and images of her from the last ten years swam through his mind.

Shruti was plagued with feelings of guilt since she had been rude to Catherine just the day before. Why on earth did she have to 'test' Catherine with this risky assignment, which was laden with dangers to her life?

Even as people arrived to pay their last respects to Catherine, the news that the Delhi Sessions Court had passed a landmark judgment on the Nirbhaya gang rape case, awarding death sentence to all the four accused, also filtered in.

It was an eerie coincidence that Catherine's rape and death coincided with this judgment – a stark reminder that crimes against women were quite unrelated to the quantum of punishment they got. Would Catherine's rapist and murderer ever be found and punished? Daivik had a strong suspicion who was behind this ghastly crime but he could make no accusations till more evidence was in hand.

Catherine's body was flown back to Mumbai. She was buried according to Catholic traditions. Strangely, it was her ex-husband Armaan Kapoor who performed the last rites, with Daivik standing close by. Two cousins of Catherine's had also flown in from Austria, along with a maternal uncle. Others who attended Catherine's burial included Shruti Ranjan; party-bearers of the ABP; Ravi Nehra; Ratna Pandey; almost all of Bollywood; media persons and several thousand fans – nearly half of whom had travelled from outside Mumbai to bid her a final farewell. The Government was represented by the Information & Broadcasting Minister. The next day's papers carried a poignant photograph of Catherine's innocent little daughter placing a rose on her mother's grave.

Much after everyone had left the cemetery and darkness had fallen in the secluded Versova graveyard, Daivik sat alone looking blankly at the spot where Catherine had been buried, tears flowing down his face.

'What wrong had Catherine done for happiness to always elude her? Her life was as tragic as her death…' he mumbled to himself.

At that moment, he felt a hand on his shoulder. It was Shruti.

'Daivik, you need to be brave.'

Daivik, in the troubled and conflicted state of mind he was in, did not respond to her. When a concerned Shruti insisted that he come with her, he finally shouted: 'Listen Shrutiji, please just keep out of my life! You did not treat Catherine well in her last days! For God's sake, don't treat us all like immature kids!'

Shruti was taken aback by Daivik's outburst. But then she thought, if yelling at her would help him, she was more than okay with it. She left Daivik alone and returned to her hotel.

The next evening Shruti and Daivik returned to Delhi. As they were on the same flight, sitting separately would have made people suspicious and so Daivik was forced to sit next to Shruti to keep up appearances. He didn't talk and stared out of the window into the clear starry sky.

Daivik was terribly shaken by Catherine's death and it showed on his face. Shruti put her hand on his arm and initiated the conversation: 'You know, when Sharad died I used to look up into the sky and try and seek him out among the stars. Are you trying to find out which of the stars Catherine is?' she smiled gently.

'I know which one she is. The one over there that looks different from the others,' he said without looking away from the star.

Indeed there was a star that seemed a bit bigger than the others and whose light twinkled with a soft surreal glow.

'You were in love with her, weren't you?' Shruti asked him, out of the blue. The candid question made him forget his anger at her.

Daivik's eyes filled with tears: 'It's so obvious to everyone. I wonder why only she never understood how I felt for her. If only she had given me one chance. Why did she always fall for men who mistreated her? Men like Armaan and that bastard, Nehra?'

Shruti was quiet, letting him speak.

'You know what, Shrutiji, I always felt that I had her in my life, yet did not have her at all…I mean it just baffles me how she could have got close to Ravi Nehra…'

'Do you think they were involved? I mean…'

'No, no,' Daivik cut her short. 'No way. Catherine was kind-hearted enough to believe in sob stories and allow people into her life. But she had a strong sense of what was right and what wasn't…'

'Could Nehra have got her murdered?' Shruti asked him point-blank.

'Yes. I know that bastard is involved. But how do we prove it?' Daivik said his eyes brimming with tears. 'I want to kill him! How could he do this to her? Poor Catherine… why didn't she talk to me? Why couldn't I have been there for her?' Daivik broke down completely. Shruti caressed and consoled him like a mother would a child.

When they landed in Delhi and were in their car, Shruti got a message on her cell. Immediately Shruti turned on the TV-news app on her phone and streamed in a live feed. Delhi's Commissioner of Police, Ranjit Shekhawat was holding a press conference. Shekhawat shared an important and rather incriminating breakthrough, which seemed certain to change the case completely.

'There was only one CCTV at the gate of in the D-4 block of Safdarjung Enclave where Catherine lived on rent. This camera has revealed the entry of a white Maruti Swift at around 12:45 a.m. The car left the compound five minutes later, which indicates that it had come to drop someone. However, twenty minutes later, the car came back and this time it left only two hours later at around

3:15 a.m. Quite shockingly, the number plate of the car has no registration records. While we have launched a manhunt for the driver, as you can make out from the hazy visuals that we have, there was possibly a man on the back seat as well, the first time the car entered the compound. When the car returned twenty minutes later, the man on the back seat was missing. This man's face can't be made out by the camera as both the back window as well as the rear window were tinted.'

The police played out the video of the car entering and leaving the D4 block four times as also some still images of the driver, and requested information about him from the public.

The news galvanized Daivik out of the despondency that engulfed him. 'I think we can get more answers than the police,' he said grimly.

Chapter 35

Daivik called up Faisal wanting to meet him immediately and asked him to come over to Shruti's place. That whole night, the three of them stayed awake, watching the videos – that they had obtained from the police on a DVD – over and over again, trying to work out the leads. The next morning, Faisal took the DVD to a studio where they could pause and zoom the video beyond normal parameters. On doing so, they just about managed to see through a small portion of the tinted glass and get a somewhat clearer view of the wristwatch that the person on the back seat was wearing. It looked like a designer brand: 'Faisal, can you obtain video footage of all the public appearances Nehra made last year?' Daivik said excitedly.

Realizing that Daivik and Faisal were headed on a dangerous trail, Shruti, issued a word of caution: 'Listen, from today you guys will stop talking to each other on the phone on this matter. In fact, none of us in the ABP team will talk to each other on the phone at all. We will either SMS or email and then meet face to face if it's urgent.'

'Why, are our phones being tapped?'

'I suspect so.'

Over the next few days, Daivik and Faisal scanned close to a hundred videos of Nehra obtained over the last year. These included public rallies of his party, press conferences, his presence at public events, and of him in Parliament. Surprisingly, Nehra seemed to sport a different wristwatch each time, but, yes, on at least three different occasions, he sported a watch that looked very similar to the one they had seen on the video.

'This isn't admissible proof. There are at least 22 different watches that we have already spotted.'

Even as Daivik and Faisal brainstormed, Daivik thought of another idea. 'Can we see all the footage again?'

'But why?'

'Maybe we might find the man driving the car in one of these videos.'

Faisal wasn't too convinced about the idea, but upon Daivik's insistence he agreed to help. For the next 34 hours, Daivik and he watched the videos non-stop on one TV screen, while on the other they played the video released by the police. Finally, Daivik turned to Faisal. 'Any breakthrough?' Faisal asked.

Rubbing his eyes, Daivik showed him a snatch of footage that had Nehra addressing a public rally in a village near Amritsar. Just behind him, on the stage, were at least a dozen local party activists. 'Look at the man in the green turban...second from left, standing behind Nehra...Take away his turban and beard and the features match the guy driving the Swift.'

Faisal paused and zoomed in the video and was stunned by the resemblance. 'Have we cracked the case?' he asked, still confused about whether they'd nabbed the killer.

'Not yet. But Rhea is supposed to land in India in the next one hour. She will be able to help us nail it.'

That evening, the ABP office-bearers met in their office to review the investigations into Catherine's death. In fact, Rhea who had just landed in India a few hours back and looked terribly jetlagged, also attended the meeting on a very special request from Shruti. Given the brutality of the assault on Catherine, she took it as a call of duty to help book the culprits.

'The Government agencies have been sluggish in investigating the case – like they usually are in such high-profile cases. But we have been running a parallel investigation and think we are very close to cracking it,' Daivik said.

Daivik and Faisal then took everybody through their findings.

'So it's all pointing towards Nehra's involvement,' noted M.P Singh.

'Yes, except that we need clearer information on the wristwatch and the driver. In fact, that's where Rhea, you can be of great help.'

For Rhea, it was awkward to testify against her ex-husband, but realizing the magnitude of the crime, she was determined to help. For the next few minutes Rhea watched the footage closely until she had some answers. 'Yeah, in fact that sardar looks very familiar,' she said. She thought hard before finally giving out more information. 'I think he is a local karyakarta of the party in one of villages in Punjab. Three years ago, the Jan-Hit party held a huge rally near Amritsar to launch a welfare programme for the farmers' wives. It being a women's scheme, Nehra had persuaded me to attend the rally. I remember this guy because he garlanded all the leaders present on the podium, including me. In fact, that's when he had introduced himself as the karyakarta. I think he introduced himself as Trilok…or was it Jaslok?… Singh.'

Daivik and Faisal were thrilled. They now had a very strong case against Nehra! He had probably used this guy to commit the murder hoping that his clean-shaven look would conceal his identity and fool the investigators.

'And what about the wristwatch? Can you tell me for sure that that's Nehra's?'

'Well, Ravi is definitely fond of watches. From what it looks like in the video, it is probably a *Patek Philippe* watch. But then he has over 50 top-end brands in his collection.'

'Is there some way we can reach this Trilok Singh, or whatever his name is?' Shruti asked Rhea.

'Give me a day. Let me see if I can obtain any information about him from a couple of people I know in Amritsar, without Ravi getting to know.'

Meanwhile, Faisal decided to send one of his decoy reporters to the Amritsar village right away, just to be doubly sure that the driver of the Maruti Swift had indeed been a clean-shaven Trilok Singh.

The next morning a major shock awaited them: a man bearing a strong resemblance to the driver in the video was found dead on the railway tracks in an isolated stretch near Sahibabad, between the New Delhi and Ghaziabad railway stations. He had supposedly jumped in front of a moving train. Without much effort, the police shockingly seemed set to dismiss this as another suicide.

The ABP members were aghast. The death of the 'driver' had confirmed two things: one, that he was indeed Trilok Singh and two, that the ABP members were being snooped upon big time.

'I'm really scared now because the next targets might be one of you,' Shruti cautioned Daivik and Faisal.

Right then, Faisal received a call.

'Who was that?' asked Shruti as he disconnected the call.

'The reporter whom I had sent to the Amritsar village is saying that Trilok Singh left his home nearly a month ago and they had not been in touch with him since.'

Daivik was furious when he heard this: 'I think that's enough! We must announce our findings right away. In fact, we must exaggerate and play up our suspicions in such a way that it provokes people against Nehra. We should make people so angry that they are incited to violence; and the Government is forced to arrest him,' said Daivik, exuding a new belligerence.

Shruti smiled when she heard this from Daivik.

'I'm glad, Daivik, that you are no longer caught in debating ethics. Just go all out and finish off Ravi Nehra,' she told him.

Two hours later, Shruti, Daivik, Faisal and Rhea held a press conference that almost directly accused Ravi Nehra of being involved in Catherine's murder.

'So many things pointing towards Ravi Nehra's involvement can't be mere coincidence. First, the driver of the car bore a striking resemblance to a party-activist of the Jan-Hit party in Punjab, Trilok Singh. Before we could reach him, he was also murdered...ooops sorry, he committed suicide. Then the person on the back seat of the car that entered Safdurjung D4 block that night was wearing a watch that Nehra owns. Doesn't this point towards Nehra's involvement in the murder? Shouldn't the police at least be investigating Nehra's role in the murder?' Daivik roared at the press conference.

That evening Nehra was indeed questioned by the police. By then, his wristwatches of that particular brand had gone missing; Nehra's cell records did not indicate any calls between Nehra and Catherine for seven days preceding her death.

Nehra defended his visit to Junagarh saying he was just being humane and wanted his friend Catherine to meet her father. However, upon realizing that his 'friendship' with Catherine was hurting both of them professionally, he had decided to stay away from her and had conveyed the same to her. On the question of Trilok Singh, he denied any knowledge of him.

Surprisingly, Nehra was let off after two hours of mild questioning. At the same time, the man who was found dead on the railway track was hastily identified as a local drug peddler. The Home Ministry showed a clear disinterest in finding out the whereabouts of Trilok Singh, who had been missing for a month.

The ABP was once again left shattered. 'This is unbelievable! I mean, after all the proof that we have furnished, how shameless can this Government be to still do nothing? What else do they want us to do? Do they expect us to arrest the culprits and prosecute them as well?' rued Daivik, tired after yet another failure at getting the Government to take action.

'Well, that leaves us with just one option,' replied Shruti calmly, quite certain in her head about what her next step would be.

From early next morning, Shruti sat on an indefinite fast demanding an investigation into Nehra's involvement in Catherine's death and that the case be handed over to the CBI. As it had on the previous occasion, each passing day of her fast brought her lakhs of new supporters, each vociferously supporting her demand. At the same time, Shruti's blood-pressure began to dip, giving the Government the jitters.

While Shruti's fast continued, a key ally of the IDP Government, the ruling party of U.P, withdrew its support to the Central Government, as it knew that an early election would boost the possibility of a Third Front Government – which was their perpetual dream. As such the Government was reduced to a minority.

When the PM, the IDP chairperson, and their group of ministers met that evening to take stock of the situation, they knew they'd have to do something drastic to turn the situation around in their favour.

And this seemed to turn the tide against Ravi Nehra,

'Let's face it: Nehra's days are over. We stand to gain more by acting tough with him than by colluding with him,' a minister asserted.

'Politics, after all, is all about public perception. With the elections just two months away, who knows, perhaps the junta will forgive us if we can convince the masses that we have nothing to do with Nehra.'

For the next few minutes, Mukta Prajapati thought hard about the situation. She then asked the PM for his views on the topic.

'Whatever you decide, Madam,' was all that the faithful PM had to say.

'Then let's do something that shocks the country. That's our only hope anyway,' announced Mukta, rather ominously.

In the next two hours the IDP made its intention clear: it was ready for some high-octane action to impress the voters.

Nehra was arrested from his residence at midnight and the Catherine murder case was formally handed over to the CBI. The meek PM, speaking to the media, on board his flight to China, gave some unusually assertive sound bites, 'Catherine's killers will not be spared, irrespective of the clout and power they enjoy. The Government will not allow powerful MPs to get away with crimes of such a horrific nature.'

Shruti ended her fast; this time however she did not feel any sense of achievement or satisfaction. In fact, when the ABP office-bearers met the next day, the members were all very subdued. A common grief and a common mission united them so strongly that they did not need to reinforce their thoughts with words. Each one of them had solemnly committed to uproot the IDP in the elections, which were now less than a month away.

After Nehra's arrest, the undercurrent of rebellion that had always been suppressed successfully within his party, now assumed dangerous proportions. Nearly half of his party MPs were reportedly eyeing options elsewhere – half with the ruling party and the other half with the ABP – whereas a majority of the remaining MPs favoured Ratna Pandey staging a coup and taking over as party president.

Ratna, though, wasn't sure if the time had come to usurp the leadership of the party. There were two reasons for this: the less popular but more experienced Ratnesh Prasad hadn't ruled himself out for the post; besides it wasn't clear how long Ravi Nehra would spend in jail. What if he got released on bail in the next hearing and he still clung to the post? Of course, Ratna had finally made up her mind that in a hopeless situation like that, she would simply quit the party along with her supporters. Clandestine parleys and crass bargaining among the political classes thus, once again became the order of the day.

There was a difference of opinion between Daivik and Shruti on the issue of poaching MPs from the Jan-Hit party. While Shruti favoured the move, Daivik was still opposed to it.

'These MPs are rats jumping out of a sinking ship. We will gain nothing by giving them our party ticket. It will work better for us if we accept them in a post-poll tie-up. We will also know which ones of them are capable of winning elections on their own reputation by then,' reasoned Daivik.

Shruti thought about it and agreed with Daivik's point of view. 'Well, yes, that approach actually would achieve the dual purpose of helping us strike a moralistic posture, without us needing to be so in reality. I think that makes a lot of sense, Daivik!'

Chapter 36

Ravi Nehra, given the seasoned defaulter that he was, managed to obtain bail in the next hearing with his lawyer arguing successfully that there was no evidence yet of Nehra being 'directly' involved in Catherine's death. Ravi thus managed to get out of jail by furnishing a personal indemnity of just Rs 50,000 and promising to make himself available regularly for court hearings.

Nehra knew that in the present situation, it had become virtually impossible for him to continue as party president without running the risk of his party splitting into two. The challenge for him, thus, was to let go of the president's post without losing control over the party. Hence, while Nehra would have liked to have his loyalist, Ankur Yadav, head the party, he knew that in the present situation, the massive public ire against him, would make it difficult for him to push his candidate through. Hence, very reluctantly, Nehra finally agreed to Ratna Pandey taking over as party president on the condition that the party would set up a three-member core committee headed by him and with Ratna and Ankur Yadav as the other members, which would take all key decisions of the party.

He intended to still run the party by proxy.

In a scripted press conference presided over jointly by Nehra and Ratna Pandey, Nehra lashed out at his detractors for conspiring against him. He swore he was innocent and that his decision to quit as party president was only in the interests of the party. For her part, Ratna Pandey declared as dramatically that the party stood solidly behind Nehra and would expose the Government and the ABP for the baseless propaganda they had unleashed against Nehra.

Well, in India such is the obsession to be in the reckoning for the PM's post that Ratna Pandey was merely trying to keep her faint prospects alive: after all, with Nehra heading the three-member committee, she knew that her fate would hang upon Nehra's wishes.

That evening, the Election Commission announced the dates for the elections. The elections were to take place in three phases, with the first phase of polling just about four weeks away. Nehra and Ankur sat in Nehra's living room, chatting away till night and mulling over their future prospects.

'*Bhai*, it's going to be very tough election for us…I'm afraid we may not even win fifty seats if things stand this way…' rued Ankur Yadav.

Nehra did not respond. He just kept looking into the giant-size aquarium just a few feet away. His focus was on a particular orange catfish, larger in size than the others and which moved to and fro predatorily, intimidating the other fishes around. Nehra was intently following the movement of this fish.

'Isn't this fish behaving somewhat like Shruti Ranjan?' remarked Nehra, flashing his diabolic smile. 'Mark my words, this is what the fate of Shruti Ranjan is going to be.'

Nehra then shouted for one of his servants.

'Can you see that fish – yes, that one here,' he pointed at the fish he had set his eyes on.

The servant nodded.

'Cook it for me now.'

As Ankur Yadav witnessed Ravi Nehra's descent into madness, he felt a wicked joy inside. With Nehra set to embark upon a path of breakdown and self-destruction, Yadav knew that he could emerge as the lucky underdog who stood to gain from Nehra's disgrace.

Chapter 37

With the first phase of polls now just two weeks away, Shruti was all set to embark on a whirlwind tour of the country. As she went through the itinerary which had been drawn up for her by Daivik and his team, it filled her with a sense of déjà vu. It reminded her of the time, eleven years ago, when Sharad and she had toured the country amidst the boisterous '*Sharad for PM*' clamour. It reminded her of the hysteria that the slogan had generated in towns and villages and how almost everyone had begun to believe that Sharad would indeed occupy the PM's chair and transform the country. But destiny, of course, had other plans up its sleeve.

Even as Shruti sat alone, with only her thoughts for company, a news channel telecast the results of an extensive opinion poll it had carried out across 220 of the 543 Lok Sabha constituencies.

According to this poll, 44% people wanted to see Shruti Ranjan as the next PM; only 17% were in favour of Ratna Pandey being the next PM; 14% favoured a status quo and backed the present PM, Devender Singh. Among others, Ravi Nehra had just 5% people support him.

As for the election results, a hung parliament was predicted, with the ABP ahead with a forecast of 180 plus seats. The ruling party, riding aggressively on some proactive image makeover initiatives, was predicted to get 150 seats, while the Jan-Hit party was expected to get around 100; that too only if Ratna Pandey took centrestage and Nehra kept out of the campaign.

Shruti wondered if there was a larger force at play, shaping things in just the way it would best serve the country's interests. She wondered if she was being manipulated to realize her mentor, Sharad Malviya's, unfulfilled agenda. She felt a frightful sense of responsibility as she prepared herself for another high-voltage electoral circus.

'Yes, time indeed has come a full circle for Shruti Ranjan,' mulled she, smiling at the ways of destiny, her smile just about managing to conceal the apprehensions that lay deep within.

Shruti wanted to go back and contest the Kishanganj seat where her story had begun. Daivik was inclined to contest from Ranchi where he had his roots and where his parents still lived. Pratibha Kaushal, on the other hand, wanted to contest the New Delhi seat.

The frontline IDP leaders, like they mostly did, were once again preparing a back-door entry into Parliament via the Rajya Sabha.

The Jan-Hit party, on the other hand was in particular disarray. While the ABP enjoyed a better perception on account of being untested, in several places the ruling IDP stood to benefit in triangular contests. The Jan-Hit Party, on the other hand, was carrying a huge venal baggage on its shoulders, which was bound to impact its prospects adversely.

Given all the negative publicity that Ravi Nehra had had to confront in the last couple of months, he was not very keen to contest from Rohtak – a constituency he had represented thrice. He knew how tough it was to win a seat the fourth time when the voters were restive and hungry for change. Hence, he had asked his men to hunt for another safer constituency, preferably one with a greater Jat base. After toying with several options, his chamchas finally zeroed in on Gurgaon, convincing him that Gurgaon would be his safest bet. When a news channel broke the story of Nehra planning to contest from Gurgaon, Nehra actually used it as an opportunity to make his announcement. 'Yes, I will be contesting from Gurgaon, a town where I was born and where I grew up. In fact, Gurgaon has always been my first preference...I'm glad I finally might have the opportunity to repay my debts to Gurgaon.'

When time is not on your side, it doesn't take much for things to keep going horribly wrong. Hence just two days later, Rhea, asserted that *she* would contest the Gurgaon seat against Nehra as the ABP candidate. Rhea's decision left Nehra flummoxed. It was bad enough to lose to someone one didn't know, but losing to one's wife would be the ultimate humiliation! He cursed and abused his advisors for suggesting the Gurgaon seat to him.

'But sir, if Rhea Madam was determined to contest against you, she could do it from anywhere. Why blame us for suggesting Gurgaon? Besides, since you have not filed your nomination yet, you can always back out.'

The egoistic Nehra knew that the option of backing out did not exist. He couldn't be seen as running away from facing his wife in a contest. Thus, the other viable option was for him to contest two seats – a provision that was available to those contesting the elections.

Nehra thus filed his nomination for the Gurgaon seat first and on the last day of filing the nomination, he quietly proceeded to Rohtak. He was pretty sure that his decision to re-contest from Rohtak would surprise his rivals who wouldn't have prepared for it.

But instead when Nehra reached the DC's office in Rohtak, it was he who was in for a rude shock. He was asked to wait outside as another candidate was already filing his nomination inside.

'Who is that?' he asked casually.

The name he heard left him sweating.

It was Daivik Verma!

Nehra came face to face with Daivik when he stepped out after filing his nomination. Even as Daivik flashed him a confident smile, Nehra said, 'Withdraw your nomination unless you want to lose your deposit.'

'Nehra Saab, by winning this seat, I will prove that elections in India can still be fought without black money and without any corporate sponsors,' Daivik rejoindered, before walking off.

It proved to be a tense night for Nehra. He was woken up twice by hideous dreams. In the first he saw himself falling at Rhea's feet and begging an apology; in the other he saw himself being chased by Daivik and his supporters through the congested streets of Rohtak. He hated himself for having no control over his dreams.

As the campaign reached its peak, Shruti's popularity was clearly established. The ABP did finally hire a chartered aircraft for three weeks to fly Shruti to every nook and corner of the country. And as Shruti travelled across the land she was amazed and moved by the people's support. It seemed as if the entire country was solidly behind her. Interestingly, it was also observed that the rallies that were addressed together by Daivik and Shruti got the best crowd responses as both were excellent orators. Hence party candidates from all over the country kept requesting the ABP headquarters in Delhi for joint rallies of Daivik and Shruti. Thus, keeping the sentiment of the people in mind, Daivik and Shruti extensively toured the country together.

In between rallies, on their flight from one destination to the other, Daivik found Shruti quiet and lost in her thoughts. He thought it strange that Shruti was so withdrawn, and perhaps a touch melancholy, when everything seemed to be working in their favour. Perhaps Catherine's death had affected Shruti as deeply as it had affected him.

'Shrutiji, aren't you happy? I mean, everything is apparently going so well for you,' he asked her one day. 'Why are you always so pensive and mellow?'

Shruti smiled sadly. 'I'm finding it difficult to differentiate illusion from reality, Daivik. I mean, it's so strange that just when everything seems to be going well for you, a terrible tragedy makes it all seem so meaningless. This power we gain is always at the cost of something, or someone. The memories of Sharad and Catherine still haunt me. The way they were both snatched suddenly out of my life, makes me feel that I can't take anything for granted.'

The first phase of polling, which saw 171 constituencies vote, recorded an unimpressive turnout of 48%. Though exit polls had been banned until the elections were over, Ravi Nehra got a sense of what to expect from them. From the reports that he had got from the ground, most of these constituencies had a direct IDP *vs* Jan-Hit party clash with the Jan-Hit party trailing a distant third. As such, Nehra knew his goose was cooked. And he had to do something desperate to stay in the running.

That night, when Ankur Yadav went to meet Nehra to discuss the usage of funds, he was in for a shock. Ankur sauntered into Nehra's living room, only to find Nehra, with his back to him, talking urgently into his phone.

'It has to be next Monday! Shruti and Daivik are both supposed to attend a joint rally. Make sure it is the last rally of their lives!' Nehra was talking to the Maoist leader, Somnathji. After finishing his conversation, he removed the sim card and burnt it with his lighter.

Seeing Ankur looking flabbergasted, Nehra explained his diabolic game-plan to him: 'If Shruti and Daivik are eliminated in one go, the ABP will be left leaderless and the party will collapse. In such a situation, both the IDP and our party will try to woo the elected ABP supporters into our folds. With the ABP more or less eliminated, I am pretty confident that in a bipolar draw, the people will favour us, provided we pitch a clean leader like Ratna Pandey to them…'

Ankur was aghast when he heard this. 'But, *bhai*, what if your involvement is found out? You'll spend the rest of your life in jail…'

'Don't worry. This blast will have a clear Maoist imprint to it. Besides, in a worst-case scenario, my sources will inform me much before the needle of suspicion points towards me. And in that case, I'll be off from the country forever. I'll spend the rest of my life in some distant beautiful land that does not have an extradition treaty with India,' Nehra said airily, not caring to even find out if what he spoke made any sense. He was clearly drunk. But more than drunk, he seemed headed on a trip of self-destruction.

Ankur's disenchantment with Nehra was complete.

Chapter 38

Next Monday arrived.

The second phase of polling was to start on Wednesday so it was the last day of campaigning. The previous evening, Shruti and Daivik had attended a mammoth rally at the Mohrabadi ground in Ranchi. Shruti was canvassing here for Daivik. The incredible turnout and the enthusiasm of the crowd indicated that Daivik was headed for a comfortable win. After the rally, both of them had stayed back in Ranchi for the night.

That Monday they were supposed to attend what was being touted as the biggest gathering of tribals in a small town called Chaibasa, some 60 km away from Jamshedpur, in Jharkhand.

For reasons that weren't particularly clear to Daivik, it had turned out to be a rather disturbed night for him. His sleep had been fitful and restless. He dreamt that Catherine and he were walking hand in hand on the beach, into the sunset. She was reassuring him that everything would be fine; that they would soon be reunited. The dream had left him shaken. Daivik had too much on his mind to be able to go back to sleep. He spent the rest of the night surfing the net and reading all the latest articles on the elections.

At 9 a.m. on Monday morning when he met Shruti on the plane, he heaved a sigh of relief. Battling his uncertain thoughts all alone, he really needed to talk to her. Daivik shared his dream with Shruti and she responded with a reassuring pat on his shoulder. Hoping to distract him from his unhappy mood, she tried changing the topic of conversation: 'Are you satisfied with the way our campaign has shaped up?'

'Well, yes and no. What we have achieved as a debutant party is quite phenomenal. The crowd response vouches for it. But I am not sure if it will be sufficient to help us win. I dread the prospect of a hung parliament,' Daivik said, sounding his usual pragmatic self.

'Hmm, we've done what we could. Let's leave the rest to the powers-that-be…' Shruti said.

A thoughtful pause preceded Daivik's next sentence. 'I don't know why I get the feeling that the powers-that-be will do something extraordinary to shake things up in the next few hours.'

An hour later, when their copter landed at Chaibasa, two senior police officers were standing by, waiting to talk to them on a matter of utmost importance.

'Ma'am, we have some bad news. Two low intensity blasts have occurred at the site of the rally in the last half hour. We fear that your life is in danger. We'd advise you to call off the rally,' one of them told Shruti.

Shruti looked at Daivik.

'Shrutiji, let me do this rally alone. Your life is too precious to be lost at this stage,' Daivik pleaded.

'For all you know my martyrdom could get us an absolute majority,' Shruti replied, unfazed, and casually ignoring his suggestion. 'Have there been any casualties so far?' she asked the police official.

'Two dead and four seriously injured. So far we've not informed the gathering that it was a bomb blast. The people there think it was an accident started by a firecracker or at the most a cylinder blast. The entire area is being covertly combed as we speak. The moment the crowd gets to know that this was a bomb blast, there will be huge panic. It could result in a stampede.'

Shruti thought for a moment before spelling out her decision: 'I will go ahead with this rally.'

'But, Ma'am...'

'When the crowd gets to know the reason why I am not coming, they will anyway get restive. This will trigger a bigger stampede and result in more deaths. Rest assured, my speech will not have a mention of the blasts at all. But I have to go ahead with this rally. I can't disappoint the people waiting for me.'

When Shruti reached the podium to address a one-lakh strong crowd of tribals, she realized that she couldn't abandon her fears. Beneath her facade of courage, she was very worried. It was scary to think that there was also no barricade between the crowd and her. More than her death, it was the thought of seeing people die in front of her eyes that really disturbed her. Three blasts had occurred by now; more were likely. Would she survive the next half an hour? Would some of her hardcore supporters live to hear her complete her speech? Would Daivik, for whom she had developed such protective instincts, be safe? She set aside her fears and began to speak:

'Friends, we live in rather uncertain times, with the spectre of violence always looming over us...Sadly, evil has always been an important force across history and mythology. Perhaps evil exists for good to vanquish it and hence reassert itself. Even in the Ramayana and Mahabharata, evil wins over good far too often, before the good finally vanquishes the evil forever… and so it's been happening in contemporary India. As if corruption, black money, inflation, crimes against women and terrorism weren't issues obnoxious enough, political intolerance has now reached shocking levels. How else can one explain the murder of Catherine? Just because you disagree with someone and see him or her as a threat to your political position, would you have him killed? Is that the *raj dharma* which our present set of rulers wants to bequeath to the future generations of politicians?

'Every politician wants to be in power someday. But power needs to be won and commanded rather than be usurped and demanded. Let the country not have to pay the price for your naked ambition…' With all the surrounding anxieties, Shruti was clearly not in her element. Her speech was impassioned but the effort showed.

Even as Shruti spoke, she heard an explosion rip through the vicinity towards the eastern end of the ground. Even though her heart pounded in her chest, she chose to ignore it, lest the crowd panicked and caused a stampede.

Given the high threat perception to Shruti, four police officers stood at the podium sweeping the crowd with their binoculars. While Shruti spoke, Daivik watched the crowd.

'…In the Ramayana and The Mahabharata, Ram and the Pandavas fought against Raavan and the Kauravas. In today's India, Ravi Nehra is Raavan, while the ruling IDP are the kauravas who have always supported the illegal and the corrupt for their vested interests and to somehow cling to power. Like Ram and the Pandavas, we, the ABP are few in number. But our numerical limitation does not restrain the strength of our spirit.'

Just then, Daivik noticed some unusual movement between the second and third row of people seated diagonally in front of Shruti. He snatched the binoculars from a policeman standing close by.

'We, the ABP, will always be there to confront evil, till evil exists in this world...And that's the reason I am standing in front of you, staring at possible death...I am told my life is in danger. I don't care if I am killed. Remaining alive to see you all suffer at the hands of IDP or Jan-Hit party is worse than death. Even if I am no more, promise me that you will uproot the vices of the present regime. Make sure that you will vote for change!

'Brothers and sisters, say with me thrice...Bharat Mata ki Jai...' she exhorted the crowd. 'Bharat Mata ki –'

At that moment Daivik hurled himself at her and pushed her so hard that had one of the police officers not held her, she would have fallen off the podium. Turning around to see what had happened she saw Daivik standing in the spot where she had stood just a few seconds ago, taking the bullets meant for her, in his chest.

A few hours later, Shruti found herself outside the operation theatre of Ranchi's Apollo Hospital. Daivik had suffered serious injuries and was bleeding profusely. He was hit by three bullets fired from a country-made pistol that had been aimed at Shruti. Had Daivik not snatched her away from the jaws of death, Shruti's life would have been over. Why did Daivik do this for her?

As Shruti waited outside the operation theatre, she was reminded of a similar situation when Sharad had been shot at and was battling for life in Kochi. Why did her life throw up unending tragedies like these? As Shruti sat there, numb and devastated, mumbling her prayers, Daivik's words just before the rally echoed in her ears: 'I don't know why I get this feeling that the powers-that-be will do something extraordinary to shake things up in the next few hours.'

Shruti hated the powers-that-be for always making her the sufferer, in politics and in relationships.

The serial blasts at Shruti's rally and Daivik's condition sent shock waves through the country. People were enraged at how violence was being unleashed as a means to suppress the challengers of a flawed system.

If Daivik died, his death would mean the death of their last hopes of resurrecting a failed polity. After all, Daivik symbolized the power of the common man. Within hours of the blast, even as Daivik was being operated on by leading doctors of the country, large sections of the people had immersed themselves in mass prayers, hoping fervently that he survived.

Shruti stayed by Daivik's side, shutting herself away from everybody else. Virtually shattered, she just wanted to be left alone. The remaining phase of polling did not interest her one bit.

Several hours passed, with the situation remaining as fluid. Daivik was still critical; Shruti was still incommunicado.

Far away in Delhi, Ravi Nehra sat over a drink with Raghunandan Gupta, mulling over the situation. 'Bloody bitch, she's got such a long life. How could she escape the bullet?' he mumbled, anxiously flipping news channels.

When he didn't find any favourable news, Nehra flung the remote on the floor.

'Relax, Nehra Saab. Life and death are destiny. So what if Shruti is alive. Daivik will be off,' reasoned Gupta.

'That's precisely my problem, Gupta. There's a hell of a difference between Daivik dying and Shruti dying. If Shruti would have died, people would have perceived her party to be leaderless and voted against them. But if Daivik dies, I am afraid it will only get sympathy votes for Shruti's party. It will make Shruti emerge far stronger. Dammit!'

'Oh, I see, then we should pray that Daivik survives. I will organize a hawan,' suggested Gupta, only partially comprehending the complexity of the machinations going on in Nehra's head.

Nehra wondered where Ankur Yadav was. He had been trying to call Ankur but his phone was switched off. An hour went by. It was midnight now. Nehra was several pegs down, blabbering indiscreetly and hurling invectives at anybody and everybody. Suddenly, his drinking partner, Raghunandan caught something on a news channel that left both of them aghast. Ankur Yadav was addressing a press conference, along with the Home Minster, S.K. Patil. The very sight of both them together sent shivers down Nehra's spine. By the time, Ankur had begun to speak, Nehra knew that his downfall was complete.

About an hour earlier, a secret meeting had been held in Mukta Prajapati's Teen Murti Lane residence: Prime Minister Devender Singh, Home Minister S.K. Patil and Ankur Yadav had sat in Mukta Prajapati's exotically designed living room, waiting for her to arrive. Ankur had looked nervous even as Patil and Singh wore victorious smiles. Finally Mukta had walked in and all three stood up to greet her obsequiously.

'*Boliye,*' she ordered Patil, at whose behest the meeting was taking place.

'Ma'am, Ankur Yadav has divulged information about today's blast. He says he overheard Ravi Nehra talking to a Maoist leader instructing him to carry out the blast. The plan was to kill Shruti and Daivik together…'

'Hmm…'

'Ankur has also revealed that it was Nehra who had Catherine murdered.'

'So what's the deal?' asked Mukta in her typical businesslike way.

'The deal is that Ankur Yadav is willing to spill the beans and expose Nehra. In other words, he will turn legal approver against Nehra.'

'What does he want in return?'

'He says he will join us with thirty MPs of his and wants to be Railway Minister if we form Government.'

Mukta thought it over. 'After today's blast, the ABP has been left rudderless. If we strike off the Jan-Hit party as well, people will have little option but to vote us back. It therefore indeed makes sense to be ruthless on Nehra. He has anyway outlived our utility.'

Mukta complimented Patil on this deft move. She was filled with new hope that with both the ABP and the Jan-Hit party down, the IDP could well get a majority on its own.

'Just be quick. Make Ankur Yadav hold the press conference today itself. But make sure Ankur talks only about Nehra's role in today's blast… his announcement to join our party should happen only after the election results. He is anyway not allowed to change parties in the middle of an election.'

After Mukta left the room, Devender Singh hugged Ankur Yadav in gratitude. 'God is great! Without me putting in any effort, he always sends angels like you who help me continue as PM.'

By the time Ankur was done, Nehra was sweating profusely. Ankur had revealed everything about the plot to murder Shruti and Daivik. He had exposed Nehra's old links with the Maoist leaders and how it was a mutually beneficial one. Nehra was soft on the Maoists; in return the Maoists were supposed to return him a favour or two – like they had today. More shockingly, Ankur had revealed that Nehra had confessed to him that he had Catherine murdered.

Even as a dazed and devastated Nehra watched the fallout of Ankur's revelations on TV, a grim-faced peon walked in to inform him that a police team led by the Delhi police commissioner was outside the door with a warrant for his arrest. Nehra was handcuffed and dragged to jail as per a specific instruction passed on by B. C. D'Souza to the police commissioner.

Chapter 39

For Shruti it was one of the most terrible nights she had ever spent. Daivik was still unconscious after an eight-hour long surgery. His vital parameters were still way out of control, with the BP fluctuating rather wildly. As such he was still critical.

Even as Shruti continued to chant prayers for Daivik's survival, doctors pegged his chances only at 50:50. As Shruti sat all alone in the corridor outside the ICU, her eyes chanced upon the muted TV set fixed on the opposite wall. A news channel was playing out the latest developments in Delhi.

While Shruti had never underestimated Nehra, she couldn't believe that he could stoop so low as to actually conspire to have her killed. Shruti wasn't sure whether she was lucky to survive the attack, because given a choice, she would have happily traded her life for Daivik's. She couldn't bear the thought of losing him.

Finally, unable to stay away from Daivik, at 3:10 in the wee hours, Shruti insisted to the medical team that she be allowed to visit him.

For the next one hour, Shruti sat by Daivik's side. She couldn't hold back her tears seeing him in this condition. She started talking to him. She bared her thoughts to him. She chided him for taking the bullets that were meant for her. She told him about Nehra's arrest. She told him how miserable she was feeling.

At 4:30, Daivik finally regained consciousness. Apparently, he mumbled Catherine's name a couple of times. Shruti responded to him urging him to talk. By this time, the doctor and the nurses had also rushed into Daivik's room.

'Sh-Shrutiji, don't worry about me...go and fight for our dream...for the cause we all have sacrificed so much for...' Daivik urged her in a feeble voice.

The next phase of polling took place a day later. During the course of the day, the Home Ministry issued a press statement saying that the evidence against Nehra in the blast case at Chaibasa and his collusion with banned outfits was so incriminating that the ministry would press charges against him under the National Security Act. Hence, Nehra would hold the unenviable distinction of being the first national-level Indian politician to be charged under the Act and the chances of him coming out of jail anytime soon were bleak.

The dramatic incidents of the last two days altered the dynamics of the elections significantly. One, Ravi Nehra stood exposed and damned. In fact, such was the people's anger against him that they hated anybody who was remotely connected with him. Ratna Pandey, thus, was completely out of favour. And so was the Jan-Hit party – which was predicted to suffer massive losses at the hustings.

The other significant change was the sudden surge in the ABP's support. Shruti's fiery speech at Chaibasa and the subsequent shoot-out were played on news channels ad nauseum. History is replete with instances where impassioned speeches by leaders have achieved the virtually impossible and the stark honesty in Shruti's words and her courage in the wake of threats to her life, left the masses moved and touched. Shruti was seen as a sufferer, a victim and a crusader. And this evoked huge sympathy for her.

Shruti, for her part, stayed close by Daivik's side, refusing to meet the media or her party. 'I have nothing else to say to the people. If justice still exists in the world, they'd ensure that our fight does not go in vain.'

On the night before the final voting day, the common refrain across three news channels was: *Will the nation fail Shruti Ranjan yet again?*

The next morning, the country's leading newspaper carried a rare front-page editorial piece titled, 'Don't Fail Shruti Ranjan'. The article went on to say that if the people did not back Shruti at this critical juncture, they would be squandering a rare historical opportunity; in which case they would have nobody but themselves to blame for the continued failures of the country.

These last two phase of polling, thus, became the game-changer. The voter-turnout for the last two phases, which covered 362 Lok Sabha constituencies, was at least 20% higher than the first two phases. There was a general hunch that after the last two phases, the ABP would improve its tally significantly.

Finally, it was D-day. The counting of votes was to start in another half hour. Shruti had visited the Hanuman temple early that morning and brought in prasad for Daivik, who by now, had shown a marked improvement in his health.

'What's your hunch, Shrutiji? How many seats do you think we'll get?' a still weak Daivik asked Shruti from his hospital bed.

Shruti was rather philosophical in her response. 'I don't know about the numbers. But I do believe in something called poetic justice.'

And so it was! By noon, it was clear that Indian psephologists and pollsters had got their calculations all wrong. The election results had thrown up a clear surprise. Riding on Shruti's impactful Chaibasa speech and visuals of the shoot-out, it seemed that the ABP had performed exceptionally well in the last two phases, winning nearly 180 out of the 362 seats that went to polls in the last two phases!

As such the ABP's total tally was a staggering 227, much higher than what it had expected, but 45 short of the magic figure of 272. The Jan-Hit party won a meagre 70 seats, the public anger against Nehra's politics clearly evident in the results. The IDP, on the other hand, managed a not-so-bad tally of 138, mainly due to some last-minute corrective action in the last two weeks.

Ravi Nehra had lost both his seats; Rhea had defeated him from Gurgaon and Daivik from Rohtak. Shruti had once again won the Kishanganj seat with a record margin, whereas Mukta Prajapati had lost her deposit from the constituency that her family had represented for ages.

'So poetic justice it indeed is,' said a triumphant Daivik, as Shruti sat alone with him in his hospital room until a nurse informed them that there were hordes of people waiting outside the hospital to catch a glimpse of their possible future PM.

Shruti, given that she had stopped taking anything for granted, refused to let herself believe she could actually be the next PM. But then destiny often finds ways to make things happen.

Given that no party or coalition had got to the majority mark on its own, the Jan-Hit party with seventy MPs had a crucial part to play in the formation of the next government. When the elected MPs met to decide their stance they had two options: one, form a minority government with outside support from the IDP and hope to buy out Independents and other smaller parties; or two, to support the ABP from outside and help provide a more stable government to the country.

Ankur, who had begun to act as a stooge of the IDP, preferred the former option but was shocked to realize that not even a dozen MPs supported him.

'We've done enough damage to ourselves by constantly compromising our position under Nehra. Now it's time to make amends...We must rightfully honour the sentiments of the people,' remarked Ratnesh Prasad.

The veteran MP's words reflected the sentiments of most of the Jan-Hit party MPs. They wanted to make a fresh start and exorcize the wrongdoings of Nehra forever. As such, Ratna, her personal dislike for Shruti notwithstanding, decided that she would support Shruti Ranjan and help her form the Government that the people had voted for. In a press conference an hour later, Ratna Pandey declared that her party would extend unconditional support to the ABP in forming the next Government. The opportunist Ankur Yadav knew that his calculations had gone horribly wrong. Just twelve MPs by his side and with the IDP's tally reduced to what it was, he would gain nothing by joining the IDP. Instead it made sense for him to keep a low profile and not embarrass himself.

Three days later, it was time for Shruti to be sworn in as the new PM. By now, Daivik's condition too was much more stable and he was able to move about in his wheelchair. Given the historical significance of the occasion, Daivik wasn't going to miss Shruti's swearing-in as PM for anything.

Shruti and Daivik flew into Delhi for her tryst with history. Daivik had not yet been discharged from hospital. In fact, after the swearing-in, he was once again going to be shifted into the Apollo Hospital in Delhi, where he was going to be subjected to more restorative surgery.

As Shruti stepped forward to take oath as PM, a gamut of memories – some sweet, some bitter – filled her mind. She vividly remembered the day when it all began: when Sharad Malviya had first offered her the Lok Sabha ticket; her first swearing-in as MP, then as a deputy minister, then as CM of Bihar and then as Minister of State of Home. She had a vivid recollection of the day Sharad had died; she remembered her stay in jail. She remembered the formation of the Nationalist League (Sharad) with Rhea. She remembered the humiliating defeat in the 2009 polls which had left her so dejected that she quit politics. She remembered Daivik and Catherine coaxing her back to the world to which she possibly had a karmic bonding. She remembered Catherine's unfortunate death and Daivik's fortunate victory over possible death.

As Shruti cleared her throat to take her oath of office, she could see Daivik sitting in the front row. Beside him she sensed the presence of Sharad Malviya and Catherine cheering and applauding her. The images distracted her but she knew now, more than ever before, that she owed this post to all of them. That every decision she took henceforth would always be one that met with their approval and respect. They had sacrificed their lives for her to be where she was, and she would ensure that she would never let down the trust they placed in her.

With eyes glistening with tears, but in a voice that was steady and full of conviction, she said:

'I, Shruti Ranjan, do swear in the name of God that I will bear true faith and allegiance to the Constitution of India as by law established, that I will uphold the sovereignty and integrity of India, that I will faithfully and conscientiously discharge my duties as Prime Minister for the Union and that I will do right to all manner of people in accordance with the Constitution and the law, without fear or favour, affection or ill-will…'

Acknowledgements

I am grateful to my editor, Nandita Aggarwal for her unflinching belief in my stories and to the entire team at Hachette India for their support through my last three books. It's been a thoroughly enjoyable and fruitful journey with them.

I wish to thank my wife Ramyani for her constant feedback on the manuscript and for always helping me with thoughts and suggestions for marketing and promotions of the book. I also wish to thank a dear friend, Rahul Sharma, for reading through the book and offering some invaluable suggestions.

Last but most importantly, I owe a debt of gratitude to my readers. Without your continued faith, I would not be able to experiment as much with my stories as I do.

PRAISE FOR TUHIN SINHA

The Edge of Desire

'Shruti Ranjan is an apt representation of today's Indian woman, living on the cusp of modernity and tradition and dealing with the multitude of problems which come with this...In many ways, Shruti represents the formidable modern day Draupadi.' – ***The Asian Age***

'*The Edge of Desire* is worth a read to understand the quirks of fate, the machinations of politics and what a combustible combination the two can make.' – ***The Hindu***

'The book's immensely pacy – mirroring exactly the frenetic developments in Indian politics where a split second can transform people's lives. Sinha's made good use of real-life events as markers in Shruti's political and personal life. The Mahabharata metaphor is thought-provoking and Sinha's also done a fair job of showing the different, often clashing sides of his characters' personalities.' – ***ibnlive.com***

'The book has an interesting plot, considering the immensely political times we live in...Sinha covers a wide swathe, keeping his narrative interesting while portraying Shruti's "it's complicated" status, be it her rocky personal or professional life.'– ***rediff.com***

Of Love and Politics

'Indeed, in today's age of monosyllabic phrases and grammatically horrifying SMS-lingo, it is commendable to have a writer like Sinha who can so adeptly weave Shakespearean phrases like "phlegmatic propensities" and "puerile denials" with Shashi Tharoor-esque aplomb in his work.' – ***The Hindu***

'The book throws up well-researched and lesser-known trivia about Indian political history that is very illuminating. Tuhin represents a breed of young Indian authors who are conscious of their roots and who keep an eye on their political surroundings.' – ***Deccan Herald***

'One of the most critical areas which the books delves into and which I liked very much is the connect between one's personal beliefs and his/her political ideology... the book celebrates democracy.' – **Ravi Shankar Prasad, Senior Politician**

'...very interesting characters and some brilliant passages' – **Rimi Chatterjee, Author**

'The best part about the book is that it provides a distinct perspective on almost every important political event of the last century' – **Piyush Jha, Filmmaker**

'Politics makes strange bed-fellows and this book aptly proves it.' – **Abhijit Bhaduri, Author**

'Thought-provoking, easy flowing, yet deep. Not only does it raise questions about the flaws in our multi-party democracy but also makes an attempt at offering solutions.' – **Gul Panag, Actress**

That Thing Called Love

'Set at a good pace, debutant novelist and scriptwriter Tuhin A. Sinha weaves a contemporary story of a bunch of well-etched out characters' exploring expectations, disillusionments and fragility in relationships.' – **Indiantelevision.com**

'...an urban metropolitan reader may easily be able to relate to the dynamics governing the rising complexities in relationships.' – **Shaaditimes.com**

'...the book touches several social issues and deals with them in a manner that has hitherto not been dealt with before.' – **Screen**

'A subject, currently explored in films, coupled with flowing language and generous use of the first person, makes this book an exciting read.' – ***Afternoon Despatch & Courier*, Mumbai**

'A journey of discovery through disparate spectrums, Tuhin waxes eloquent on the choices that lie before the typical urban Indian male and in an odd way strikes a chord that is unmistakable.' – ***The Sunday Indian***

***The Captain* (formerly *22 Yards*)**

'Setting the cats among the pigeons, *22 Yards* steers dangerously close to uncomfortable facts surrounding cricket today' – ***Financial Express***

'The book is the first of its kind – it embarks on a course that is based on some real life incidents in Indian cricket.' – ***The Hindu***

'The plot is extremely interesting and would find favour with all cricket lovers. The writing is swift and lucid.' – ***The Statesman***

'A breezy non-stop read with some excellent passages which bring out the issues that confront modern day cricket.' – **Charu Sharma, cricket analyst**

'All the passion and pain of cricket, all the glory and gloom; the need to be a loner and share a field with twenty-one other loners; the swing and spin of success, greed and lust... *The Captain* is alive with that feeling, that comprehension.' – **Tom Alter, actor and cricket expert**